FALLING ON A DUKE

Stefany Nunes

Copyright © 2025 Stefany Nunes
Originally published as *Um duque do passado*.

The moral right of the author has been asserted.

Apart from any fair dealing for the purposes of research or private study, or criticism or review, as permitted under the Copyright, Designs and Patents Act 1988, this publication may only be reproduced, stored or transmitted, in any form or by any means, with the prior permission in writing of the publishers, or in the case of reprographic reproduction in accordance with the terms of licences issued by the Copyright Licensing Agency. Enquiries concerning reproduction outside those terms should be sent to the publishers.

This is a work of fiction. Names, characters, businesses, places, events and incidents are either the products of the author's imagination or used in a fictitious manner. Any resemblance to actual persons, living or dead, or actual events is purely coincidental.

The manufacturer's authorised representative in the
EU for product safety is Authorised Rep Compliance Ltd,
71 Lower Baggot Street, Dublin D02 P593 Ireland (www.arccompliance.com)

Troubador Publishing Ltd
Unit E2 Airfield Business Park,
Harrison Road, Market Harborough,
Leicestershire. LE16 7UL
Tel: 0116 2792299
Email: books@troubador.co.uk
Web: www.troubador.co.uk

ISBN 978 1835741 948

British Library Cataloguing in Publication Data.
A catalogue record for this book is available from the British Library.

Printed and bound in Great Britain by 4edge Limited
Typeset in 11pt Minion Pro by Troubador Publishing Ltd, Leicester, UK

To Karina, for the friendship and tenderness with my sweet steamy stories.

And to my loving family and husband, for knowing I could do this.

Author's note

This book contains themes that may be sensitive for some people, such as **depression and grief**. It contains explicit erotic scenes.
Recommended reading age: 18+.

E nosso amor, que brotou do tempo, não tem idade, pois só quem ama escutou o apelo da eternidade.
Carlos Drummond de Andrade

1

Suddenly, everything disappears

Bath, England
1817
Benjamin

I massage my temples as I listen to my assistant speaking.

Today must be the most tumultuous day of my year. And the hottest too. The sun pours through the window without mercy. Closing the curtains seems to make it worse, as the air becomes even stuffier. I want peace and quiet, God damn it. I deserve it after this insane week. But first, I need to make an important decision.

"Then what, Your Grace? What do we do?"

Jacob Howard, the middle-aged, balding man with a broad moustache in front of me, is a practical and efficient man; that's one of the reasons I hired him. As a duke, I have many commitments and deal with endless bureaucracy – investments, meetings in Parliament, and tenants' affairs… the list goes on.

Apart from that, I own a promising newspaper in Bath, the *Daily Bath*, although nobody knows about it. My position requires discretion, so the *Daily* is a secret I share with only three people: my sister Abigail, my best friend Jack, and my secretary, of course, who keeps looking at me with an anxious expression.

"I'm thinking, Howard." I hold out my hand and reach for my glass of Scotch, taking a long sip. We're in my study since I don't go to the newspaper – I wouldn't want to give rise to gossip.

My secretary shifts his weight from one leg to the other.

"I didn't say anything."

"But you thought it," I say, cracking my neck in an attempt to relieve the tension.

The problem we're facing is serious. My decision cannot be rushed. As much as I want to give the order and make tomorrow's front page denouncing that treacherous scoundrel, I can't do it without the evidence in hand.

"We need the documents," I say. "Letters, notes, something signed by Cornell to prove his betrayal."

"We don't have it yet, but James is confident that he will succeed."

"Trust isn't enough." I take another sip of the Scotch, putting the empty glass aside. "Look, I want to turn him in, but you know me. I do not do things in a hurry. That never works."

"What could possibly go wrong, Your Grace?"

"A lot of things. Raoul Cornell is a marquis; he is close to the King. If the newspaper publishes that he betrayed the Crown by handing over information to Napoleon without proper proof, that could get us into trouble."

"Not when the owner of the newspaper is the Duke of Waldorf."

"When it comes to the *Daily*, I try to be anything but a duke," I correct him. "You know that no one is aware of my involvement with the paper."

Howard twitches his moustache and nods, but I know him well enough to know that he is unhappy with the way the conversation is going. I decide to end it once and for all.

"I will think about it, and we will talk tomorrow. Abigail is waiting for me for dinner. We will have to discuss it another day."

"But, Your Grace, it's still early, and—"

I raise my hand, with a grim expression.

"My sister ate dinner alone every day this week because we have been so busy. I am tired. I will think about our dilemma tonight. Tomorrow morning, a decision will have been made."

As much as I want to end this conversation, I'm not lying. I have been remiss in my duties to Abigail. My sister, the only family I have, is my priority. She always has been, even before the death of my father and Barney, my twin brother.

"There are rumours that Cornell is going to America soon," Howard says insistently.

I frown, puzzled. Is Cornell on the run? It is quite possible. If that's the case, the coward must know he's at risk and that also explains Howard's urgency to make a decision. Even so, the complaint is too delicate to act on impulse.

"Twelve hours, my friend. Tomorrow, I'll tell you what to do. Go home and rest. You are in too deep."

I understand his motives, and I share his feelings. Howard lost a son to the war. The exposure of Cornell's crimes would, in a way, reinforce that all those men didn't die in vain. Including Barney.

Despite his annoyance, Howard gives up arguing. He turns his back to me, and I relax in my chair, sighing heavily. On my desk, piles of papers demonstrate the chaos of my own mind. There are at least eleven different issues that need my attention.

I'll have to sort them out tomorrow. I am overcome with doubt as to how Abigail spent her day. I have been cooped up in here for the entirely of it. Yesterday, she was not very well; I could tell by the sadness in her eyes. It has been like this for the last few months, ever since our father passed. I just wish I knew what to do, how to ease her pain, even though I feel it in my own chest.

I push the chair away and stand up, straightening my jacket. Nothing's going to change, so there's no point in complaining. I pull my watch out of my pocket and look at the time: 3.56pm. I open the drawer to put some papers away, but something glinting catches my eye. I reach out to pick up the intriguing object.

It falls to the floor, so surprised am I. The sound of metal fills the silence of the room. Near the foot of the table, on the wooden floor, an antique cameo locket finishes tinkling. What runs through my veins is more than strangeness. It's astonishment, unbridled surprise.

I know this cameo. I haven't seen it for a long time, but I know it. It's mine. I did not even know it was here.

One day, you will understand, my boy.

The weather is still hot, and the air is still humid, yet a shiver runs down my spine at the memory of my grandmother's words. I shake my head, shaking them off. God, I must really be tired. In the last few minutes, I have remembered absolutely everyone I have lost over the years: my mother, my brother, my father, my grandmother. Basically, my entire family. No, not all of it. Abigail is still here, and she's waiting to dine with me.

I have been dealing with a lot lately. The grief, the duties, the title. Sometimes, I wonder what it would be like to disappear for a while. I could very well disappear.

Ignoring my thoughts and the emptiness inside me, I bend down, approaching the item, ready to put it back in the drawer. I stretch out my hand, reaching for it. The silhouette of the delicate mother-of-pearl face, carved on the rounded stone, is the same as I remembered. The metal around it looks more aged, but it's still a beautiful, elegant, and distinctive locket. Involuntarily, the tip of my thumb brushes lightly against the small pink stone set into the female figure's neck.

And that is when the impossible happens.

I cannot explain the next few seconds. They do not seem real. They cannot be.

As soon as my fingers wrap around the cameo, a peculiar light switches on in the palm of my hand. I don't have time to ask questions, or even to think.

One second, I am in my study.

The next, everything disappears.

2

Writer's block

London, England
2022
Isabella

I need you like I need air to breathe.

What a load of rubbish!

I press the *delete* button even harder than usual. This cliché is so cheesy it makes my eyes roll back in my head. Holy Tessa Dare of clever phrases, forgive my sins. This author is not in her normal condition.

Calm down, Isabella, it's just a phase. It'll pass.

A very long phase, but that's OK. I consider myself an optimist, although lately it's been hard to keep my spirits up with this horrendous writer's block. I haven't published anything for a year now. Not a single short story. Every time I face the blank computer screen, it's as if my ideas are suffocated by a giant mental wall, and I end up typing these meaningless words.

With a frustrated sigh, I close the laptop screen, putting my "novel" to one side, and massage my temples, feeling the twinge of a headache. I don't deny that sometimes I feel like giving up for good. To let it go, to carry on working in a café and paying my bills as I have been doing for the last few months, to go out and explore London without thinking about my stories. The problem is that I love writing, and I don't *want* to give it up.

I reach for my phone. This delicate moment deserves an upbeat song. There's nothing an inspiring lyric can't solve. I click on my "Sunshine" playlist and choose the first song that jumps out at me. "Here Comes the Sun". OK, The Beatles should do the trick. As soon as the beat starts, I push back my chair and stand up with the device in my hand, stretching my aching back. Duke, my corgi dog who is lying in the corner of the room, just lifts his head and looks at me, wagging his tail slightly. He settles back down as soon as I let out a low moan, moving his neck slowly. Everyone had told me that when you're in your thirties everything starts to hurt, but I'd never really believed it.

Well, it's true, especially for me, as I'm basically just sitting around at home on these colder days.

I walk into the kitchen singing. I open the fridge, pull out a can of Coke Zero, and leave it on the counter to get a glass from the cupboard. Look around, believing I've left a chocolate bar here. I can't find it. Cinthia, my flatmate, must have got hold of it this morning.

Leaning my back against the sink, I stare at nothing as I sip my Coke, reflecting on how I came to this unfortunate situation in my writing career. I don't want to put all the blame on Matheus, but it's a bit difficult considering that my inspiration to write ended along with my relationship. How can I write romance novels when I find myself deeply wounded by love?

I thought I'd laugh about it one day, but it's been over a year and a half now, and I still can't laugh when I think about how my ex ended things. And what a bad ending, since he called me with the cliché that he had met someone else. I've never been a big fan of clichés, and now I officially hate them. I'm Brazilian, and Sorocaba, my hometown, is close to São Paulo, where Matheus works in a law firm on Paulista Avenue. It's only an hour and a half by car, so it's undeniable that, after almost three years of relationship, he could have driven there to do it looking me in the eye. What a fool I was to consider spending the rest of my life with a guy who can't drive a hundred kilometres for me.

The rest of my life. It's ridiculous.

As always happens when I think about it, I feel my stomach lurch, so I put the Coke aside after just one sip. No point trying to drink the rest. I put the can away in the fridge, go to my room, and throw myself on the bed, opening my Instagram feed without stopping the music, which is now playing "Love On Top" by Beyoncé. Duke follows me, his paws making a *clack clack* on the wooden floor. He jumps onto my bed, settling at my feet. I must like torturing myself. I can't resist getting Matheus's profile up on Instagram. I stopped following him as soon as we broke up, but that doesn't mean I've stopped following what he posts. Glancing at his latest photo, I already bitterly regret having given in to my impulse.

There he is, with that broad smile I loved so much, at a barbecue with his new girlfriend, Julia. I don't know her, but she seems perfect. Beautiful, a lawyer, and from what I saw on her feed, they have a lot in common.

I used to be an "opposites attract" enthusiast. I like contrasts. Today, I'm not so sure it really works. I started dating Matheus out of a genuine desire to make it work, even though we were different in many ways. So much so that, after a year of dating, I started saving most of my salary as an English teacher, already thinking about our marriage. The money at least enabled me to fulfil a long-held wish: to live abroad for a while – a wish I had put aside for him, in fact. I've got my job, my papers are in order, and I don't have a date to return.

I open my playlist again and stop the music. The silence immediately feels good. I guess I was wrong – no positive lyrics seem to be helping today. As soon as I put the device away, I hear the keys in the front door and Duke jumps out of bed to meet Cinthia.

"Bella?" Cinthia calls.

"I'm in my room," I reply.

Not even two minutes later, Cinthia appears at the door. Her curly hair is tied up in a stylish ponytail and she's wearing a black T-shirt, denim trousers, and boots. Her mauve blush is the perfect shade for her dark skin and discreet gold eyeshadow emphasises her big brown eyes – elegant, as per usual.

"With sunshine like this on your day off, you're lying there?" She leans against the doorframe with a careful expression, her British accent as charming as ever. "I wish I'd been able to get out earlier to go on a walk."

She's a make-up artist and works in a shopping centre in Canary Wharf, near our home.

"It's cold, and I decided to try writing." I sigh.

"Did you manage to?" She seems excited. Cinthia is one of my only friends here, so she knows my whole story and how I've suffered from writer's block.

"Nothing. Just rubbish."

She frowns.

"Oh, what a shame. But don't beat yourself up. It's a phase. All writers go through it."

"I thought the same thing, although we have to admit that this phase is already too long."

"A lot has happened, Bella. You're too hard on yourself."

Yes, I know. Cinthia always reminds me how drastically things have changed in my life since I moved to England eight months ago.

"Do you think it could be the panic years – the thirties crisis?" I ask her.

"Of course not. Thirty, flirty and thriving, don't you remember?"

I laugh. We watched *13 Going on 30* last week as part of a marathon we did on films about time travel. I don't know why we chose that theme, but it was nice. Every now and then, when we're both off and don't feel like going out, we take advantage of our passion for films and spend hours on the sofa. The films we choose are usually romances or comedies, and we have a lot of fun munching on popcorn while chilling in our PJs.

She looks away and bends down to pick Duke up when he jumps on her leg. "My God, this little beast is getting bigger and heavier."

I agree with a smile, gazing at my dog's happy expression.

Duke came into our lives by chance. A friend of Cinthia's, who lives in Brighton, was surprised to discover that his pair of Welsh corgis had bred. Some misunderstanding about castration. As he is against buying and selling animals, he offered one to my friend, asking if she wanted to adopt it. Cinthia didn't want that responsibility, but I accepted Duke immediately.

"You spoil him." I point to the two of them. "He's got used to it."

"*Oh*, but he's a darling," Cinthia speaks in a cutesy voice. "Isn't he, Your Grace?"

Duke wags his tail frantically, and my friend promptly puts him down.

"Seriously, Bella. Apart from writing, what have you been doing all day?"

"I rang my father to see how he was."

"Has he arrived in Tokyo yet?"

I nod in confirmation. My father, Tadeu Kato, has Japanese heritage. He's been living in Japan for a while for work and took the opportunity to go to Tokyo to visit his paternal grandfather, the only living relative he has apart from me. He and my mum, Janete Souza, divorced when I was three. He lived in São Paulo; she lived in Sorocaba. I also have a younger sister, Laura, from my mum's second marriage. She lives in Quebec, Canada, with her husband and works for his company. Basically, we're a family spread all over the world.

"OK, what else?" Cinthia asks me again. I think it's cute that she's so concerned about me. At thirty-three, it's like she's the big sister I never had.

"I haven't done anything else," I reply.

She crosses her arms. Here comes the lecture.

"Go out for a walk. It'll do you good."

I look out of the window, seeing the sun shining through the curtains. It really isn't a bad idea for me to go for a walk; it's been a few weeks since I've been to the Tower Bridge area, and even though it's busy, I really like it there. I look at the clock. It's 2pm and it's November, which means I still have a couple of hours of sunshine.

"Do you want to come along?" I ask, sitting down on the bed.

"I can't. I have to pack." Cinthia rolls her eyes.

"Oh, yeah."

Cinthia is going to spend a month in Paris studying French. She's excited, especially because her boyfriend will be keeping her company during this time. I don't know him personally, but I've seen a photo, and the guy is hot.

"So, things are progressing between you guys?"

She shrugged.

"We're having fun. I don't think it's serious yet."

"Wow, keeping your cards close to your chest?" I tease.

She denies it, laughing.

"You're very romantic, I don't want you to get excited for nothing."

I roll my eyes, joking around. If there's one thing I haven't been in recent months, it's romantic. It's kind of hard to be when your heart is being held together with glue and tape.

"I get really excited. How could I not, with a beautiful French man to—"

"Belgian." Cinthia corrects me. "Paul is Belgian."
"Oh, fancy."

"See? *One comment* and those little eyes are shining," Cinthia teases me.

Maybe she's right and I really am an incurable romantic.

"OK, I admit I love romance."

"I know. You write only that."

I frown softly. I *used to* write. Now, it's a bit difficult.

"You know what?" I sigh because thinking about my writer's block only makes me more upset. "I'll do what you suggested. Maybe seeing a few people will really help." I stand up, looking for my pair of trainers.

"That's it. And I'm going to get something to eat and start packing up."

She leaves me alone while I finish putting my trainers on. Duke doesn't make a point of following us this time, but I look at him anyway.

"Do you want to come along?"

Faced with the silence of Your Grace, who must be the laziest puppy in the UK, I decide not to insist.

"Nice, but your tummy is growing…" I laugh, leaving him behind.

I walk through the living room and stop in front of the coat rack, picking up a yellow woollen scarf that is hanging there, along with my pink coat. Cinthia is sitting on the sofa chewing something and lets out a laugh.

"For God's sake, woman, it's not that cold."

"Yeah. You know, where I come from, we're not used to cold weather." I put my coat on, shrugging.

"You Brazilians…" she murmurs good-humouredly,

as I check that I have my phone and keys and say goodbye.

I hurry down the stairs, feeling the cold wind as soon as I open the door to the entrance hall. To get to Tower Bridge, I just have to take the DLR, as it's only fifteen minutes from where I live. It's a good location, close to Underground lines and several bus stops.

The train isn't full, probably because of the time of day. As soon as I press the metal button and get on, I sit down in the nearest empty seat. I don't pick up my phone. Instead, I do the exercise I learnt on a writing course: observing the other passengers and what they're doing. After all, that's why I left home, isn't it? Trying to overcome the block. There's a gentleman two seats to my right, reading today's newspaper. His dark skin is almost wrinkle-free, but he has a few grey hairs in his curly mop. Discreetly, I notice him mumbling something to himself as he reads the articles.

I then shift my gaze to the front seat, where a boy, probably under twenty, is fiddling with his phone. On his pale, acne-ridden face, he scratches with his index finger what looks like an attempt at a moustache but looks more like a shadow over his lips, so thin. The kid frowns at the screen, coughing generously without covering his mouth. Ew. That's enough to make me lose interest and change my focus, and I continue people-watching until the train arrives at Tower Gateway station.

Unlike my neighbourhood, the streets near Tower Bridge are a little busier. As soon as I leave the station, I'm about to cross the road when I see three electric scooters standing on the edge of the pavement. I like to walk; I don't usually rent them, even though I got my driving licence for that very purpose. But today I feel like using them. As I'm already registered with the app, I use my phone and scan the QR code on one of them. In less than two minutes, I can feel my hair fluttering as I guide the scooter through the streets of London.

Getting out the flat is good for me, I won't deny that. Just getting out of my tiny flat makes me think more clearly, and this, combined with the imaginary soundtrack I attach to the situation and the magnificent cityscape that London has to offer, can be defined as synonymous with inspiration. I don't take too long because I want to get back before it gets dark. On the way back, I pass by the Tower of London, stopping at a red traffic light on Tower Bridge. The crossing is clear, but I wait anyway. The green light appears, and I look to my right, just in case. There's no one coming, so I move on.

I just didn't expect the thud that was to come, sending me crashing to the ground on top of a strong, warm body.

3

What the hell is a scooter?

Benjamin

Beep... beep... beep...

What kind of bloody noise is that?

I open my eyes slowly, feeling my head throbbing. The room is so bright that I feel like I'm facing the sun itself. The lights on the ceiling are white, a lot of them. Apart from the annoying noise, it's cold and the pungent, unfamiliar smell, which is not unpleasant, gives me the impression that I'm not in a familiar place.

"You're awake! Oh, my goodness!"

The soft, feminine voice sounds relieved. It takes me a few seconds to focus on the stranger's face. Her dark eyes show concern.

But who is she?

"What..."

"Thank God you're awake. Jesus Christ, I'm so nervous," she says, staring at me intently. "I'll call the nurse. Don't move."

She practically runs out of my sight. Nurse? What is she talking about?

My limbs are heavy, without strength, and my mouth is bitter. I look down at myself and realise I'm wearing strange clothes. In fact, what covers my body is more like a sheet with sleeves. There's a thread on my left arm, which ends in a transparent pouch filled with a liquid – I have no idea what it is – tucked into a metal holder. On my chest, more wires, these ending in a rectangular box. I realise that the annoying whistle seems to come from there, from this unknown object.

I blink once more, trying to understand. Where am I? What has happened? Why am I not in my study?

"Look! He's awake." The unknown girl returns, this time accompanied by another older woman. My eyes wander over them both. They are also wearing unusual clothes. Masculine, I'd say, considering they're wearing trousers.

The lady approaches me, her eyes attentive.

"Hello, I'm Nurse Sam. How are you?" she asks me, checking the beeping box next to me.

It's a difficult question to answer, not just because I'm tired and confused, but because I have no idea what has happened.

"Where am I?" I ask and raise my arm with the thread. I pull it and feel the area burn with the movement, bleeding. "What is this?"

They both look in the direction of my arm with alarm. The nurse is quick to press the place that hurts.

"Don't move like that, you'll hurt yourself. I'll have to take another vein."

I don't have the energy to move around much.

"Where am I?" I repeat.

"You're in the hospital," Miss Sam replies.

In the hospital? Why? How did I get here?

"I was in my study…" I stop talking, trying to remember. My eyes meet those of the first girl, the young woman. "Who are you?"

She swallows dryly, her cheeks flushing in what I think is embarrassment.

"I'm Isabella. Isabella Kato. Don't you remember what happened? We had an accident, I…" She sniffles, blushing more. "I hit you with the scooter."

With what?

"What the hell is a scooter?" I mutter quietly.

They look at each other again. Why are they looking at each other like that?

"Well?" I say again.

"What's your name?" the older woman asks.

What kind of dialogue is this?

"My name is Benjamin Gerard Waldorf," I say slowly. The words come out slurred, but I have no control over my weakened voice. My arm is still throbbing, but the nurse is still holding it.

"And you remember what happened, Benjamin?" Miss Sam asks me.

Why is this woman calling me by my first name? We're not intimate. I don't know her, and she doesn't know me or my name, or she wouldn't call me that.

Not that I'm a snob. I'm not. I wish I didn't have to be His Grace. But I'm a duke, and society has its rules.

"I…" I said, "I was in my study, and…"

I stop again. They wait a few seconds until Miss Isabella starts.

"We were on Tower Bridge. I looked the wrong way down the street and ended up hitting you. You know, I'm not from here. You do everything the other way round."

"You?" I ask.

She nods, pushing her long hair out of her face.

"You English people," she explains, as if it were obvious.

So, she's not from around here. Well, obviously not. Miss Isabella has an accent whose origin I don't know.

Apparently, I'm completely unaware of everything around me.

"Try to remember, Benjamin," the nurse asks, her voice very calm. "Take your time."

I close my eyes, feeling a twinge of headache. I'm trying. Just now, I was in my study. Howard was talking to me about a complaint. It was noisy and hot. I thought about Abigail. I wanted to be free sooner.

And then the memory hits me.

The cameo. The cameo my grandmother gave me a few days before she died.

I remember hearing it falling and reaching for it. I remember the light, and…

God in heaven, I remember that everything went dark.

"Where am I?" I ask again.

"In hospital," the nurse repeats.

"Where?"

"London," Miss Isabella answers.

"London? I was in Bath!"

"Calm down, Benjamin." The nurse touches my arm.

"Let's calm down, please. You're in London, at Guy's Hospital. You're safe, don't worry."

It seems they do not understand me.

"How did I get here? Since when? What day is it today?"

Miss Isabella's frown intensifies. She is still very pretty, though. Not that I should notice *that* in a moment like this.

"Today is Tuesday," she says.

I frown. My last memory is of a *Saturday*. I was unconscious for three days?

"What day of the month?"

Isabella Kato takes a deep breath.

"29 November 2022."

I freeze. I can't be listening properly. Did she say *2022*?

"I asked a serious question," I say, irritated.

"She's telling the truth, Benjamin." The nurse looks at me, taking a rectangle of dark glass out of her pocket. Something lights up on the surface, a coloured light. Even though I'm intrigued, that's not what I'm paying attention to right now. "Look, here's the date. 29 November 2022."

Yes, that's what it says on the strange object. But it doesn't make sense. I am from 1817. *1800s!* The date these two women tell me is two hundred years after my time.

They tell me I'm in the future.

Suddenly, I can't breathe. I can't even think.

"I need to get out of here..." I mumble, trying to get up.

"Benjamin, calm down," the nurse says, trying to contain me.

I'm not sure what I'm doing, I just want to leave. I want to understand where I am, who these people are, these things around me. My chest is tight; my lungs are squeezing inside my chest. I'm suffocating, desperate like never before.

The movement in the room increases. Within seconds, there are more people there, and I feel someone holding me back, restraining my movements, and a pinch on my other arm. I lose control of my own body.

I can't speak; I can't ask them to let me go.

My eyes close against my will. Even in agony, I fall into a deep sleep.

* * *

Isabella

I watch Benjamin close his eyes and stop moving as my heart squeezes.

Oh, my God, what have I done?

Bloody English streets where everything is the other way round. Even after months of living here, I still get confused. But he also came out of nowhere – the people who stopped to help us at the time said so, that they didn't see where he came from.

It was like magic, like some special effect.

Wow. *That* would make an excellent scene for a romantic comedy.

Come on, for God's sake, creativity, now's not the time to show up. But she's been absent lately so… I'll save the idea for later, just so I don't forget.

I open my phone notepad and type, feeling my knee sting. Apart from a scrape, I wasn't hurt by the impact. He, on the other hand, hit his head and didn't wake up from the moment of the fall until just now, even with all the paramedics' efforts.

I was really worried.

From what the nurse told me, he's fine. They did tests, put him on an IV to hydrate him, all while I took care of the bureaucracy of this kind of situation.

I was so nervous that I even forgot to text Cinthia. I've been out of the house for hours, so I'd better let her know.

I go back to typing on my phone while the nurse goes back to dealing with Benjamin, now asleep. I open the messaging app and request a video call.

My friend answers two rings later.

"Wow, Bella. I was worried," she says, as I sit down on a chair in the hospital corridor.

"Girl, I ran over a man." The words burst out.

Cinthia's dark eyes widen in amazement.

"How did he get hit?"

"With the scooter. I was practically on Tower Bridge when I looked the wrong way and nearly ran over him. I'm here at Guy's Hospital."

"My God, Bella. Are you alright?"

I sigh. "I am, but he hit his head. He woke up super anxious just now, and they injected him with a sedative."

"Have you already spoken to the police?" she asks me.

"Yes, I did. Actually, I could leave, but I don't want to leave him until he's well. It was my fault."

"Wow, that's a lot…" Cinthia grimaces in disbelief. "Do you want me to come?"

"No, you don't have to. You're travelling tomorrow, better not to leave Duke alone." I glance quickly at Benjamin. "He's asleep now; maybe I'll pop home to change and have a shower."

"I think that's a good idea. Shall I order you something to eat?"

I think for a moment. I'm not hungry, but considering I've only had lunch today, it's not a bad idea to eat something.

"You can order a burger, please. I'll speak to the nurse and be there in about thirty minutes."

"Fine, I'll order it. Oh, and who's the guy? Do you know him?"

I shake my head.

"He only told me his name. They didn't find any documents on him." I stop talking and Cinthia notices my expression.

"What's wrong?"

Only then do I realise that the man was dressed as a nineteenth-century lord. A *handsome* lord, by the way, the kind you imagine dukes and viscounts in Regency novels, like Jonathan Bailey in *Bridgerton*.

Not that I noticed, of course.

"He was wearing a lord's costume. And what a handsome lord, God in heaven. I wonder if there's an event here."

It wouldn't be unusual, after all, we're in the land of Jane Austen and *Bridgerton*.

"Not that I know of, but this city is kind of nuts. Since

you know his name, see if he has Instagram." She shrugs. "Sometimes it's easier to track down someone in the family, and you're free right now."

Great idea. I hadn't even thought of that.

"But, Bella, don't get too involved."

"What do you mean?" I ask, frowning.

"I know that guilty look. You hit the guy, but it can happen to anyone. Make sure he's OK and move on."

Argh, I know that. You'd think I'd get involved with a stranger. I already have my own problems to deal with, for God's sakes.

Although such an unlikely encounter could make for a good story…

"Bella, what are you thinking about?" Cinthia asks me.

"Let's say the walk worked to spark creativity, at least." I shrug. At least one good thing in the midst of chaos. "I have to go now. Kiss, kiss."

I thank my friend and hang up the phone. Nurse Sam has her eyes fixed on a clipboard.

"Is everything alright?" I ask.

She nods, not looking worried.

"Yes, he is OK. He's going to sleep for a few hours. When he wakes up, we'll try again."

"Is it normal for him to be so anxious?"

She smiles amiably.

"Yes, it could be. Even though the CT scan is normal, he could just be confused and disoriented. It happens sometimes."

I sigh heavily. I feel a little lost, not knowing what to do.

"I think I'll go home and have a shower and come back. I want to talk to him when he wakes up."

The woman agrees, jotting something down on a clipboard.

"He'll be discharged tomorrow, no doubt. As soon as he wakes up, we'll try to locate his family."

Thank goodness. But even knowing that the hospital is keeping a close eye on the guy, I don't feel comfortable abandoning him. I'm going to take advantage of the fact that he's asleep and go home. I just need to change and eat something, and then I'll come back here.

The nurse says goodbye, and I take one last look at the victim of my stupidity. Oh my, how handsome he is. Even with his tired face and hospital gown, he looks like a model. Strong and masculine, an angular face, square jaw, and stubble. His brown hair falls over his forehead, and his nose is straight, very aristocratic, just like I write about in my novels. His voice, which I heard earlier, is baritone, thick, and elegant. I didn't see him standing, but I'm sure he's tall. Very, very tall. I shouldn't be noticing his beauty now, but I have eyes and needs – what can I do?

All the single ladies who have suffered from this problem before, please, raise your hands.

I shake my head slightly and walk out of the room into the corridor. A little lost, I remember that I need to get to the nearest tube station. I walk out the door, feeling my knee throbbing and my head heavy. Wow, I'm exhausted. Who would have thought that one little walk would end up in all this?

When I get to the Underground, I get on and go down the escalators automatically, just checking which way I should go. I manage to sit down in a free seat in the carriage. On the way, with my mind still on the handsome guy I hit, I do what Cinthia suggested and open Instagram to look up the guy's name.

Benjamin Gerard Waldorf.

A suggested post pops up on my screen, with a recent photo of my ex and his girlfriend. I've seen it before, but the open smile he shows continues to intrigue me. He never smiled like that when he was with me. Not once.

Blergh, I won't think about my ex. I turn my attention to the search, which shows me several Benjamins, some Bens, a few Waldorfs, but none of them are *him*. I decide to try Googling the name. Maybe the guy is one of those people who doesn't have social networks.

Again, nothing. Well, unless he's a duke from the 1800s, which is the only result I can come up with.

I put my phone back in my pocket and get off at my station.

All the way home, I can't stop thinking about what a disaster today has been. I just hope that Benjamin will be OK, despite everything.

And then, life goes on.

4

He thinks he's a duke

Isabella

Two hours later, I'm back at Guy's Hospital. I haven't mentioned the accident to anyone in my family because I'm fine and I don't want to worry them. Plus, they'd ask a thousand questions, and I don't have the energy for that. I'll tell them eventually, when it's all over. Or not, who knows?

I had a quick shower, changed my clothes, ate a sandwich while Duke stared at me with his tail wagging, and told Cinthia everything that had happened.

She also searched for his name on social media. The result was the same as mine: nothing. Cinthia realised how guilty I was feeling and advised me not to get upset, that these things happen. But... I don't know, it's not that easy. Someone was hospitalised because of my carelessness. It could have been serious. It wasn't, but it could have been. My Virgo ascendant won't let me forget that detail. And

I know myself, and I know that I'll only feel calm when Benjamin is well.

That's why I'm here, to take a closer look.

I speak to the girl at reception and see a familiar figure at the desk. The nurse is the same one as before, Sam. She recognises me straightaway, smiling as I approach.

"You're back."

I nod, smiling at her. "Is he awake?"

"Not yet. If you want to stay with him, visiting hours are until 9pm."

I look at the clock. It's 7.15pm.

"Of course, I'll stay here."

The woman agrees and beckons me into the wardroom. Benjamin is still asleep, and I'm not sure what to do. I pull up a chair next to the bed and sit down. My palms are slightly sweaty, even though I'm not hot. I once again analyse his masculine face, his thick, drawn eyebrows. However, staring at Benjamin makes me anxious, as if I'm pushing him to wake up. I'd better do something else. Before leaving the house, I decided to bring my e-reader with me. I open it to my latest read and start flicking through the pages.

The story I'm reading is a marvellous book with a *Romeo and Juliet* vibe, but even that can't distract me. Every five seconds, I look away from the screen and check on the man lying in front of me. Time passes, seeming to drag on. Soon, visiting hours will be over and I'll have to leave, which means it's going to be a long night, because I doubt that I'll be able to sleep peacefully without knowing how he's doing. I'm lost in thought when I notice him move.

Benjamin opens his eyes very slowly. He's sleepy, and it takes him a while to focus on me. He stops for a moment, seeming to recognise me.

"Wasn't that a dream?" Benjamin mutters.

I get up from my seat and approach him, quietly. I can't work out whether it's a question or a statement, but I don't want to frighten him.

"Benjamin, you're in hospital," I say as calmly as I can.

He jumps and reaches to pull out the drip again, but I touch his forearm.

"No! Don't do that, or they'll put you to sleep again."

I sound like a mum talking to a naughty little boy, not a big man like this. Benjamin stops again, looking calmer than before, although frightened. Very frightened. His gaze meets mine in a mixture of confusion and despair. Something touching, which goes straight to my heart.

"I know it's confusing, but…"

"I don't understand," he mumbles.

I'm the one who stops talking now. Has he forgotten what happened before? My God, is his recent memory impaired?

"I'm…"

"Isabella Kato," he adds. "I remember. Your name is Isabella, and you ran me over with a…" Benjamin hesitates, "scouter, smooter…"

"Scooter," I say, holding back the urge to laugh. Poor chap. He's confused and it shouldn't be funny, but it is.

"Yes, that's right," Benjamin continues. "And you also said that it's 2022. That's impossible."

"Why?" I frown.

Benjamin takes a deep breath, his gaze lost in his

surroundings, staring at every corner full of astonishment and indignation.

"Because I'm not from that era. Because I have duties, a title, a sister who needs me!"

OK, now I don't understand anything. What is this madman talking about?

I sit on the edge of the bed.

"What do you mean?"

Benjamin rubs his eyes, then his messy hair. Bending reveals his muscular arms. For God's sake, the man is panicking in front of me and I'm noticing his fit body.

I need a man yesterday.

"Benjamin, talk to me," I ask once again.

His brown eyes meet mine again.

"I am Benjamin Gerard Waldorf. I was born in 1785, and I am the Duke of Waldorf."

A shiver runs down my spine. Jesus, I've broken the man with my scooter. He's out of his mind.

"I think you're confused, and…"

"I'm not confused! Stop repeating that word. I am who I say I am," he insists.

"A duke from the past?" I ask. "Like Kate and Leopold?"

"Who?"

OK, it's hard for a man to understand a reference to a romantic comedy, so I'll overlook this serious offense.

"Are you telling me you're a two hundred-year-old duke?"

He nods. I remember the research I did on the tube and then at home. The man I found with his name was indeed a duke, although I didn't pay attention to the name of the title.

"Wait," I say, taking my phone out of my pocket. I open Google once more and enter his name. The same result as before appears on Wikipedia, and yes, this Benjamin was the Duke of Waldorf. There's hardly any information on the page nor any images. I hold out my hand, showing the phone screen.

"This one?"

Benjamin squints, looking lost.

"How do you do that? What kind of book is it that has no pages?"

Book?

"This is a *mobile phone*." He still doesn't understand. I insist, "A phone."

"What?"

Wow, this guy is taking this thing about being from the past very seriously, to the point of pretending not to recognise objects.

But… he doesn't seem to be pretending.

I scratch my head. I don't know what to do or how to respond. I'm still thinking when Nurse Sam appears at the door.

"Ah, you're awake! How do you feel, are you calmer?"

Benjamin takes a deep breath before answering. "No, I'm not. How can I be calm if I'm in the future?"

The nurse nods slowly up and down. "Future?"

"Yes!" Benjamin continues. "I'm not from here, nor am I from this year. I don't recognise anything around me; I'm in indecent clothing; and I need to go home!"

She presses her lips together in a thin line, looking at me.

"It's 9pm. You need to go, but the doctor is here if you want to ask him anything."

I want to. I have all the questions possible and imaginable.

"Well, I've got to go, but I'll be back tomorrow."

His expression flinches. "To go?" Benjamin asks.

"Yes, Benjamin. Visiting hours are over. Stay here and I'll be right back to talk to you." The nurse touches his arm and then leads me down the corridor.

Benjamin and I exchange one last look, and it's as if he's asking me to stay. As if I'm the only person he trusts. And then I realise that, if it were up to me, I would stay. That if visiting hours didn't exist, perhaps I would stay all night so that we could talk calmly until he felt better.

I'm a silly woman, but I can't help it.

Nurse Sam and I reach the corridor. She walks up to a middle-aged doctor and waits until he has finished talking to another nurse.

"Doctor, I've just spoken to the guy who was hit by the scooter," Sam says.

The grey-haired man looks at her from behind his glasses, taking the clipboard she holds out to him.

"What happened?"

"He thinks he's from the past," she tells the doctor. "The tests are normal, but I think he's confused after the crash."

The doctor nods, looking at the spreadsheet. He doesn't seem surprised. If the hospital's daily routine is anything like those medical TV shows, I imagine this kind of situation is common.

"And you're with him?" he asks me.

"Yes... well, I was the one who ran him over, so... I guess so."

"He'll be discharged tomorrow morning; there's no reason to keep him here."

It takes me a while to understand, but the way he talks, it sounds like I'm his chaperone or his carer. Only… I don't stop being one, do I? At least, until they find some contact details for the guy.

"I'll be back tomorrow. Don't worry about it."

He doesn't seem the least bit worried.

"And what do we do if he thinks he's from the past?" I ask.

"There's nothing you can do. The best thing is to wait and, if he doesn't improve, it's best to book a psychiatrist and a neurologist."

So much information. And I can't help thinking that he's alone and scared.

I look at Benjamin's room once more, determined to take a chance.

"Can I talk to him for another fifteen minutes?" I ask the doctor. "I promise not to push it."

I at least want to say that I'll be here tomorrow.

He looks at the nurse, then at me again. "Fifteen, and no more than that."

I let out a breath, agreeing. When I come back into the room, Benjamin is still looking lost. He looks so disorientated that I immediately feel the urge to hug him.

"Benjamin…" I say, and he looks at me. The doctor says there's nothing we can do but wait, but I wonder if it's better to help him at this difficult time. Maybe it is. It doesn't cost me anything to ease his burden. "Or would you prefer me to call you Your Grace?"

He seems surprised by the question and equally relieved. As if someone finally understood him.

"Do you believe me?"

I'm not comfortable lying, but I'm not the priority here.

"I think so. If you want me to treat you like a duke, Your Grace can rest assured."

The hope that shone in his eyes died instantly. He lets out a humourless laugh.

"No, you don't."

Damn it, why do his words touch me so much?

"I believe it," I insist.

Benjamin just shakes his head.

"Look, I can't stay here for long, but I wanted to say that I'll be here tomorrow for your discharge."

He frowns. "Discharge?"

"Yes, they'll let you go home."

Benjamin lowers his gaze, clenching his jaw. "My home is in another city, in another century."

Silence. Jesus, what a situation. How am I going to console this man? "Where do you live?" I ask.

"The city of Bath. 52 Brock Street."

I take out my phone and type the address into Google again. The information is that the house is a museum and has been for the last forty-five years. In other words, he doesn't know where he lives, just as he doesn't know *who* he is.

"Right. Look, it says here that it's a museum… nowadays."

Benjamin shows no reaction, as if he had already been hit with so much bad news that one more wouldn't make any difference.

"In other words, I have nowhere else to go."

Yes, that's right. Unless…

No, that would be crazy. I may be feeling guilty, but offering to take the guy home would be too much. He's a stranger who could attack and kill me. Do I want to be in tomorrow's news? God forbid.

I look at him again. Damn it, why can't he look dangerous? Why does he have to look so… gentle? And why, God, do I feel like it might not be a bad idea to help him?

Life goes on, I remember Cinthia's advice.

Life goes on? You'd think so.

What a pain in the arse. That look of disappointment on his handsome face is my undoing.

"You've got it," I say. "Tomorrow, when you're discharged, I'll take you to my flat."

* * *

Benjamin

I stare at Miss Isabella for a moment before speaking.

I really hoped that I was dreaming. That when I woke up, that jumble of names, smells and things was just a delusion of mine. That I would be home, safe, with my sister who is now alone. For heaven's sake, I need to go back.

I'm not someone who gets carried away by my emotions, even though I'm desperate. I'm trying to act with reason, even if nothing, *absolutely nothing*, makes sense. How can I deny everything that surrounds me? I don't recognise these objects, these clothes, this accent. If it's not a dream, I'm crazy. But am I really? No, I don't think I am.

I just want the girl in front of me to believe me.

"Your Grace, did you hear me?" she asks me, after a long pause.

The weight of being called that has always had a certain impact on me. In a perfect world, that title would never be mine. However, hearing her treat me in this condescending way causes a bitter taste in my mouth. As if I were a child being spared of the cruel reality.

"I heard you," I reply. I don't want to be rude to her. It's not her fault that I disappeared into time. If someone came up to me and said they were from another time, I wouldn't believe them either.

I'm not going to insist that she believes me either. I don't even have the energy to do that.

"You don't have to try; you've been through a lot." Miss Isabella touches my arm. "Tomorrow, when we get home, we'll—"

"I can't go to your house, miss." She tilts her neck to the side, a gracefully confused gesture. I continue, "I'm not going to bother you or your family."

"Ah, it won't be a bother at all. And I don't live with my family; I live with a friend."

My eyebrows furrow. "Is your friend a woman?"

"Yes."

"Is your friend married?"

"No."

"And you expect me to take shelter with two single women?" I can't believe what I'm hearing. "I know you feel guilty about hitting me with a… scooter? But I won't allow your honour to be ruined. That would be absurd."

Miss Isabella seems to have realised what she said.

"Wow, that's true. There's this honour thing… look, here in the future, you don't have to worry about that. Nobody cares."

"Doesn't anyone care about *honour*?" What kind of fate has humanity taken?

"No, that's not it. We care, but not like we did back then. Today we can live with whoever we want, without worrying so much about reputation," she explains. "I know it sounds confusing but trust me. Taking shelter with me won't harm anyone, I promise." She touches my skin again.

Once again, as much as it doesn't make sense, I can't feel anything in her words other than honesty. A shiver runs through my body at the warm touch. A touch of comfort. I don't know her, but I want her around. Even though she's lying, she seems to be the most real and tangible thing around me.

She seems to be… worried about me. Really worried.

"Why do you care?" My gaze meets hers. "You're not responsible for me, miss."

"I *want* to help you. I'm sure you'd do the same for me."

Would I? Yes, I would. I would never let a woman get into trouble if I could help it. The thought reminds me once again of Abigail. I wonder how she is, what she's doing without me. I'm the only family she has left.

The annoying noise of the overhead box next to me gets faster.

"What happened?" I ask Miss Isabella.

"Are you nervous?"

Yes, of course. How could I not be?

"I thought about my sister. I thought..." I stop talking. Nothing I say will make any difference.

She comes closer, attentive to my face.

"Benj... Your Grace, let me help you. We'll find your sister or someone from your family, and we'll sort everything out."

Isabella doesn't know what she's saying, but I understand why she's saying it. She doesn't believe me, and I know that because I see pity in her beautiful eyes. But what can I do? If this is a dream or a nightmare (although I strongly suspect it isn't), one day or another I'll have to wake up. And if not, what will I do on my own in a totally different world from the one I know?

I'm proud, but not stupid. She's offering me help, albeit out of pity, and I have no choice but to accept it.

I want to scream, pull my hair out, and punch a wall. But what good will that do? I need to think clearly about how to act. How to find out what the hell happened, and then how to get home to Abigail.

Now, Miss Isabella is my only chance. If pretending to believe that she believes in me is the way back, then so be it.

"That's fine. I'm very grateful for your help."

She smiles, a smile that lights up her delicate face, full of relief.

"Excuse me?" The nurse's voice sounds at the door. "Time to go," she says to Miss Isabella.

"Right. I have to go, Your Grace, but I'll see you

tomorrow." She takes her hand and starts to walk away. "Rest, and don't worry – everything will be fine."

I agree, even though I'm not so sure.

5

And what's this?

Benjamin

"*This, my dear, is yours.*"

Without understanding, I looked at the locket that my grandmother, Mary Waldorf, was holding out. When my father asked me to come, I knew I would find her in a bad way, but I didn't realise how bad. The woman in front of me was weak, pale, and her eyes were dull. Only then did I understand my father's call: my grandmother was dying, and perhaps this was my last chance to see her.

"*A cameo locket?*" *I asked, grabbing the object. It was beautiful, elegant. A feminine silhouette in mother-of-pearl, with a pink stone at the top of the figure's neck. A cameo like many I'd seen before, although I had the impression that there was something different about it.* "*But, Grandma, don't you think Abigail would make better use of it?*"

My grandmother, even without her strength, gave me a sweet smile.

"No, Benjamin. This cameo is yours. I've always known, ever since I got it from your grandfather, that I would pass it on to someone else one day." She closed her eyes, sighing heavily. "I didn't imagine it would be you, my naughty boy."

I felt a knot in my stomach and tears sprang to my eyes. She and I had always been close. Grandma was loving to all her grandchildren, but there was something extra with me. Something special. She was different from the other women in the family. Mystical, I would say. My father always joked that if we lived in the 1600s, she would definitely be accused of being a witch and would die at the stake.

"I'm glad it's you." She looked at me again.

"I don't understand." I took her warm, wrinkly hand.

"You don't have to understand for now." Grandma shook her head gently. Her eyes showed such certainty that it gave me goosebumps. "Just accept my gift. One day, you'll understand."

I open my eyes, jolting upright in bed. I'm sweating and can barely breathe, my grandmother's words as clear as water.

The cameo locket. It was after the cameo that everything disappeared. It was after reaching for it that I woke up here, in this strange world. How could I have forgotten that detail?

"Nurse!" I shout, the beeping next to me accelerating even more than yesterday. The room is bright, which makes me realise that it's already dawn.

It doesn't take long for an unfamiliar woman to enter the ward. She has her blonde hair up in a bun and is wearing the same baggy, masculine clothes and a pair of very thick-rimmed glasses. I've never seen such a model.

Well, I've never seen much around here.

"I need my things," I say. "Where are they?"

"Calm down." She touches my forearm.

We're in a time when touching seems to be normal, even between strangers. I've seen marriages happen for much less than that.

"I want my things!" I repeat. "I had a cameo with me; I can't lose it."

"Calm down, Benjamin. Your things are safe."

"Where? I need them!" I insist.

The blonde woman takes a deep breath, as if seeking patience. I understand. My manners have been lamentable ever since I found myself in this place, a real insult to chivalry. I should be ashamed, but there are too many emotions for me to deal with right now.

"I'll get them," she says.

I nod in agreement, waiting anxiously as I watch her turn. I run a hand through my hair, my chest tight with anguish. I still have no idea what happened, or how, but it must have something to do with the cameo.

First, it suddenly appeared in the study. Then, I saw a light come out of it just before it went out. Now I've dreamt about my grandmother, Mary, something that hasn't happened since her death four years ago.

And there's the feeling. This voice that seems to whisper in my ear that what she said to me that afternoon, about me finally understanding why she was giving me the locket, has something to do with this madness.

"Here, Benjamin." The nurse returns. "Your things."

I take the parcel she hands me, a strange, transparent cloth, and open it. My clothes are there: the jacket, the shirt, the tie, the trousers. I start groping in the pockets, and an immediate relief runs through my veins when I feel a bulge under the cloth. It's there. I haven't lost the cameo.

"Ah, thank God…" I mumble, taking the item out of my pocket and staring at it.

I run my hand over the mother-of-pearl, over the pink stone. Nothing happens. That's what I did last time, wasn't it? Well, I don't know for sure because I'm still here in this hospital bed with an unknown woman staring at me as if I'm a lunatic.

Probably because I really am. I don't know anything anymore.

"Can I take your drip so we can discharge you?" she asks me.

"Drip?" I have no idea what that is.

The woman replies without looking at me. "Yes, that liquid that's been keeping you hydrated."

Hmm. That makes sense.

I notice the woman's blue clothes and open necklace around her neck.

"What's this?"

She looks where my finger is pointing.

"A stethoscope. It's used to listen to your heartbeat."

Interesting. Very, very interesting.

"And what's that?" I now point to the noisy rectangle that has been chirping out of tune next to me all night, sounding like a dying bird.

"A monitor. These..." she points her finger at the scratches that appear on the surface, rising and falling, "are your heartbeats."

"Does everything here have to do with my heart?"

She opens her mouth, thinking. Before she can answer me, Miss Isabella enters the room. She has kept her word and is here, smiling as soon as she sees me. Suddenly, I feel safer.

I can't explain the reasons for this reaction.

Beep. Beep. Beep. Beep. Beep.

The annoying beeping gets faster. I look at the nurse, who looks at Isabella and holds back her laughter.

"What's wrong?" I ask.

"Someone's affected by their companion..." Is she making fun of me?

"Good morning," Isabella greets the nurse. Just like yesterday, her long dark hair is loose, and she's wearing a long-sleeved yellow shirt and blue trousers, very tight against her thighs. My eyes are involuntarily caught on them. I never imagined that a woman could be so sexy in men's clothes. I probably shouldn't be noticing anyone's curves in my current situation. Well, I may be crazy and lost, but I'm still a man.

Beep. Beep. Beep. Beep. Beep.

The damn whistle blows again.

"But what the..." I start to say, but I'm interrupted by the woman next to me.

"Good morning. Are you his carer?" the nurse asks Miss Isabella.

"Yes, it's me. Good morning, Your Grace." The pretty girl turns to me.

The nurse lowers her gaze, her expression still amused.

I'm glad other people are enjoying my tragedy. Marvellous.

"Good morning, Miss Isabella."

"Are you ready to go?"

"The doctor should be by soon," says the nurse. "If you want, you can change now, Benjamin."

I look at my arm and only then realise that she has already released me from the drip thing.

"Of course. Where can I do that, please?" I ask. I don't usually dress myself, but I don't see any valets available who can help me, and respectable ladies can't fill that position either.

"There in the bathroom." She points to a door at the far end of the hall. "Can you stand up?"

I nod because I feel physically well. At least there's that!

"Do you want to sign his discharge papers in the meantime?" the nurse asks Miss Isabella.

"Hmm… do I do that?"

"You could, since he doesn't have an identity card."

Once again, I wonder what they're talking about, but I decide not to voice my doubts.

Realising I want to urinate, I carefully bend down. These clothes are the height of indecency to look for a potty. There's nothing under the bed.

"What do you need, Benjamin?" the woman wants to know.

I shouldn't talk about this with a lady, but I don't see any other way. I have no other choice.

I sniffle, a little embarrassed. "I was looking for a chamber pot."

"Chamber pot? Oh, because you think..." She stops mid-sentence. "I'm going to introduce you to something better than a chamber pot. Come with me."

She heads towards the bathroom, waiting for me to follow. I exchange a look with Miss Isabella, who just nods, as if to encourage me.

God, I'm not a child.

I take the parcel with my clothes and follow the nurse into the tiny room.

"Look, you can use the toilet." She points to a crockery seat with a hole in the middle, very similar to the wooden toilets I know.

I tilt my body, analysing it carefully. There's a bit of water inside the toilet. How did they do that?

"After use, flush it." She points to a button on the wall. "Like this."

The nurse squeezes it, and immediately the water inside the toilet begins to swirl, only to disappear, and new water takes its place.

"Does this 'flushing' mean that the waste is eliminated without us having to deal with it?" The question jumps from my lips.

She smiles and nods. "Practical, isn't it?"

Impressive, that would be the right word. But indeed, practical.

"Don't forget to wash your hands here." She presses another metal button, this time over the sink next to it.

I'm still fascinated. Everything in the future works with buttons.

"Can you manage, or would you like some help?"

I stare at her serious face, wondering if I've heard correctly. Is she offering to *help me* relieve myself? What kind of question is that?

"I can do it myself. Thank you, miss."

Minutes after being alone, I'm still shocked by the freedoms of this time when, for the first time in my life, I flush a toilet.

* * *

Isabella

I'm just finishing signing the hospital documents when I see Benjamin emerge from the corridor and walk towards me, dressed in his Regency duke outfit, riding boots and all.

My God, what a handsome man. I love these Regency boots so much.

Yes, he's a bit mad, and yes, I have my part to play in this, but any reader of Regency novels would be thinking the same thing as me right now: Your Grace is a hot Greek god, drop-dead gorgeous.

Not to mention… I noticed his monitor speeding up when I entered the room. Coincidence? I ask you guys. I really don't know.

Well, I'd better watch out for my fanfic. I'm helping the man, not living an only-one-bed trope. Which, by the way, is another idea that could well be adapted into an interesting plot.

The maiden finds the wounded gentleman; he doesn't remember who he is. She takes him home against all social conventions. The man is beautiful, a temptation. They get closer, and...

"I suppose my clothes are inappropriate for the occasion," he says as soon as he reaches my side, interrupting my reverie.

I smile and leave the pen on the counter, handing the papers to the clerk. I was right before. Benjamin is quite tall and stronger than he first looked. I could easily wear heels next to him. Matheus was almost my size and didn't like me wearing them.

I'm amazed at the thought. I don't know why I've thought of it now.

"Not at all," I reply. "They're *vintage*, but we're in London. People won't even notice."

He doesn't seem to believe me, but he doesn't answer.

Last night was hectic. I got home late, and Cinthia was already in bed. It took me a while to get to sleep, but my creativity was still running high, so I managed to get a few ideas down on paper. Cinthia went to the station early to catch the train to Paris. Considering that taking a stranger home goes beyond the bounds of prudence, I decided not to tell her that Benjamin would be staying with me while we sorted everything out. I know, it's wrong of me, but if she were against it, I would never have been able to take him in.

And I feel I should, even if I don't understand why.

This man is... unlike anyone I've ever met. He's bruised and a little lost, but he's sincere. I can't see any danger when I meet his gaze. Even though he's a stranger, he treats me better than any other man ever has. Including my ex.

Not to mention that, since the accident wasn't serious,

it shouldn't take him long to get back to normal. Maybe he just needs to rest in a quiet place. I'll do my best to help him in any way I can. Of course, I have my work at the café, good thing I was off today, and he'll probably need to stay at home alone, but how long will that be? A day? Two days? A week at most?

It'll all work out, I'm sure. We'll be laughing about it soon. I don't doubt that this whole mess will give me ideas for a new book. It would be a good reward, and I could still use this piece of mischief as my avatar.

"Ready to go?" I ask, looking up.

Wow, he really is tall.

"Yes, miss." Benjamin straightens his posture and the lapels of his jacket.

"That's great. I live nearby, just five stations away." I wave my hand, and we start walking side by side.

"Stations?" he asks, following me. "What is that?"

What's that? Oh, that's right.

Right, I have to remember that, considering who he thinks he is, Benjamin won't recognise or understand anything I say.

"Our world has changed, Your Grace. Transport has become faster, and we have… stagecoaches of different kinds."

"No more carriages, then?"

"There are, but not to get around like we used to. And we don't use horses anymore. It's faster now."

Benjamin frowns but seems to understand.

It will be interesting to use my Regency knowledge to understand him. When I was writing, my research was so extensive that it sometimes took weeks. I admit that

Benjamin sounds *very much* like a true lord of the time, which indicates that he must have studied a lot about the period. Once he's recovered, I'll make a point of writing down his sources.

Benjamin nods, looking like he's going to ask me something. I wait a moment.

"You can ask me anything," I tell him as soon as we reach the hospital door. We're still inside.

He stares at me, moistening his plump lips.

"How do you know so much about my time? How do you know to call me Your Grace and what stagecoaches were?"

"I'm a writer of historical novels. I do a lot of research on the subject."

Benjamin lifts the corner of his mouth.

"Writer? Have you published any books?"

"I have, but they're online and self-published."

Once again, he doesn't understand what I'm saying.

"I'll show you when we get home. I think it'll be easier. I've even had a few ideas. Would you mind, with all your English manners, helping me?"

"Help how?"

"I don't know, can you tell me some interesting things about your time, so I can write them down in case I want to use them one day?"

Another nod.

I don't know if Benjamin really knows anything about the Regency period, but it seems that he does. At least he acts like it. I don't see a problem, if that's the case, in exchanging ideas, asking him a few questions. Maybe he'll inspire a character of mine or something.

"I'm a little afraid of the world we'll find outside," he admits.

I understand, and I think it's cute that he confesses his fear to me.

"Everything's going to be fine. Just… try not to get carried away."

We walk out of the hospital doors, and I immediately notice Benjamin's wide eyes as he takes in the outside world: the cars, the red double-decker buses, the crowds of people, each with their own style. The noise is intense – horns, music, and engines. He looks at the ground, the sky, and to the sides. He jumps when a bicycle passes us at high speed and curses at the cyclist. It's an impressive scene. If I didn't know that he'd hit his head, I could easily believe that he doesn't know any of this, given the panic in his eyes.

"Your Grace? Are you alright?"

Benjamin meets my gaze, swallowing dryly. "It's… a lot." He's breaking out in a cold sweat.

Yes, handsome duke. This whole situation is too much even for me. Lucky for you, I don't like to complain. "Can we go?"

He nods and follows my lead. We walk in silence through the bustling streets towards London Bridge station.

"I'll need to buy you an Oyster card," I say as we approach the entrance to the Underground. "It's a card so you can ride the Underground, which is the type of transport we're going to use now."

"Alright, what do I need to do?" he asks me, but I'm not sure Benjamin has understood me. His gaze is disorientated.

"Nothing." I stop in front of one of the refill machines. "Just wait and I'll arrange it."

I'm just finishing the operation when I notice a group of people walking past us, whispering and pointing at him.

Benjamin is immediately embarrassed.

"You said nobody would notice me."

I shrug, reassuring him. "They're tourists; they must think you're an actor or something."

He denies it with a sniffle. "I'd be terrible at it. I've been in theatre before, and it was a disaster."

I hold back the urge to laugh, imagining him in a play. I'm sure he'd be a hit. *And the Oscar goes to Benjamin Waldorf and his impressive performance.*

"What if we went to buy you some clothes? Current clothes like…" I look around for a reference, "that man over there."

Benjamin turns in the direction I've indicated. The guy standing in the corner of the station is wearing jeans, a T-shirt, a long brown coat, and white trainers. A basic look, but one that won't cost me much money if we buy everything at Primark. I don't consider myself an overspender, so my spending basically comes down to food and rent, which my father pays half of. That's why I'm able to put a little money aside each month in case of an emergency.

The curious case of Benjamin, the man who thinks he's come from the past and has only one sexy lord's outfit to wear, seems emergency enough.

"I don't have any money on me," Benjamin says.

"I do, don't worry about it."

He lets out a frustrated sigh. "I feel like I'm abusing

your kindness. Will you house me, pay for my transport and my clothes? How will I ever repay you?"

"Don't think about it now." I touch his arm. Benjamin follows the gesture with his gaze, and I wonder if I'm overstepping here. If the man thinks he's from the Regency period, he must think I'm a cheeky little bitch. I pull my hand away and continue, "Then, we'll think of a way for you to repay me. But I really think it's a good idea for us to buy you a change of clothes."

As much as it pains me to get you out of those boots, my lord.

"Very well, I'll do as you say. I won't make things any more difficult."

Satisfied, I hand him an Oyster card near the little automatic door.

"Here."

He looks at the card with a frown. I hold mine up to the reader and go through the turnstile, waiting.

Benjamin looks at me without moving.

"What's wrong?" I ask.

"I... I don't know what to do. Every time I needed to be transported, it was my coachman who took care of everything."

I take a deep breath, nodding.

"Tap the card like I did and go through."

He looks at the card again, obeying my command. The little door opens abruptly, and he jumps in fright.

"Good Lord, that's very aggressive," Benjamin comments.

Going down the escalators is another challenge.

"Hold on to the handrail," I say. He watches the steps

go down but doesn't go any further. There are people waiting behind us. "Benjamin, come on."

"I'm going to fall." Benjamin shudders.

"You won't." I try to calm him down, but it's no use. We decide – I decide – to take the lift.

Benjamin seems more frightened with every passing second.

"This room is moving."

"Yes, and the Underground will move too, but forwards."

Arriving at the line, Benjamin almost falls backwards as the train approaches.

"Damn, this is too fast."

"Yes, and that's why it works." I take his hand before the door closes. It's crowded; there are people everywhere. Benjamin frowns, looking at them in astonishment. If he carries on like this, he's going to get some permanent wrinkles.

As soon as the tube starts moving, Benjamin falls over a scowling man.

"Careful, boy!" the old man complains.

"Oops!"

I grab his jacket, making him hold one of the iron cylinders.

"Miss Isabella," he tries to talk over the noise of the tracks. "I…"

"Just hold on. Whenever there's a spare seat, you sit down."

He thinks for a moment but does as I say. Well, almost. Benjamin not only holds onto the bar, but he sticks his whole body to it, clinging for his life.

The people near us stare at him, some laughing, others shaking their heads. He doesn't seem to notice. He's too scared for that.

I glance at the carriage panel, checking the remaining stations. Six, considering that now we're going shopping and not straight home.

It's going to be quite an adventure.

6

Your Grace, meet Your Grace

Benjamin

Today's world is chaos.

Noisy, too fast, and surprisingly diverse. We're leaving the shopping centre after buying my new clothes. I feel scared and sweaty, but I try to calm down in the midst of the euphoria. However, I've managed to see some advantages in all this hubbub. Although I'm still wearing my own clothes, I like the jeans, for example. An elegant and comfortable fabric, although I found them a little revealing because they were tighter. Miss Isabella, however, assured me that they weren't, that I looked good in them. She even gave me an unseemly look.

I liked it too. More than I should have, I suspect.

I don't know exactly what this lady does to me. Over the last few years, a lot has changed in my life, not as radically as waking up in the future, but I think I've ended up becoming a man who doesn't even know himself.

Before Barney went off to war, I was just a second son, with no titles to inherit and a great desire to enjoy life's pleasures. I did, in fact, for years. Women, bohemian nights, gambling on friends' estates… God, it seems like ages ago. Well, it was, considering my current situation. After my brother was killed on the battlefield, everything changed.

Not immediately. My father was still alive; the weight of the title was still only in the distant future. Nobody expected the Duke of Waldorf to die suddenly. But he did, so I had to abandon my libertine life and assume the mantle of responsibility. After all, I had a sister in my care.

Abigail… I wonder what she'll think of all this madness, if she'll believe me when I tell her what happened. If I tell her… because revealing this adventure would be risky. They might think I'm mad and send for the doctor. Then, there's the chance that I won't be able to return. No. I can't be pessimistic. It's better not to think about that possibility.

"I still don't understand," I say to her. "Don't they wear boots anymore these days?"

"No. I mean, they do, but not these riding boots, unfortunately. They wouldn't go with today's casual style."

"Casual? Is what we bought for me casual?"

Miss Isabella nods. "Yes."

"Even my undergarments?"

She starts laughing. "That word is so funny."

Is it? I don't see why. "What could be funny about undergarments?"

"If I introduced you to the elephant underwear, you'd be surprised."

Elephant what? Miss Isabella notices my expression and struggles to stop laughing.

"What you'll be wearing now are boxers, Your Grace." She runs her eyes over me, tilting her delicate neck to the side. "I imagine they will look excellent."

I frown. What a rude and impolite comment for a lady. Not as rude as the shiver it caused in my body, but… well, she provoked it.

It seems I have no choice but to accept modern clothes. At least I'll be dressed like everyone else while I figure out how to get back. The stares from others bother me a little, even though I'm used to being the centre of attention – ever since I became a duke, of course.

But I'm not being discreet in my stares at her, either. I try not to show it, but the clash of realities is too great. Immense. How could I have imagined that shopping centres would spring up, full of shop windows and strange lights, which I discovered were connected to electricity? According to Isabella, some people today don't even know what a gas lamp is.

She told me that England has a new king, after more than seventy years with a queen, Elizabeth II. And that there was another great queen before her, Victoria, during whose reign much of modernity began. I also saw a giant metallic bird in the sky as we left the shopping centre, which she told me was an aeroplane, where people travel to all the corners of the world. Boats now are only for cargo or luxury, and journeys that used to take months are completed in a few hours. I think it's a big step forward.

Society has also changed a lot, and that's what pleases

me the most. It's shocking, but it's progress. Parents walk with their children without servants around; there is no longer any issue with showing affection in public; and couples are formed in all kinds of ways: people of different races or the same sex. Women are free, more independent. They work; they don't need to be married to guarantee a secure future, nor are they their husband's property if they do. Miss Isabella gave me a brief summary of the history of the fight for these rights when we were on the Underground on the way home. I was very pleased with what I heard, and I definitely want to know more about it later. Which reminds me again of Abigail and why I *need* to go back to her, because in our time, things unfortunately don't work like that.

"Tell me more about your writing career," I ask Miss Isabella, in an attempt to distract me from my anxieties.

She sighs. "Well, I've been writing for a while; I started with fanfic on the internet." I have no idea what fanfic or the internet are, but I don't want to bother her with my questions again. "I studied, improved my writing, and published a few novels independently. At the same time, I was teaching English in Brazil, working two jobs. Then life happened and… well, creativity decided to take a holiday with no return date."

I'm not sure what happened to her creativity, but she seems very upset about the situation.

"I live here," Miss Isabella says as soon as we arrive in front of a brick building. I'm carrying bags for the first time in my life. If it hadn't been for Isabella reminding me, I would have forgotten them inside the shop.

The task is not so bad.

"We'll have to take the stairs because the lift broke down."

She's already explained to me what a lift is, and we even used one in the Underground. I also know about escalators, mobile phones, and Kindle, a formidable pageless library. If you told me one day that we could carry as many books as we wanted in our pockets, I would certainly have laughed.

This whole story only makes me realise that I know absolutely nothing about this strange world.

I stop as we reach the stairs of the flat, giving way.

"You can go up," she says.

"Please." I hold out my hand.

We climb the stairs to the third floor. I try to be a gentleman and not notice the buttocks in front of me, even though they are in evidence. I don't want to be rude. Miss Isabella is always attentive to me, to my reactions. She would notice. I'd like to know what I'm feeling, what this whirlwind in my mind and this storm raging in my chest mean. At the same time, I try my best not to lose my head and throw myself into the Thames. I want to be grumpy, but how can I be if the woman keeps smiling at me?

She is the gentleness in all my chaos. How can someone I've only just met become my synonym for security?

"We're here," Isabella says as soon as we stop in front of flat 34. "Come in." She gives me room to pass, but I hold out my hand.

"Please, you first."

She blushes in an adorably sweet way. A way that makes my body wake up, suddenly anxious. Once again,

I shouldn't be thinking about her like this. Once again, I don't mind doing it.

As soon as Miss Isabella passes me, I go in and pull the white door shut. The corridor is dark, and the room smells good. Sweet, soft… her house smells like home.

"Duke?" she calls.

Is it me she's talking to? Why is she calling me by my title?

"Duke, wher… oh, there you are, Your Grace."

I'm very confused by her talking to me without looking at me, but before I can ask, I notice the four-legged ball of fur running towards us. The small dog, a Welsh corgi, also sees me. Dogs have remained the same in the future. I confess I'm happy to finally recognise something without difficulty.

He walks past Isabella, his eyes riveted on me. I've always loved animals, so much so that I felt uncomfortable when they made me go hunting. I'd go, but I didn't put in any effort. I never saw the point in killing an animal for fun.

Leaving the bags on the floor, I bend down and pick up the little creature. He's heavier than he looks, but he's still a puppy.

"Hello, dog," I say.

"Duke."

"Yes?" I turn to Isabella, feeling a lick on my chin.

She laughs. I've heard many sounds today, but her laughter is the most beautiful.

"His name is Duke." She points to the pet with a nod. "He seems to like you."

I look at the dog, and then at her again. "Is the animal's name Duke?"

She nods. "Yes. As well as being fancy, I once read a novel in which the coachman was called Duke, and I liked the idea." She approaches and picks up the furry paw. "Your Grace, meet Your Grace."

Fancy... centuries have passed, but the fascination with the title remains intact.

The dog blinks its round eyes and wiggles its ears at me.

"Pleased to meet you... Your Grace." Dear lord, I am talking to a dog.

I leave the puppy on the floor, following Isabella into the living room. With a few exceptions, I can identify most of the furniture in the small space.

"What do you think?" she asks me.

"It's great. Of all the places we've been, this is the most normal."

She smiles again. "Make yourself at home. I'll just show you..." Miss Isabella stops talking and takes her mobile phone out of her pocket. The surface, which I've learnt is called a screen, is lit up with various numbers and a portrait of a person. She explains the many functions of the object, but I'm confused about some of them.

"Is something wrong?" I ask, noticing her startled expression.

"No, nothing. It's my father." Isabella walks away from me, disappearing down the corridor. "Hi, Dad."

I can't see her, but I can hear her.

"Hi, darling. How are you?" The male voice sounds distant and clipped.

"Fine. The connection's a bit poor – where are you?"

"In the street. I'm going to visit my grandad, but he's not well."

At the mention of her family, I realise that I know nothing about Isabella. Just the basics: that she lives with a friend and that she's not from here. She told me she's Brazilian when I asked about her accent.

I'll have to correct that later. She's giving me too much attention, and I think showing an interest in getting to know her is the least I can do.

"I'm sorry, my dad called." She returns.

I must have got lost in my own thoughts because I didn't hear the rest of the call.

"Are you alright? You look worried."

She sighs, pushing her hair out of her face. "My great-grandfather is unwell, and my father is nervous. The man is already very old."

"Allow me to ask you about your great-grandfather's health."

The lady presses her lips together. "Permission granted."

"Is he bedridden? In a hospital? I can accompany you, so you don't go alone," I offer.

She denies it with a half-smile.

"He's in Japan. There's nothing to be done."

"Do you have family in Japan *and* Brazil?"

"Yes. My parents are divorced."

Divorced? That is a very rare situation.

"Divorces are common nowadays," Isabella explains. "There's still a legal process but without the difficulties of previous centuries. My mum and dad have been separated since I was a child. It was better that way, believe me."

Well, what else could I do?

"Would you like to take a shower?" she offers. "You must be tired from all the excitement today."

I'm not denying it, although I suspect I won't sleep. "Can I have a bath?"

"Of course." She stops, and her expression turns mischievous. "One question: are you used to showering every day?"

I frown at the unseemly question. "It's not necessary every day, though…"

"Oh, no, no, no. As long as you're here with me, Your Grace will bathe every day!" The dog reappears, jumping on her leg. "No, Duke. I didn't call you. I'm talking to him, the other Your Grace." Isabella laughs.

I continue, "I was going to say that, although it's not necessary, I like to bathe every day. There are rare exceptions."

She seems truly relieved. God, baths are nice, but for her, they seem like a vital necessity.

"So it's agreed that we'll both smell nice."

No problem for me. I've already noticed her perfume. Isabella Kato smells of vanilla, which I like a lot.

She speaks again, "Come on, get your clothes and I'll show you the bathroom."

I obey the command without question. I'm an unexpected guest, and I really don't want to be a nuisance. I take a change of clothes from the bag, choosing to wear pyjamas since it's late afternoon. Miss Isabella guides me to the bathroom, switching on the light as soon as we enter the cubicle. The little animal with the noble name follows us.

"The bath is here. This towel is clean, and you can use the shampoo and soap all you like."

"Shampoo is…"

She understands immediately. "A hair soap. Liquid, which is more practical. Take your time to relax and I'll make us something to eat while you wash."

Isabella starts to leave the bathroom, but I move.

"What?" she wants to know.

"I…" I shiver, crossing my hands behind my back. "I need someone to prepare me a bath."

Miss Isabella presses her lips together in a thin line. Is she holding back a laugh? That's the third time that's happened. But I'm being honest. I don't know how to prepare a bath. I've never had to.

"Of course, because you're used to having your baths prepared. Here's what we'll do: I'll prepare this one, and you watch so you can be independent and prepare the next ones."

It makes sense that she wouldn't want to carry out tasks like that.

"Of course, whatever's best for you."

"Fine, then watch this manoeuvre."

She bends down and slowly turns a handle on the bath. As soon as the water starts to flow, I realise that the strange spout is a tap. And the water is probably thermal because the steam indicates that it's hot.

I didn't realise there were hot springs in London. It must be another change in the passage of time.

"And that's it, Your Grace. Your bath is ready."

In other words, all I have to do is turn on the damn tap.

The dog wags his tail as soon as he hears the two magic words.

"Considering that the dog is also called that and that nowadays you no longer use formalities, can we call each other by our first names?" I suggest. "I think it will be less confusing for the poor animal."

She smiles, holding out her hand for me to shake. "Well done, Benjamin. Call me Bella, then."

I return the handshake. "Too intimate. I don't usually call other people by their nicknames. Well, except for my sister."

"It's three letters apart from Isabella." She rolls her eyes. "Do you think you can make that effort?"

There's a certain provocation in her voice. I like that. People, especially after I inherited the title, don't usually talk to me like that. And deep down, she's right. Three letters make little difference.

"Alright." I agree, "I'll call you Bella."

"That's great. If I feel we're unequal, I can call you Ben. I think it's... sophisticated."

Ben. I've never been called that, but on her lips, I like the nickname. It sounds nice. "No problem."

Bella bends down and picks up Duke, the dog. "Make yourself at home." She smiles, walking away. "See you soon."

I sigh as I close the door, listening to the sound of the water filling the bath, the steam fogging up the mirror over the sink. I'm so exhausted that even taking off my clothes takes a lot of effort.

As soon as I get nude and slide into the bath, I try to forget what happened to me and allow myself to relax.

7

Pizza?

Isabella

There's a handsome, naked man in my bathroom.

I know, of all the things I could think of, this shouldn't be first on the list. But it is. Because Benjamin is really handsome and he's naked, "without undergarments" as he says, taking a bath a few metres away from me.

I consider today a small victory. The poor chap freaked out every five seconds, but with an otherworldly elegance. I wonder if he's ever sat crooked before in his life, or if he's ever changed the tone of his voice. But despite everything, this noble, English behaviour baffles me.

Because every second I spend next to him, it feels like Benjamin is telling me the truth.

I leave Duke on the floor and go into the kitchen. I had a shower earlier before I went to pick him up, so I can relax. I give up on preparing anything; I'm too tired for that. I'm no whiz in the kitchen; after recent events, even less so. I decide to order a pizza. There probably weren't any pizzas in 1817, but I doubt Benjamin won't like it. A soft drink should also do the trick. I want to watch closely when he tries a Coke for the first time.

Wow, here I am believing that this is the first time the guy is going to try this drink. See how confused I am? I need to sort myself out.

While I wait for the pizza to arrive, I think about my father and the sadness I heard in his voice. His grandfather must really be ill, from what I understand. I also remember that I have to call my mum and answer the messages from my sister and Cinthia, who wanted to know how I was. I thought it best not to take my eyes off Benjamin while we were in the street. Firstly because it was nice to look at him. But also, what if I lost the man? It was better not to get distracted on my phone.

I pull it out of my pocket now and see a new notification from my friend.

Cinthia: Darling, I'm home. How are things going over there?
Cinthia: Oh, I left a piece of chocolate cake in the fridge – you have to eat it or it'll spoil.

I sit on the sofa, typing.

Me: Hi, hun. I'm sorry I didn't answer – it was a bit rushed. Don't worry, I will eat it. How are you? Did you get there OK?

She comes online a few moments later.

Cinthia: I'm tired, but fine. I'll tidy up tomorrow; today I'm going to relax. What about your unknown subject? Have you managed to find out anything about him?

I could tell you the whole story, about him thinking he's from the nineteenth century, about having nowhere to go, but that would mean saying that he's a guest here in the flat, and that I'm crazy.

Both things are true, but I prefer to avoid the sermon.

Me: I managed to sort it out. Don't worry about it.

I'm not exactly lying. Although I don't know anything about him yet, things are moving along, so… I can consider this a kind of resolution.

Cinthia: Good. I'm going to sleep because my eyes are closing. We'll talk tomorrow.
Me: OK. Sleep well and enjoy France. Eat lots of sweets for me.
Cinthia: Lol. You got it. Kiss. I'll speak to you soon.

The pang of guilt is present. I don't feel right hiding all this from her, but something tells me to. I'm not used to having secrets. I wear my heart on my sleeve; I've never had any reason to keep anything to myself. The most interesting thing that's ever happened to me was being dumped for someone else. Benjamin, however, is not like that.

He's… different. Not just because of the situation, but

because of his manner too. Maybe it's my fascination with lords and gentlemen, but the guy, from what I've seen so far, is perfect. Kind, polite, and clearly concerned about not bothering me.

It's nice to have someone care about me for a change. I don't like to complain, but this time alone has made me realise that I had been dating – for over a year – a guy who was... *not so great*. Matheus was decent, hard-working, and studied to get good enough grades to pass his exams, but that's it. He wasn't the type to give you the runaround, but neither to ask about your great-grandfather's health. He didn't look at me with attention or interest. Sometimes, he didn't even seem to hear me.

I instantly feel melancholic. Matheus, the arsehole boy, is in the past. As for Benjamin, "the magic man", what's done is done. Then, if necessary, I'll bear the consequences. I'm about to type a message to my sister Laura when I hear a strange noise in the bathroom. With a frown, I go over, stopping in front of the closed door.

"Your Grace?" I knock on the door. Duke lets out a low bark, approaching happily. "Not you, sweetheart. Ben?" I correct myself.

"Yes?" the muffled baritone voice replies.

"Are you alright?"

A second of silence.

"Yes. I..." He hesitates. "I tried to empty the bath, but the drain won't come out."

I let out a little laugh. If he thinks he's a duke, he must imagine that he has servants even to dress him. Let's not forget that he asked me to prepare his bath. So here he is, struggling to empty it. Cute.

"Are you dressed? I can show you how to empty it if you let me in."

The handle turns and the door opens. I almost lose my breath at what I see.

Unfortunately, Benjamin doesn't have a towel tied around his waist, showing off his muscular body. The scriptwriter in my life failed miserably in this scene. He has already put on the pyjamas I bought him: light-grey joggers and a basic white T-shirt. However... the fabric is glued tightly to his strong chest. Tight enough that I can see he has a six pack. A duke from the past with a six pack.

Oh my God, that's delicious. I wouldn't mind dressing that little body.

"Bella?" The question makes me look away from him. I'm still mesmerised. His dark hair is damp, wet, and messy. Beautiful. I conclude that Benjamin is hot no matter the era, from the Stone Age to the year 3000.

"Yes, I'll show you." I stand next to the bath. "Just turn here."

Benjamin nods as the water begins to flow down the drain. "Where can I hang this?" He shows me the towel.

"Leave it to me." I take the towel and leave the bathroom, and he follows me. "Are you hungry? I ordered us some pizza."

"Pizza?" I hear the confused voice behind me.

"Yes, it's a kind of bread with cheese and pepper..." I remember that perhaps he has no idea what pepperoni is. "It's an Italian delicacy. Very tasty," I complete, hanging the towel on the rail near the kitchen.

"If you say it's tasty, I'll believe you."

I look at him, and Benjamin is standing in the middle of the room, his arms folded behind his back. Very formal.

"You can sit down." I wave my hand. "Make yourself at home."

"You first, miss."

I obey because I want to put him at ease. And because my little dreamy side likes to be treated like this, with such kindness. Benjamin settles into the armchair opposite the sofa. Duke comes up to him, wagging his furry tail. Ben smiles as he picks him up.

Wow, how cute is this man holding my little ball of fur.

"Do you like dogs?" I ask.

"A lot. I like animals in general."

"Do you have a pet back home?"

"My sister had a cat, but it died a few years ago. He was rather skittish, and…"

The sound of the intercom makes Benjamin stop talking.

"The pizza." I stand up. "Just a moment."

A few minutes pass before I return to the living room after picking up the pizza from the delivery man. As soon as I enter the room, Benjamin puts Duke on the floor and stands up, nodding slightly.

A true lord, no doubt about it.

"Would you like to try it with a soft drink? It's a fizzy juice."

He thinks for a moment. "Do you recommend it?"

I nod. "I really like it."

"Very well, I accept. Thank you very much."

I go to the kitchen, get two cans of Coke Zero, two

glasses, and the paper napkins. "If you're going to eat pizza, you have to eat it with your hands."

I settle into my seat and Benjamin sits down too. I serve the pizza to him, and he analyses the slice with a frown.

"It smells good." He takes a bite. As he chews, his expression changes. It's clear that he enjoys the pizza.

"Well?" I ask, eating a piece too.

"Very good. Simple and tasty." He keeps eating.

"Now take a sip of Coke." I open the can and pour him a glass.

Benjamin is still chewing as he stares at the bubbling liquid. "Fascinating…" He grabs the glass and smells the drink. "Sweet, isn't it?"

I nod, watching Benjamin drink his Coke without even blinking.

He swallows and grimaces. "That's different…"

"Good different?"

He looks at me, one corner of his lip lifting. "Good different. I was right to trust you."

I wasn't expecting this phrase, and I know he's referring to food, but it touches me. Because not only am I trusting him not to be dangerous, but Benjamin is also trusting me with his difficult dilemmas. It's very rewarding to know that I am making a difference in someone's life. To be appreciated, even for a meal suggestion.

We eat in silence for a few minutes. I realise that Benjamin is deep in thought, a little lost.

"Do you want to talk?" I suggest, as soon as I've finished eating. "Tell me about yourself, about what you…" *think*, "you remember."

He wipes his mouth with a napkin, nodding. "Well,

I don't want to bother you, but I don't mind telling you who I am."

And I don't mind listening to him. "Tell me about it."

"I'm the second son. My twin brother, Barney, was the eldest, the heir to the title. Our mother died when my younger sister, Abigail, was three. Our father was a serious man but loving in his own way." There's a lot of sadness in his words. An intriguing nostalgic tone. Benjamin continues: "My brother went to fight in the war against Napoleon. I imagine you know about that period."

I agree. I've studied so much about the Napoleonic Wars that I could write a book about it. "Yes, I know enough."

"He died on the battlefield. My father died not long after him, having sunk into sadness. When they'd both gone, it was just me and my sister. Now… now Abigail is alone."

My heart feels like it's tied up with string. My God, the way Benjamin tells things seems so true. Honest. Where is his subconscious getting all this drama from?

This also explains his despair when he mentioned his sister earlier. We're talking about 1817, a time when women were completely helpless. Thinking about Abigail, even though I don't know her, fills me with anguish. Thankfully, this story isn't real. Right?

"Why did your brother go to fight?" I ask.

"Barney was different from me," Ben continues. "Responsible, honourable. The best man I've ever known."

"You're honourable, Ben. All I've seen since I met you is honour."

Which is true. Considering that he thinks he's in the wrong century, Benjamin hasn't raised his voice or exploded around me once since he opened his eyes in hospital. Matheus blew up at me for much less. I chase the thought away. I don't want to think about Matheus.

"I've become honourable, Bella." Ben shrugs. "If we can become that. I was a bon vivant, an irresponsible libertine. Barney was honour itself. He went to war proud, and I'm sure he died that way too. After I took over the title, I changed because I thought he deserved such consideration."

"What do you mean?" I ask, trying to ignore the images my mind wants to form when I think of him as a rake.

"I started acting like a duke, like a responsible man. I kept some things from my life before, but the fun, the nights of pleasure… I didn't take part in that anymore. I didn't even have time, really. My sister suffered their loss a lot. It was… difficult. Abigail spent months in bed."

Depressed, probably. And how could she not be, after losing her father and brother?

"You're close, then."

Benjamin nods. "Very. It's funny because I only realised it when I lost my brother and father."

I know what it's like. I'd never stopped to think about it until I found myself far away from everyone on an island on the other side of the world.

"I'm sorry, Ben. You've been through a lot."

He takes a deep breath, trying to smile.

"What about you? So far, we've only talked about me."

I tell him about my family, about how my parents split up, and about my mum's second marriage. When Benjamin asks me why I decided to come to London, I don't reveal my break-up with Matheus. That would definitely spoil our conversation. But I do tell him about Laura and her noble Canadian husband, about how my sister unexpectedly fell in love with the man she met in a coffee shop. Benjamin finds it curious and says he's friends with a guy who had a baroness cousin in Quebec, in the 1800s, of course. It's funny how he has a very solid background for this mental confusion. There are no gaps or holes in the stories he tells me; everything is perfectly aligned.

Absolutely easy to believe.

I'm not sure how long we talk. I know I could spend hours here, listening to his words, even if they are fantasy. A fantasy that seems more real than anything I've ever heard.

"You must be exhausted," I say when Benjamin can't help yawning. "Do you want to lie down?"

He apologises and nods, running his hand through his already dry hair. Apologising for yawning... my God.

"I think it's a good idea," he says.

Looking at him like this, in his normal clothes and relaxed, I would never have said that he was the same madman I hit yesterday.

"Is it OK for you to sleep in the living room? My friend isn't here, but I think it's unfair to offer her bed since she doesn't know you're here."

"She doesn't know?" He frowns. "You didn't tell her?"

I shake my head. "No, because I was afraid that she wouldn't agree. Let's face it, we don't know each other, and you could be a murderer or an abuser."

He lets out a laugh. I think it's the first time I've seen him laugh. I hope this happens more often.

"You're right, miss. I apologise for you having to lie."

"Don't worry, I'll tell her later." I stand up. "I'll get a pillow and a blanket." I return a few moments later and hand him his things. "You know how to cover yourself, don't you?" I ask, as the man doesn't seem independent.

"Yes. Thank you." Benjamin nods again, and I look at Duke, standing quietly at the foot of the sofa.

"Is Your Grace coming with me or staying with Your Grace?" I ask him.

The puppy doesn't even move.

"Come on, even he can't resist a duke," I joke, and Benjamin laughs again. Our gazes meet and something jumps in my chest. Deliciously disturbing. "Good night, Ben. Sleep well."

I'm halfway down the corridor when I hear a thick voice.

"Bella?" he calls me, and I turn round again.

"Yes."

Benjamin sighs, before saying, with heartbreaking honesty: "Thank you for helping me. I'm eternally in your debt."

I'm suddenly emotional. "There's no debt. I'm happy to help you, believe me."

I leave him alone and lie on the bed, staring at the ceiling and thinking about everything.

I know that some would say that I'm crazy for harbouring a stranger, that I'm reckless. That's probably true, but I can't help it. Knowing that he's there, sleeping on the sofa, brings me nothing but peace of mind.

With a soft smile, I let my heavy eyes close and fall asleep peacefully. Helping Benjamin seems to me to be my best decision in the last few months.

8

I could be right

Benjamin

"What is it, Your Grace? What are your dilemmas?"

At the sound of Bach's notes, Duke the dog blinks his round eyes and wiggles his ears, staring at me.

That's what we did today. We faced each other.

Bella had to work, so I was left alone with the dog. She looked worried when she left the house, but I made sure I wouldn't cause any problems. Very quickly, Bella introduced me to the fridge, the microwave, and Netflix, where I can watch plays through a screen.

Everything in the future has screens; it's exhausting.

I also asked if there was a way of using the computer to do research. If I'm in the future, there must be some document that can give me some information about what happened, how they dealt with my disappearance, or what my sister's fate was. Bella has done at least twenty searches since we met, according to her on a Google thing, a huge repository of information on the internet. I didn't understand a thing, but I know it works. However, I couldn't search for anything because I must have pressed the wrong button, and the computer didn't obey me.

The result: idleness, without moderation.

"Alexa, please stop the music."

The little round box lights up and the music stops playing. I was impressed by this modernity, an object that obeys voice commands. I realised that everything in the future is easier but also lazier. From what I've seen, most things require minimal physical effort. That can't be very good in the long run.

"I'm home." Isabella's voice catches my attention, as well as the dog's. "Hi, sweetheart. Hi, Ben, how are you?"

I stand up and nod slightly. "Bella. Welcome back. Yes, I'm fine, and you?"

She smiles at me. "Good. You don't have to get up every time I enter the room."

"Ah, I think I do. I'm a gentleman."

She tilts her neck to the side, her eyes flashing something I can't identify.

"Yes, you are." Bella sighs. "How was your day?"

Discouraged, I sit down again. "I stared at His Grace to the sound of Bach's notes."

Duke wags his tail and seems to smile.

"Hmm, I see you, him, and Alexa got up to something," Isabella jokes.

If you'd told me last week, in the midst of all that intense newspaper work, that today I'd be wasting time with a dog and a… strange round box, I would never have believed it. It's my turn to laugh. Better that than crying.

"I couldn't do my research," I tell her.

"Why?"

"I pressed something wrong, and the computer didn't obey me."

Bella puts her bag aside and walks over to the computer on the coffee table. "Can I sit next to you? If you like, we can do some research together."

The question bothers me. She's in her own home; she shouldn't be asking my permission for anything.

"Of course, please." I gesture with my hand, standing up again until she settles down. "How was work?" I say as soon as I sit down again. I can smell the soft scent of vanilla as we get closer. Lovely.

"Good. Normal. Every day at the café is the same."

"Do you work in a café? Tell me more about that."

She seems surprised by my interest, but agrees, switching on the computer.

"Yes, I do."

"I thought you were a writer."

Which, when I found out, really amazed me. I've always loved writing, and I've never found someone with whom I can share my passion.

"I am, but I'm an independent one. I publish on the internet on a specific website. And I haven't written in over a year now."

"Why not?"

Isabella smiles humourlessly, suddenly uncomfortable. "It's a long story; I'll tell you about it sometime," she says.

I feel there's something more there because I realise there's a twinge of pain in her voice. God, do I already know her that well?

"Forgive me, I didn't mean to invade your privacy."

"You didn't, it's just that the subject is really unpleasant. Tell me, what are we looking for?" She is talking about the research we are doing now.

I think for a second, putting my doubts about Isabella's personal life to one side. There's so much I'd like to find out. About me and about her.

"Well, I think we can start with my name."

"Right."

Isabella types so fast that I can barely follow the movement of her fingers.

"Look, this is your Wikipedia page." She turns the screen towards me.

"What?"

"Wikipedia. Were there encyclopaedias in your day?" Isabella wrinkles her brow.

"Yes, in various volumes, in alphabetical order. They cost a small fortune."

She seems more animated. "So, it's the same, but on the internet, for free, and people can edit and add information."

That easy? How curious and practical. The modern world never ceases to amaze me.

I stare at the computer screen, squinting against the bright lighting, and analyse the information about myself. There are no images, just a brief summary of my being the fifteenth Duke of Waldorf and some random data.

"Look, it says you were born on 4 November 1785, but there's no date of death." Isabella points her finger at the screen. "Are you a Scorpio? Wow, I would never have guessed."

I think it's funny that she guessed my astrological sign so easily. These mystical subjects aren't usually discussed by women.

"Why not?" I ask.

"I don't know, I just thought it would be something else. Although, thinking about it now, it makes sense. You have some Scorpio characteristics."

"Like what?" Only Isabella could arouse my curiosity about something as illogical as the zodiac in the midst of a time-travelling crisis. Jesus, Mary, Joseph, who have I become?

"Ah, you seem loyal, attentive, sensual…" She stops talking, blushing immediately. "I'm sorry!"

I can't help smiling, and I don't blame myself for it. Let's not forget that before becoming a responsible, commitment-phobic duke, I had my naughty days.

"No, no, please continue," I tease.

Isabella nudges my arm. "Benjamin, stop embarrassing me! You're doing it on purpose."

We start laughing together, and I feel normal and light for five seconds. "You started it."

"You must know you're handsome – it's no secret."

Yes, I'm not falsely modest. I'm vain, and I really appreciate women enjoying my company and looking at me with desire. But Isabella… it's different when I think she's attracted to me.

"You're beautiful too, Bella. Don't think I haven't noticed."

She's really blushing now, a flush creeping up the skin of her neck. And God, what the hell am I doing flirting with her? Still, I can't take my eyes off her pretty face. I've got used to her loose hair, her sudden touches. I like them. I like *her*, because it's impossible not to.

"Let's get back to the research." She clears her throat.

At least one of us has good judgment.

"Right…" I look at the screen again. "Why isn't there a date of death? Do you think it might have something to do with my disappearance?"

Isabella opens her mouth, then closes it. "No, maybe they just didn't register it."

I don't think so, and it seems to me that she's trying to deny something very obvious. I continue to read the tiny text. I stop, my heart racing at the sight of my sister's name.

"This is Abigail Melissa Waldorf! Is there any information about her too?"

Isabella denies it immediately. "Not here, if the letters are in black, there's no link." I don't understand anything at all. Bella adds before I can ask, "Let me open another tab."

Isabella types my sister's name into the bar at the top of the screen. Unfortunately, we don't find anything apart from a few, according to Bella, social media profiles of some Abigails who aren't her. I still can't get over the fact that nowadays people have long-distance relationships. How can you live in society if everyone is in their own home?

While some advances are fantastic, others are very inconsistent.

"There really isn't anything, Ben." Isabella checks the screen once more.

"God in heaven, what happened to her? If Gustave handed her over to anyone, I swear…"

"Gustave?" Isabella asks me.

"My cousin. He's the next heir to the title, considering I have no children or nephews. The man is a scoundrel; he only thinks about taking advantage of others. He would certainly spend my fortune on courtesans and drinks, if not on something worse. And he would be legally responsible for Abigail in my absence, but I'm sure the bastard would try to get rid of her at the first opportunity, marrying her off to anyone or something worse. Abigail would be lost in his hands."

The mere thought of what Abigail might have suffered makes my heart drop into my stomach. If I don't return, it means that she's lost all of us, that she's left alone. I don't even know if there's anyone she could ask for help. Maybe Howard could help her, but…

Wait, Howard! The newspaper!

"What's wrong?" Isabella realises my epiphany.

"I own a newspaper in Bath. Can't we get some information about it?"

"We can check. What was the name of the newspaper?"

"*The Daily Bath.*"

She goes back to typing on the small keys. Several results appear on the screen. On the right-hand side, I recognise an image of one of the newspaper's front pages.

"Here, this seems to be it."

Bella clicks on the image. The page that appears is confusing, a bit of a mess.

"Wow, your newspaper was famous back then," Bella comments, her eyes still on the screen.

"Famous?" I find that strange. The *Daily* was well known in Bath, but famous is too strong a word to define it. "What do you mean, famous?"

"It says that the newspaper was a tradition in the city from 1813."

It's still strange to think of this information as something from two hundred years ago. After all, for me, that time feels like yesterday. Literally.

"Yes, the year I founded it in secret."

She looks at me. "In secret?"

"Yes, only a select group of people know that I'm involved with the newspaper. It wasn't my choice but my father's request. It could have been complicated for him if the family name was involved if any of the stories were about Parliament or its members. Later, when I inherited the title, it was a relief that I had followed his request."

"But if nobody knows, how do you get to work?"

"My office is in the front house, and I visit there with the excuse of talking to my secretary, 'a friend'," I explain.

Isabella blinks her dark eyes, seeming to think.

"Right…" She looks at the screen again. "Well, it was only after 1817 that the newspaper came to prominence in the country, following the denunciation of a traitor to the Crown."

I move my face closer to the computer, looking for the familiar name. Cornell! That traitor has really been exposed, which means that Howard decided to denounce him. Although I feel satisfied in a way, I wonder how things went on without me. If the paper was prestigious, someone had to finance it, and I doubt that my cousin would have done that, even if they had revealed my occupation to him.

"What else?" I ask Isabella, and she lowers the screen a little.

"Look, the name of the man in charge of the *Daily* until 1848: Jack Spencer."

Jack? My best friend took over the newspaper? Why would he do that when he never wanted to take on any responsibility in life?

"What's with the face? What does it mean?"

Her eyes are curious and intrigued. It's not like she's pretending to believe me.

"Jack Spencer was a good friend of mine. He was also the second son of a duke. We were friends with other rakes. But he lived in London; he had no interest in journalism. It doesn't make sense."

And here I am, referring to everyone in my life as if it were really in the past.

"Spencer," she says. Bella bites her lower lip. "Let me see."

Isabella opens a new tab and throws Spencer's name up on the screen. We find little information. There is something about William Spencer, Jack's father, and his successor, Flavian, who by the way fought in the war alongside Barney; they were close friends. I was surprised to discover that he had married. Flavian Spencer returned from the battlefields a completely different man, broken in every way. He came to us once to apologise for my brother's death. As if the poor chap was to blame for something...

Apart from that, there's nothing more detailed about them in the article. Damn, that's hard.

"There's nothing else, Ben. I'm sorry."

I drop my body onto the sofa, running my hands over my face. I feel so tired and disappointed. "It seems that the more I search, the less I find. Is this lack of information normal?"

Isabella nods. "Yes, not everyone has their entire life published on the internet. But don't be sad. Maybe, if you want, we can look for the information offline." Bella tries to console me.

"Where?"

She shrugged. "Libraries, museums…"

The mention of the word reminds me of something she said earlier. "Wait a minute! You said my house became a museum, didn't you? That day in hospital."

"Yes, Google Maps showed that."

"Could there be more detailed documents about my family there?"

Isabella moistens her lips. Even though I'm a bit agitated, the movement catches my attention. They're plump and full, perfect for kissing. For God's sake, I can't be thinking about kissing Isabella in a situation like this. But I am. A lot.

"I don't know, Ben, but the house is in Bath, right?" she asks, helping me to refocus.

And yes, Bath is a long way from here. I'd forgotten that detail. I fall silent again, trying not to despair. What am I going to do now? Not only do I not know how to get back, but I also have little idea what happened.

"Look, what if we go there?" Isabella suggests. "I could see about a train or bus ticket. Bath isn't that far away."

"The journey from London to Bath takes days, Bella."

"Before, with carriages, it might have done. Not now, with modern transport." She smiles again.

The room becomes brighter and my chest a little less compressed. I take a moment to stare at her beautiful face so determined to make me feel better. But tickets, as far as I know, cost money. She doesn't seem to lead a miserable life, but I realise that I'm an unplanned expense.

"Bella, I need to ask you something, but please don't get angry with me."

"Of course, what is it?"

I pause for a moment, measuring my words carefully. "Why are you doing all this if you don't believe in me?"

She blinks, looking embarrassed.

I continue. "I don't blame you," I explain. "If someone came up to me and said they were from… I don't know, 1500, I wouldn't believe it either. But I know you're treating me well out of pity."

"It's not pity…" she retorts.

"Nor is it because you believe I am who I say I am."

Isabella lets out a breath, brushing her straight hair out of her face.

"OK, I admit you're right. I think you think you're telling the truth, but it's all just some mental confusion from hitting your head."

I laugh without humour. "Is that what the doctor said?"

Isabella nods. "He said it will pass, and if it doesn't, we can book a doctor. But I really believe you'll get better!"

No, I won't, because I'm not confused at all. However, Isabella won't believe me, so I think I'd better be honest.

"Bella… I don't know what else to say. You can stop trying so hard, stop coming up with ideas."

"What are you talking about?"

"Everything. You don't have to listen to my stories, ask questions as if you're interested, suggest going to the museum, that sort of thing. It'll just generate more expense for you, and I really don't want to take advantage of the situation."

"But I really think that going to the museum will help you."

I turn on the sofa. The movement causes my knee to touch hers. "How would that help me?"

"I thought that seeing everything up close, you might realise that you're not Benjamin Waldorf. That you'd remember your name and your family. I just want you to get better, Ben."

Yes, I know that. The poor girl's been devoting her whole time to me ever since she hit me with the scooter.

"What if it doesn't work? What if I leave even more convinced? What if you are convinced? If you realise that I'm telling the truth and that all this crazy sorcery is real?"

Isabella laughs, and it's not the kind of laugh I like.

"I'm serious, Bella."

"I know, but you have to admit that the chances of that happening are almost zero."

"Why is that?" I'm a bit annoyed now. "Why are the chances *zero*? If I believe that I'm here, that you're from the future, that you live in 2022, why can't you believe that I'm from 1817?"

She doesn't reply. I feel like an arsehole for my words, but I'm really frustrated.

"You're right; it's not fair on you," she says. "Let's make a deal: I'll buy the tickets to the museum. We'll go there and see what happens."

"What if nothing changes?" I ask.

"At least we tried something. We can't just sit here and do nothing, Benjamin." Isabella reaches for my hand. The warm touch causes a different tremor in my body. Something good that I don't want to end. "Please don't be angry with me."

"I'm not angry, Bella. Forgive me, I just…" I turn my palm over and her fingers caress my skin. "I'm just exhausted, worried about my sister. I don't know what to do."

Isabella now entwines her fingers in mine, giving me reassurance and comfort. Our hands are a perfect fit, firm and soft at the same time.

"Let's find your origin. Whether it comes from the past or you're confused, it doesn't matter. Everything will work out; trust me."

Even against all logic, and probably only because this request comes from *her*, I trust that it will. It's all I have left.

9

Abs are good for your health

Isabella

I sit on one of the café's empty sofas, holding my latte cup and feeling the tiredness of the day. The last few days, in fact.

Today is Thursday. It's been almost ten days since I went out to enjoy the sun and ended up running over a handsome English lord: Benjamin, the man who has been my companion, my flatmate, and the guy who attracts me more and more every day, no matter how much I try to control myself.

I always knew that the disappointment with Matheus would pass and, at some point, I wouldn't think about him for days. Well, it did, because my thoughts are now occupied by Benjamin, his height, and his gentlemanly manners.

Only he's not a gentleman! He's lost and confused, and soon he'll realise who he is and disappear from my life, just as quickly as he arrived.

I managed to buy tickets to go to Bath next Saturday, on my day off. Tickets there are expensive in December, but I've found a good price if we go by bus and return by train. I'm having adventures with Ben, that's for sure. When all this is over, at least we'll have stories to tell.

And I hope we can stay friends afterwards. I don't know, I think he likes me too, because we get on really well, even in this mess. Benjamin is someone I feel I can trust.

Which reminds me that I need to do something. As much as I don't regret hiding it from Cinthia that I invited Benjamin to stay at the flat, I think it's time to clear things up. Ten days is a long time, and I'm bothered by this lie.

Finding courage, I finish my coffee, put the cup aside, and pick up my phone. Two rings later, Cinthia answers the video call.

"Hi, Bella!" She smiles at me.

"Hi, darling. How are you?"

"Alright, I've just got back from class. I'm going to take a shower and go to a happy hour with the guys. What about you? Are you feeling better about your great-grandfather? How's your father?"

I'm always touched by her concern for me and my family. As we all imagined, my great-grandfather really was in his final days. My dad rang me five days ago to say that he had been laid to rest. Even though the old man was close to a hundred years old, that's never happy news. Especially for my father, because now he has no other family apart from me.

"He's fine," I reply. "He's upset, of course. I invited him here to maybe go for a walk for a few days, but he's swamped with work."

"Ah, yes. Well, mourning is like that. Time heals everything."

I nod and swallow, trying to look as natural as possible. I love talking to Cinthia about everything, but I have to tell her straightaway that we have an unexpected guest.

"I… I need to tell you something."

Her eyebrows furrow. "Bella, what's wrong?"

"Remember the man I hit a few days ago?"

She nods. "Yes, what about him? Is the guy giving you a hard time?"

Poor chap. The last thing Benjamin does is give me a hard time.

"No, it's not. But…" I shudder and decide to say it all at once: "Well, he's living with me temporarily."

Cinthia brings the camera closer to her face. "Whaaaat? Is this guy in our house?"

"Relax, I can explain."

"I'm counting on that."

Yes, yes, I know. Let me just clear things up.

"He's mentally confused. He thinks he's someone he's not, and we can't trace his family." For some reason, I don't reveal that Benjamin thinks he's from the past. "The doctor said it would pass, but I couldn't leave him there, helpless. It was my fault that he hit his head."

"But, darling, what if the man was a thug? A rapist, a…"

"I know, and I agree. It was a risky invitation. But I swear, he's harmless. Absolutely nothing about Ben is dangerous."

"Ben?"

"Yes, his name is Benjamin."

"But you're calling him Ben, are you already that close?"

"Well, not close, but he's nice. And he needs my help, I wouldn't do this crazy thing if I didn't need to."

Cinthia sighs, cocking an eyebrow. She's not the type to lose her temper over anything, nor does she get angry easily. Lucky me.

"OK, I believe you. But why am I only finding out now?"

The guilt makes me grimace. "I know, I made a mistake. Forgive me, but I was afraid you'd say no and…"

"I'd say no!" she speaks.

"Yeah, I couldn't go against your wishes and bring him home anyway. So I thought it was best to hide it. But I promise everything is fine. He's sleeping on the sofa; he's organised, clean, and polite. He's even been helping me round the house – he did the hoovering yesterday. Duke loves him! You'll have to see."

She laughs, and I follow suit.

"That dog doesn't have a lick of sense, just like its owner." She's probably right. "OK, but what now? How long will he stay?"

I don't know, but my hope is that the trip to Bath will solve our dilemma.

"Not too many days, I don't think. Before you get back, everything will be sorted out – don't worry."

"Um, about that, change of plans. I won't be back until the 2nd of January."

My eyes widen slightly.

"Why?"

"To enjoy a few days without studying. As it's

Christmas and my holidays don't end until the 1st, I've asked a friend to swap days with me at the shop. That way, I can wander around Paris and take a quick trip to Bordeaux."

"Oh, how chic…" I say, and she laughs.

"Everything is chic for you, darling."

I smile too, and a new call appears on the screen: Laura LeBlanc.

"My sister is calling me."

"Talk to her. Thanks for telling me about Ben, you crazy woman."

"Thanks for not sacking me as a friend and flatmate," I joke.

"It's only because I've become attached to His Grace," Cinthia teases. "And, Bella?"

"Yes?"

Cinthia takes a deep breath. "Be careful, OK?"

I frown, not understanding. "What do you mean?"

"I know that sparkle in your eyes. Don't get attached to him."

Oh, that. I mean, I don't know what she's talking about. Benjamin is in my life for now. I know he's not going to stay, that what we're experiencing is something temporary.

"Don't worry, I'm just helping him."

We say goodbye and I answer my sister's call.

"Hi!" I say in Portuguese.

Two little faces appear on the phone screen, Laura's and my mum's.

"Oh, my two daughters who've abandoned me together again."

We laughed, as we always do.

"It's not unusual. I'm a married lady, and I have to accompany my husband," Laura replies.

"Yes, maybe." My mum shrugs.

"I'm not going to be lectured for being single," I retort.

Conversations with my family are always lively. Me, Laura, and my mum couldn't be more different. Janete Souza is blonde, green-eyed, and slim. Laura was born a redhead, like my stepfather, and has honey-coloured eyes. I look like my father, dark eyes and hair, and I'm taller than them. Anyone who doesn't know us would never guess that we share the same blood, but we do have one thing in common: we like to chatter.

I'm not sure how long we talked, but there's some great news. Pierre, Laura's husband, has some paperwork related to his family's paintings to sort out here in London, so they're coming here next week to spend five days in the city. I haven't seen my sister since her wedding four months ago. I have no doubt it will be fun.

My mum's fine; she asked about my dad and said she spoke to him this week. Despite their distant relationship, they get along. As for me, when they asked me about news, I quickly told them about a friend I met at the café who is staying at the flat. I didn't see any reason to mention the scooter incident, and I have no idea why I brought Benjamin into the conversation, but, well… that's that. They also wanted to know if I'd been writing anything, but I changed the subject.

It wasn't as if I had anything new to tell, although a few plot ideas have occurred to me. As usual, I've jotted them down in my notebook.

I switch off my phone and look at the time: 5pm. It's time to go home.

I put on my headphones to walk back to the flat. Today's playlist is a mix of Taylor Swift, Adele, and Selena Gomez. I barely notice the time passing, engrossed in the lyrics. The next thing I know, I'm at the door of the building.

I go up the stairs, taking the key out of my jacket pocket when I reach the third floor. I open the door, singing along to "Come and Get It", close it behind me, and go into the lounge.

The world absolutely stops with what I find there.

Seriously, there's no way to describe it. The music slows down; the air thickens; and my lips dry and part at the sight of Benjamin, the shirtless Greek god, doing sit-ups in my living room. Duke is lying next to his head, quietly. But it's not Duke that my eyes are drawn to. Not by a long shot. My eyes are locked on the man exercising. And, wow, I can see every little bump standing out on his strong, hard-working torso. I want to lick them one by one.

"Bella?" He notices my presence. "My God, look at me."

Yes, yes. Look at that. So, so hot.

"Hi, Ben." I take off my headphones.

"Forgive me." He starts looking around and reaches for his T-shirt. "I went to exercise with those videos you showed me, but I got hot. I'll get dressed."

"No!" I gesture with my hand. Benjamin stops with his T-shirt in his hand, surprised. "I mean, you don't have to be hot. That would be inhumane." Just like depriving me of this marvellous view. I continue, "Carry on with your exercise; I don't mind if you're shirtless."

I try to avoid it, but I can't. He's standing up now, and my eyes run down his perfect body, his muscular arms, the line of hair that starts on his chest, heads down his torso, and disappears into his joggers.

The scriptwriter in my life has just redeemed herself.

Benjamin suddenly looks uncomfortable. He puts on his shirt and turns round quickly. "I'd already finished. I'm going to the toilet, excuse me." He disappears down the corridor and locks himself in the bathroom.

Now I'm the one who's uncomfortable. Have I been too forward?

The worst thing is that I don't even regret it.

* * *

Benjamin

I'm more aroused than I've ever been.

Bella gave me such an intense look that my cock responded instantly. If I hadn't run to the toilet, I'd have been mortified. After all, this fabric can be very revealing.

Feeling my erection throbbing, I turn on the tap, dip my hand in the running water, and bring it to the back of my neck. I already knew I was attracted to her, I just didn't realise it was reciprocal. I know a woman's debauched glances. It looked like she wanted to lick me. And I wouldn't have minded being licked by her. Or licking her in return, after she'd finished.

I let out a moan, pushing the thought away. The idea is

to leave the bathroom in my normal state, not even more aroused. God, I really am a mess of a man. I'm looking forward to Saturday when we can get to Bath and I can try to get home.

I've been thinking about it for the last few days. I forced myself to remember exactly what happened: I was in the study; I thought about what it would be like to disappear; I found the cameo; my wish came true, and I woke up in 2022.

I can't find an explanation for all this, but that's what happened. So I've made a decision. When we get to my house, I'm going to repeat, as far as possible, what I did that afternoon, but instead of wanting to disappear, I'm going to wish to go home.

I look at my face in the bathroom mirror, taking a deep breath. The guy I see in the reflection looks nothing like the one I used to know. I've changed so much in recent years, gone through so many different phases, that it's hard to define who I am now. A libertine, an older brother, a responsible duke, a time traveller. All of those things, perhaps.

I come out of the bathroom and find the dog staring at me.

"Your Grace." I nod as I pass him and return to the living room. The sound of paws on the wooden floor indicates that Duke is following me.

Bella has her back to me, preparing something in the kitchen. She realises my presence and looks at me with a smile on her face. So beautiful.

"I'm making guacamole for both of us."

"Guacamole? What is guacamole?"

"Avocado with onion, tomato, and lemon." She walks over to me and leaves a round bowl of green mixture on the coffee table. "Oh, I forgot the Doritos."

I don't even find these different foods that Bella presents me with strange anymore. With the exception of a sour worm made of gelatine, I've liked everything she's offered me.

Minutes later, that guacamole with Doritos goes on the list of approved foods. Bella smiles so sincerely as she observes my reactions every time I taste something, that I'd like to have that smile recorded in a painting. Or rather, in a photo, since that's possible nowadays.

"Are you excited for Saturday? I've already printed the tickets," Bella says, popping a nacho into her mouth.

"Yes!" I wipe my lips with the napkin. "I need to clarify something with you, actually."

Her shapely eyebrows frown when she looks at me.

"You see, Bella, I've been thinking about everything that's happened and… I think I should use this visit to my old home to try and get back."

She swallows, nodding slightly. "Back to the nineteenth century, you mean."

"I'll try to repeat what I did the day I disappeared into the house. Maybe it'll work."

"And what did you do?"

"I found an old cameo locket that my grandmother gave me."

Her expression is suddenly curious. "Can I have a look? I've never seen a cameo up close."

"Sure, let me get it for you."

I get up and walk over to a piece of furniture in the

living room where I've kept my clothes. The cameo is there, along with my jacket, shirt, waistcoat, trousers, and boots.

"Here, this one." I hold it out to her and settle back on the sofa.

Bella looks shaken as she stares at the garment. Her delicate fingers, with nails painted in blue, carefully outline the feminine silhouette, as if she were holding a precious treasure. "It's beautiful. You said it was your grandmother who gave it to you?"

"Yes, she gave it to me just before she died. I found it by chance. It's the last thing I remember before I got here."

Bella puts her hand to her face reflectively, but I know what she's thinking.

"You must think I'm more of a lunatic every second you're around me, mustn't you?"

She denies it, handing the cameo back to me. "It's not that. I just… do you think this whole story is about a play you're in? A film? A book you've read?"

I laugh. Bella has already told me about her theory that I'm an actor in a film or a TV series.

"Bella, I'm not an actor. And no, it's not from a book."

"Yes, I know you think it's not…" she mumbles. "OK, everything you've told me makes sense. But we agreed to consider both options, yours and mine."

"I know. For you, I'll get there and realise that I was just confused. But if I'm right, and I know I am, I need you to know that I can disappear."

She swallows dryly, sighing. "Which means we'll never see each other again."

"Precisely."

Only then do I realise what my return means. As right as it is, the thought of never seeing Bella again makes my chest tighten. I'm... attached to her, something deeper than physical desire or the friendship we've formed.

"OK, Ben. On Saturday, we'll see what happens. And if you make it back to the past... well, I'll miss you."

I love the way she takes me seriously, even if she thinks I'm mad.

"Yes, we'll see. And I'll miss you too."

More than I imagined, I suddenly realise.

10

Finally, the truth comes out

Benjamin

As soon as we get off the bus, I realise that Bath, like London, is not the same city it was two hundred years ago.

Streets have become noisier with modernity. There are shops everywhere, stalls dotted around with a variety of food and products, and Christmas decorations non-existent in my day adorn the pavements and the fronts of houses. The smell in the air is sweet, with a hint of peanuts. Some of the buildings and facades have been modernised. Almost all the doors are now coloured blue, black, and red. There's an arrangement of leaves in the centre.

But even though everything is different… it's still Bath, my home.

"Do you recognise it?" Bella asks, smiling at me. She's wearing a pink coat, and her hair is tied up in a high bun, making her face stand out. The tip of her nose is flushed from the cold weather; her lips are coloured with pink lipstick; and her eyelashes are discreetly lengthened.

"Yes and no," I say, putting my hands in my jacket pockets, where the cameo lies waiting to be worn.

I wondered whether to wear my own clothes but decided against it. It would be strange to come back in different clothes to those of my time, but it would be very uncomfortable if someone stared at us the whole journey, thinking I was a *Bridgerton* actor, as Isabella says, or someone famous. In today's England, people in Regency clothes attract attention. Isabella herself seems to have a very significant thing for riding boots.

"What are we going to do?" she asks me. "Go straight to the museum?"

"I think it's better, don't you?"

I don't want to be rude to Bella. I'd like to go round the town, see what's changed, maybe even tell her a few stories, but I really need to sort out my situation. Not to mention that I'm too anxious to see the house to find out more about what happened.

"Let me see where it is on the map." Bella starts to pick up her mobile phone, but I gently stop her.

"It's not necessary. I remember the way home."

She tilts her head, pretending to be impressed. "Wow, how proactive. Come on, then."

I take a step but stop, looking at her. Considering that there's a chance I'll be saying goodbye to this lovely lady for good, I extend my arm in a chivalrous gesture.

"Shall we go, milady?"

Bella seems delighted and accepts my arm, wrapping herself around me.

"You really are a dream."

I laugh again. I've laughed so much alongside her over the last few days that I wouldn't be surprised if my face were sore. Life in the nineteenth century was not about happiness. Not with the prolonged mourning and all those duties. Now, despite being completely lost, I can smile with a strange ease.

I walk alongside her, guiding us through the streets of Bath. We see the abbey, on York Street, with its medieval architecture and three-pointed arches. Next to it, the Roman Baths. Bella says she visited them the last time she was in the city and was surprised by the hot springs and their history.

"Did you use the Roman Baths?" she asks me.

"Roman baths were used as spas but also as healing springs in my day. The city was famous for it."

"I thought rakes and deviants used these houses as their dens of fun."

Any other lady who said such a thing to me in my day would have astonished me. Bella doesn't. With her, I have an intriguing desire to discuss, if only discreetly, my old and perverse habits.

"We went to other places."

She raises an eyebrow. "Which ones?"

"Some specific houses for what we wanted. Games, carnal pleasures."

She lets out a low chuckle. "Wow, how exciting."

We continue talking as we walk through a Christmas market until we reach Gay Street.

"Look, this is the Jane Austen Centre."

I look at the facade of the house, the pale statue of the girl in Regency clothes and the plaque on the door.

"There's a museum for Miss Austen?"

Bella opens her eyes so wide that I'm surprised.

"Beloved father! Have you met Jane?"

"Yes, she lived here in Bath for a few years and was a well-known lady."

Isabella squeezes my arm, jumps up, and screams, all at the same time. "Jesus! You're God's favourite – you met Jane Austen!"

Yes, I did, but I don't understand anything at all.

"Bella, I'm lost here. What about Miss Austen?"

She looks at me as if I've insulted her.

"She is simply the greatest writer of all time. She used the best tropes: friends to lovers, second chances, enemies to lovers. She created Mr Darcy!"

I'm even more confused.

"Mr Darcy? The one from *Pride and Prejudice*?"

I read this novel a little while after it was released because it was being talked about so much.

"Yes! That arrogant hottie."

"Did Jane Austen write that?" I'm the one who's amazed now.

Everyone, absolutely everyone in my time, wondered who the lady was, the phenomenon behind the novels of the moment, praised even by Lord Byron's own wife.

"Yes, Ben! Jane is still a phenomenon today. Here in Bath, there's a museum, a festival dedicated to her and her works, and she's even on the ten-pound note."

Fascinating. I would never have imagined it.

"But tell me, what's she like? Have you spoken to her? What did you talk about?"

Bella's questions are spoken so quickly that I feel dizzy. We walk again, while I explain: "I haven't seen her for years, but she was a pleasant lady to talk to. She was always accompanied by her sister. Abigail even commented that she was ill a few days ago. She lives in Hampshire now."

Bella thinks for a moment, opening her mouth. "Wow, you're from 1817, aren't you? That's the year she died."

"Really? What day?"

"Hmm… 18 July, if I'm not mistaken."

Wow. Less than a month after my disappearance.

"She must have suffered from that disease then."

"Probably. Poor thing, she died so young."

I find it curious how Bella refers to Miss Austen with affection as if she knew her personally.

"From the looks of it, you're a big fan."

She replies without hesitation, "All romance writers are."

"Are those the kinds of books you write?" I ask as we cross the road in front of The Circus.

"Yes and no. In Jane's day, people just rubbed fingers together. In mine, the couple do a bit more than that."

A shiver of pleasure runs through my whole body.

"Are you referring to… indecent scenes?"

Bella blushes but doesn't hesitate to answer. "Yes, Your Grace. The things you and your friends used to do in your pleasure houses," she teases me, biting her lower lip.

Once again, we're flirting with each other. And once again, I'm imagining my body on top of hers, showing with attitude what kind of things I used to do in the clubs I used to go to.

"Look, it's here." Bella points to a familiar facade.

In seconds, I go from a moment of desire to one of melancholy. I'm home. Two hundred years later, but I'm home. The facade remains identical, except for the front door, which is now painted blue. My eyes suddenly moisten, and my throat feels tight. Bella pulls away from me, touching my arm.

"Ben, are you OK?"

I nod, still looking at the house. "This is it."

"Shall we go in? Are you ready?"

I meet her worried gaze, my breathing a little heavier. I don't know if I'm ready, but I have to keep going.

We enter the house. The decor is different, and the old smell isn't what I remember either. Bella speaks to a girl behind the counter in the entrance hall.

"Hi, we want to visit the museum."

"Of course. It's five pounds each," replies the stranger.

Isabella presses a button on her mobile phone twice and brings it close to a little machine.

"What are we going to find here?" Bella asks the girl.

"The house has been practically preserved since the Regency period. The family that lived here were nobles, so there is some information scattered around, and a portrait gallery in the last room."

I remain silent, just looking at everything. We walk together to the corridor, which now seems narrower than usual. The wallpaper has been changed; the carpets are not the ones my mum chose; and everything is brighter, different.

As soon as I see the staircase leading to the second floor, I turn to Bella. The moment of truth has arrived. "Bella, my study is upstairs."

She understands me without demanding explanations. "Right. Are you wearing the cameo?"

I nod and reach into my jacket pocket, pulling out the locket. "Here."

Bella looks at my outstretched palm. "Alright. I'll give you some privacy."

"Since there's a chance I'll go back to the past, I need to say goodbye."

The words squeeze my chest. Bella, on the other hand, doesn't seem as distressed as I am.

"I understand."

"I need you to know that I'm grateful for what you've done for me. *For everything*. I… would never have survived in this world without you."

She lifts the corner of her mouth in a hidden smile. So sweet.

"I just want to see you well, Benjamin. I want to see you get better."

"You think I'll leave that room with a sane mind, don't you?"

"I don't think so, I just hope this visit helps you. But since you're saying goodbye, I understand that this is important to you. So…" She lets out a breath, thinking about what to say. "If you really do go back, know that I'm happy for you. And for me, I am happy to have met you. These last few days have distracted me and amused me more than I realised. Your company does me a lot of good. I really needed something to do me good."

"A distraction?"

She denies it. "No, not a distraction. Someone. Someone special who has listened to me, treated me well. It meant a lot."

I believe every word she says to me.

"I said goodbye to His Grace, Duke, the dog, in the flat, but send him my regards, please," I ask.

She laughs heartily. I'll miss that sound so much...

"I'll pass the message on."

I approach her, taking her delicate hand and bringing it to my lips. I kiss the warm skin for a long time, hoping she can feel my gratitude.

"I'll never forget you, Bella. Never."

Bella moistens her lips and strokes my cheek.

"Me neither. But just so you know, if you don't go back, I'll be in the back gallery waiting for you."

Always careful and kind, Miss Isabella.

"Thank you."

Letting go of her is harder than I thought, but I do it. Isabella smiles at me once more before leaving me alone and walking towards the back of the house.

I face the steps and take a deep breath, moving forward. The walk down the stairs and through the corridor seems endless. The study door is the last, and it's closed. I stop in front of my room. On the other side, on the opposite wall, is my sister's old bedroom.

That's where I go, with my heart pounding.

Abigail's room is well maintained. The wooden floor looks newer; the curtains are darker than my sister would have chosen. However, the chest of drawers is the same, the bed and the canopy, as well as the mirror on the side wall, where so many times I've seen her smiling, happy in a new dress.

There's no information about it on the few plaques scattered around in specific places. I still don't know what happened. Images of my sister sinking into sadness under the sheets come back to me. The sound of her crying, her wailing, missing our brother and our father. My chest tightens with anguish, wondering what could have happened to her. I can't ignore my dark memories of the time when Abigail lay there for days on end without even seeing the sunlight.

If I was the cause of something like this… I can't even measure the guilt that overwhelms me.

With a lump in my throat, I shake my head gently and head down the corridor to my study. No more postponing my duties, my honour. I reach into my pocket, looking for the cameo. I take it out and hold it tight.

I'll try to repeat what I did, try to return to the past in the same way I ended up in the future. And, who knows, maybe I'll have a present to call my own after all this confusion.

The room is practically intact, I can even smell the tobacco in the air and the wood burning in the fireplace. The quill and inkwell are still on the table, although the papers there seem merely decorative. Above the fireplace, a plaque tells of the Waldorf family and its line of dukes. My grandfather, my father, my brother's name, and then mine. I clench my fists as I read Gustave's name, the only one I *didn't* want to read. Damn him, he really did inherit the title, as I had feared. And, as it turns out, he ended the lineage since there's no other name written after his.

I'm enveloped in a dark emotion as I position myself in the centre of the room.

Straightening my posture, I hold the cameo, rub it, squeeze it. I make my wish: I want to go home.

Nothing happens.

I close my eyes and wish again, with all the strength in my being. I think of Abigail and my old routine.

Still nothing. I insist for a few more seconds until my temples start to ache.

I open my eyes and it's as if an anvil of disappointment has collapsed on my head.

It didn't work, and it won't work.

I've never felt so powerless, so... incapable. A frustrated sigh escapes my lips, but I don't want to attract attention.

Defeated, I leave the room and go downstairs, looking for Bella, hoping that she really has been waiting for me.

The gallery is located in my old living room. I arrive in the bright room, the light of the cloudy day streaming in through the floor-to-ceiling windows. Bella is standing there, looking at the portraits. I remember them all, but she's staring at a specific one, right in the centre of the space.

That's me there. The me of two hundred years before. My portrait, that of the fifteenth Duke of Waldorf, painted just a few months before I disappeared.

As soon as I approach, she notices my presence. Our eyes meet, plunging into each other, and I realise what has just happened: she has discovered the truth. *My truth*, that I somehow left 1817 and ended up in the future.

"It's you..." Bella murmurs. "I don't know how, but... it's you."

All is not lost today, for she finally understands. Isabella finally believes me.

"Yes. It's me."

Her eyes fill with water and her chin trembles. I get emotional too. The feeling of being understood moves me in an indescribable way.

"Ben, forgive me, I…"

"*Shh…*"

I wrap my arms around her and pull her close, comforting her with a kiss on her temple. Bella blames herself too much. I don't care one bit if she doubted me before. I don't care that she thought I was out of my mind. Bella helped me, reached out to me despite that. Without her, I don't even know what would have become of me. She doesn't have to blame herself for anything, ever. Not if I can prevent it.

"Don't worry," I whisper into her hair. The scent of vanilla envelops me, cozy and soft. "Come on, let's get out of here."

11

True love stories are worth remembering

Isabella

I'm in shock. I'm simply stunned by what I've just discovered.

Benjamin told the truth – the portrait in the gallery leaves no doubt.

He is Benjamin Gerard Waldorf, the fifteenth Duke of Waldorf. He is truly a duke from the past.

How on earth can this be real?

After we leave the museum, we walk to the park opposite the Royal Crescent. Benjamin basically places me on the first empty bench. I can hardly think.

He doesn't say anything, the gentleman that he is – because he is one! I take a deep breath, wondering what to say. Where to start.

"Tell me everything." I turn to him. "I want to know everything."

Benjamin smiles slightly. "I've already told you everything. Almost, I think."

"Tell me again. Please."

He nods, his eyes riveted on mine. "Bella, are you well?" Benjamin takes my trembling hand.

I'm moved by his concern. My God in heaven, the man came from the past; he's lost in a strange world; and he's worried about *me*.

"I am. Scared, of course, but I am. My priority now is you."

"Not at all." He shakes his head. "I worry about you too."

"Don't. I'm fine," I say again. "Tell me how everything happened from the beginning. I want to try to understand."

Benjamin lets go of my hand and begins. He tells me that he was in his study one afternoon in 1817. He wanted to disappear and found the antique cameo. He tells me about the moment when his grandmother, many years ago, gave him the locket, which had previously belonged to her husband, who had it made after a trip to the Mediterranean at the beginning of the eighteenth century. Benjamin also remembers the ray of light that came from the little pink stone at the neck of the cameo silhouette, then he woke up in hospital, two hundred years later, after I ran over him on Tower Bridge.

"OK," I say, "some things in this story seem suspicious."

"Yes. The desire, the cameo. That's what I tried to do today in the museum. I went to the study and wished I was back. I rubbed the stone like I did that afternoon."

"It didn't work?"

"I'm here with you, aren't I?" he replies in a gentle tone.

Of course, it didn't work, Isabella. I take a deep breath, thinking.

"How strange… from everything you've told me, it should have worked."

Benjamin lifts his shoulders gently. "It didn't work."

"Have you discovered anything else?"

He clenches his jaw at the question. "As I suspected, Gustave inherited the title. There is no other after him, nor have I found any information about Abigail." Benjamin rubs his eyes. "I need to know what happened to her, Bella. If that bastard abandoned her, I don't… I need to go back."

The frustration in his voice is palpable. There's pain there too. Without thinking, I pull him into a hug in an attempt to comfort him. Benjamin is surprised at first but then plunges his face into the crook of my neck. I stay there, wrapping my arms around him for a few minutes, smelling the woody, masculine scent. I wonder if this is the scent we usually describe in novels as sandalwood notes.

As we lean away, he meets my gaze.

"What was that for?"

"I don't know, but I want you to know that I believe in you and that you're not alone. We'll find a way for you to go back and look after Abigail."

"How, Bella?"

"I have no idea, but we will. We'll research the subject, watch films, series about time travel. Something will give us an idea about how to do it."

Benjamin doesn't reply. But then again, what can he do apart from agree? I put myself in his shoes, imagining myself somewhere in the past or future. It would be awful to be away from my family, from my father, who, like Abigail, only has me.

My heart squeezes just thinking about it.

"I must confess that I'm relieved that you believe me," Benjamin breaks the silence. "Not that you've done anything that bothers me, but now I won't feel like a madman."

"You understand why I didn't believe you, don't you?" I ask. I feel bad now for having doubted him.

"Of course I do. It's insane."

"Yes, but we'll manage."

Benjamin moistens his lips, scratching his unshaven beard.

"What's wrong?" I ask.

"What if there's no way?" he practically whispers. "What if it's brought me this far, but I can't get back? What if the past is already written in stone and my cousin really has taken the title and Abigail has suffered her fate, whatever it may be? What if I have to stay here, Bella?"

I slide along the bench, practically gluing myself to him, and stroke his cheek.

"Then you won't be alone," I say. "I won't leave you alone, Benjamin. Not ever."

Benjamin puts his hand over mine and presses our foreheads together. He closes his eyes, and I follow him, our breath mingling. My heart feels like it wants to burst out of my mouth, but I don't move. I just hope he believes me.

When, a few moments later, Benjamin pulls away a little and opens his eyes, I know he does.

"Thank you. Even amidst this disaster, I'm very grateful to have found you."

Me too. He has no idea how much.

We're still in the moment when a loud laugh a few metres away brings us out of our reverie. Benjamin straightens up on the bench, and so do I, noticing the small metal plaque screwed to the iron backrest as I do so. I read the inscription in cursive letters: *Mel and Jack: Two souls who met and lived a long life full of love.*

"How beautiful…"

"Why is this sign here?" Benjamin asks me.

"Oh, that's normal; there are lots of them in London. Couples, families, single people… I think it's beautiful; it's like an eternalised moment. True love stories deserve to be remembered."

Benjamin lifts the corner of his lips. "You're right. It's very romantic." He keeps looking at the sign.

"Jack… could it have been your friend?" I ask, trying to distract him. "It's not impossible, after all, we know he ran the newspaper here in Bath."

Benjamin laughs out loud. "Never. I understand the coincidence, but Jack Spencer would never get married. A romantic plaque, then, is unthinkable."

"Why is that? People do fall in love!"

"Not Spencer." Benjamin drops his body on the bench. "The man was a rake, the worst kind. To give you an idea, in the same period that I opened the newspaper, he opened an underground boxing ring in London. Believe me, this plaque belonged to someone else."

If he says it, there's no reason to doubt it, although my writer's mind has already imagined Jack Spencer as one of the brutal deviants who end up surrendering to some powerful woman.

"What about you, Ben?"

"What about me?"

"Were you thinking of getting married before you disappeared?"

I don't know why I'm asking. Perhaps, now that I've discovered that Benjamin really is a lord, I want to know everything about him.

Ben runs a hand through his hair, still silent.

"I don't mean to be nosy, but it was expected of someone in your position, wasn't it?"

"Yes, it was. As a duke, I was supposed to produce heirs, build a family. Only..." He sighs. "I knew I'd have to do that at some point, but not now. I mean, not when I disappeared. My priorities were really Abigail, the newspaper, the Parliament."

"Did you expect to fall in love?"

Benjamin meets my gaze. "Not exactly. Of course, it would be better to feel affection for my wife, but the objectives were more practical than that." Before I can ask, he adds: "But I've fallen in love before. I think I have."

"Really? With whom?"

The image of Benjamin in love is bittersweet. I can't imagine him with another woman. On the other hand, I can only think that this man in love must be such a perfect prince.

"She was a lover I had for two years. When I realised I felt something stronger, I ended what we had. It was selfish; I thought only of myself, of preserving myself. And anything between us would be impossible, so…"

"Hmm, like Anthony Bridgerton in the series."

"What?" Benjamin doesn't understand my whisper.

"Nothing, it's a character from a show. I'll show it to you later. We can watch it together."

He laughs softly. "What about you? Have you ever been in love?"

Oh, if only he knew. The first thing I think about is closing down this conversation. However, now that I know everything about this man, I don't think it's fair to hide anything from him, no matter how much I dislike reliving my failed love life.

"I was in love with a guy from my town. We dated for a while; I thought I was going to marry him. He was my only real boyfriend; before that, I only had a few flings."

Benjamin's eyes are fixed on me. "Why does this seem like a story of a broken heart?"

"Because it is." I smile sadly at him. "For me, at least. Matheus has found someone else. He seems happier with her, I have to admit."

"I can't imagine how anyone could not be happy by your side, Bella."

The words enter my ears and go straight to my heart.

"Thank you, Ben. I don't blame him for breaking things off. That wasn't the problem. I think I just… waited too long. I trusted too much; I accepted less than I deserved. Cinthia always tells me that I'm an incurable romantic, but I think that's prevented me from seeing certain things. If I'd known that we were so much less than I thought, I wouldn't have wasted so much time."

"Didn't your disappointment change your convictions about love?"

I shake my head. "No, of course not. Just because something has gone wrong with a relationship, doesn't mean love stops being real. I believe in love with all my broken heart. And I'll keep believing, even if I don't find someone to love. I just don't want to live an illusion."

"If a man refuses to love you, Bella, it's his problem. Never yours, miss, please don't think otherwise."

My heart flutters like the wings of a hummingbird. Many people have said similar words to me since we broke up. My family, friends, Cinthia. I never believed them; I thought they were telling me to make me feel better.

But Benjamin… I believe in him. I believe with all my being. If he treats me well like this… there's nothing to stop me from finding another man who does too.

"Well, let's see what happens." I push my hair out of my face. "For now, I'll just be happy to get back to writing. I've been in a terrible creative block since everything happened. But since we met, I've had lots of ideas. I've written them all down; my notebook is full."

"How long has this been going on?"

"A year and a half, a bit more. Whenever I try to write, to put ideas into words, it's a mess. Everything has been, really. You don't always have to be travelling through time to feel lost."

Because if I think about it, there's no better word to define me than lost. My life is quiet, with no major drama. I graduated from university; I had a job that made me happy; I was in a relationship; and I wanted to get married.

Suddenly, my plans for the future collapsed. I made a radical decision, used up my savings, left the country, and started living one day at a time. I have no idea what I'm going to do tomorrow; I don't have a long-term plan. Yes, I think "lost" explains my situation well.

"I know." Benjamin agrees. "I've been feeling lost ever since Barney left. Believe me."

I believe it, and I honestly hope that he finds himself, no matter what.

"That's why I decided to come to London," I continue. "I used all the money I was saving for the wedding to pay for the trip."

"Were you engaged?"

"No, I just thought we'd be." I shrug. "My romantic side couldn't resist imagining it," I joke.

Benjamin and I remain silent. I've talked too much about my past relationship; I don't want to think about it anymore. However, I realise that telling Ben everything that happened is different from the other times I've done it. It seems that… the whole story of the break-up no longer causes me pain. I feel unexpectedly indifferent.

"What do you want to do now?" I look at the phone screen. "The train leaves in two hours. We've got time."

Benjamin straightens his posture, placing his hand on the back of his neck. "I have no idea. What do you have in mind?"

"Why don't you give me a tour *à* la Benjamin?"

He laughs, with his perfect white teeth. "Tour *à* la Benjamin?"

"Yes, show me the city through your eyes, from the perspective of the 1800s."

He seems to like the idea because he smiles and stands up, holding out his hand to me. "I think it's perfect. Will you do me the honour, Miss Isabella?"

I accept the gesture. "It would be a pleasure, Your Grace."

12

A break in the chaos

Benjamin

Since we arrived back from Bath late yesterday afternoon, Isabella has been very excited about our research into time travel.

I can't tell you what a relief it is that she's finally taken me seriously. I realised that she felt bad for not believing me, even though I said there was no reason to. I don't usually hold grudges, even when people deserve it, so with her, any resentment is out of the question. Bella did everything she could to console me; her good humour was essential for me to be able to enjoy the rest of our stay in Bath without being immersed in my problems.

It was deeply satisfying to introduce her to the city through my eyes. Bella loves history, and she asked me such curious and smart questions that I didn't even know how to answer some of them. When I return – if I return – I'm sure I'll be more aware of some of the details that would have never mattered to me if it weren't for Bella's point of view.

On the train journey back, she was tired, and I told her she could rest and that I would let her know when we arrived at London Bridge station. Bella fell asleep and laid her head on my shoulder halfway. I let her stay there, smelling the delicious scent of her hair and hearing her calm breathing. I took the opportunity and held her hand, intertwining our fingers. I'm still amazed at how perfectly they fit together. Despite everything, all the frustration of not being able to return home and all the worry about my sister, Bella's presence has allowed me some measure of peace.

She's brought me peace ever since we met. It's very intriguing, a little disturbing, as incoherent as it sounds, but I'm not complaining.

Today, however, the last thing Bella is is tired. The woman has enviable energy. Since it's her day off, we started researching time travel. Our marathon was intense. We watched *Outlander*, *Back to the Future*, *Kate and Leopold*, *The Knight before Christmas*, and *13 Going on 30*.

I really liked the music from the last film. Isabella said she'd introduce me to more Michael Jackson songs later.

"OK." She picks up a notepad and a pen with a crown on the end. "Let's summarise what we already know."

I find her authoritative manner very sensual. I wonder if Isabella realises how attractive she is. From the conversation we had yesterday, about the arsehole who broke her heart, I have my doubts.

"Let's do it." Duke approaches us and I pick him up. He's getting bigger and heavier every day.

"So far, there are various possible ways of time travel." Bella taps the tip of her pen on the paper. "Monoliths, cars that must reach eighty-eight miles per hour with a specific energy, portals, wishes made near a magical powder, and sorceresses handing out enchanted objects."

"Right. But my case is none of those. I didn't exactly make a wish; no sorceress gave me the cameo; I wasn't around monoliths; and I didn't use a car. I didn't even know what a car was."

Isabella pouts, thinking. The pretty lips catch my eyes. I want to taste them.

"The light you saw coming out of the cameo," she says. "Do you think it could have been a portal?"

"Not like Leopold's."

She nods, still reflective. "We'll have to watch *The Avengers*. They travel through time too, but we'll have to plan ahead because it's going to take a while."

"Why is that?"

"Because it's a sequence of films, and they only travel back in time in the last one. Well, until phase three."

"How many films?"

"About twenty, twenty-five."

"Twenty-five *films*? That will take weeks."

Bella laughs. "We can watch more than one a day. Or we could just watch the ones with the most information."

"You have to work, Bella," I remind her. Has she forgotten that little detail?

"Oh, I didn't tell you! I'm on holiday. My colleague was going to take it, but since her boyfriend couldn't and she wants to travel, we swapped. I'll be off work until

Christmas, and I'll only work two days that week. It'll be good, as my sister will be here."

Bella commented that her younger sister was coming to London with her Canadian husband. She said they already know about me, but I have to pretend I'm a friend spending a few days here in the flat. It's true, though. According to Isabella, I'm going to like Pierre LeBlanc because he's a "modern lord", whatever that means. From his surname, I discover that he is descended from Spencer's cousin's husband. It's a small world we live in. And it seems that next week we also have an unusual engagement: a Regency ball. And I've been trying to get away from them for so long… as I understand it, it's an extraordinary event in the town, where everyone dresses up in Regency clothes and attends an old-fashioned ball, with quadrilles, waltzes, and minuets. Mrs LeBlanc was thrilled when she received notice of the party by email and bought four tickets. Isabella almost fainted with happiness – her words, not mine.

Women and dances… who understands them? Some things never change.

"I didn't realise it was so easy to miss work," I say.

"It's easy. I like it because I have thirty days to take off from April to March of the following year. They don't have to be consecutive, which makes it easier. In Brazil, the holiday period is different. You know, different laws."

No, I don't know, but I don't have the energy to ask. With a sigh, I put Duke down and relax on the sofa.

"What do we do now?" I ask. "I don't think we've made much progress with our data."

"You look tense. Would you like to relax a little?"

"Yes, I'd like that. What do you want to do?"

"What are you thinking of doing?"

To relax? I have at least thirty images of different relaxing activities, but all of them are of complete wickedness. Images that, I admit, I would like to practise with Isabella. My member pulses inside my trousers and I change position.

"Tell the lady, please." She leaves her notepad on the coffee table and picks up her computer. "Let me see if they have tickets available before I say anything." Isabella types something quickly, her eyes riveted to the screen. She smiles a moment later and looks at me. "What do you say we go to Winter Wonderland?"

"What's that?" I lean forward, my forearms resting on my knees.

"It's a winter festival. It's a lot of fun. There's good food, hot chocolate, and games. I went last year and loved it. Even David Beckham goes there."

David who? You know what, I'd rather not ask. Isabella knows too many people for my liking.

"Let's go." I stand up. "I think you and I deserve a bit of fun."

"I'll just put my trainers on and we can go."

Isabella gets up and walks away, Duke following her into the bedroom. I can't help it, and I tilt my head to the side as I watch the round, hard arse roll away from me. Isabella's, not the dog's. Always hers.

* * *

Isabella

Benjamin looks like a child at Disneyland when we arrive at Winter Wonderland. He's the perfect mix of cute and sexy, with that manly build and that fascinated expression.

A hottie indeed.

"What do you want to do first?" I ask, as soon as we go through the gates of Hyde Park.

Benjamin is still dumbfounded. "I have no idea. It's all so… colourful." He cracks a smile. "These lights are very curious."

"They're nice, aren't they?" We're walking side by side, my arm wrapped around his. "Look, there's that hot chocolate I told you about. I'm going to buy some – would you like one?"

Benjamin hesitates, looking suddenly uncomfortable. "Bella, I think you're spending too much money on me."

I tell him it's fine. Yes, some unplanned spending was necessary, but I have relatively good savings. Not to mention the fact that my father transferred a "Christmas present" for me this week. My father and his unexpected gifts…

He's much better now. We text every day, but I've made an effort to align our time zones, and I've managed to speak to him by video call twice. It may sound cliché, but my father and I have a special bond, one that isn't shaken even by thousands of kilometres. It's like that with my sister and my mum too.

I suspect that Ben will soon be on that list. Even with him returning to the past, two hundred years away from me, I doubt very much that our connection will be broken.

Because Benjamin is special. And, even though it's presumptuous, my heart seems to whisper that we were destined to meet. That he needed me.

Just as I needed him.

"Bella? Are you alright?" he asks me. I didn't realise I was silent.

"Of course, I was just wondering what to do."

"You were going to buy the chocolate."

"Oh, yeah. Listen, don't worry about money. I never spend what I don't have. Not to mention that I've set aside some money to have fun at the festival this year, so… it's all planned."

An unconvinced Benjamin nods, and I walk away in the direction of a stand serving the best hot chocolate I've ever had. The minutes pass quickly, as they always do when something is fun. Benjamin and I go on the roller coaster, the haunted house, and the ice rink. I don't think I've ever laughed so hard as when I saw him fall flat on his arse and pull me along, telling me I shouldn't be so cruel. I've got used to the sound of his laughter, the frantic effect it has on my heart.

Smiling next to him is one of the best things I've ever experienced.

"Why are these ladies holding these absolutely huge teddies?"

I laugh again as we walk through the park. "They're gifts that you win by playing at these stalls. It's a film cliché – usually the boys play and win the animals for their girlfriends."

Benjamin frowns thoughtfully. "Does it have to be a boyfriend?"

"No, it's just what's most common."

He nods again. "Can I try to offer you one?"

"A what?" I tilt my head to the side.

"A stuffed animal of enormous size."

Oh, my God. This man doesn't exist.

"Of course. What do you want to play?"

Benjamin straightens his posture and fixes the collar of his jacket, looking around. "Is that like target practice?" He points to a stall on our left.

"Yes. It is target practice, really."

"Alright, then. That'll be it then."

We walk to the stall, and I hand my chips to the boy there. The aim is to hit the cans arranged in the centre with the shots. There are six cans positioned in three tiers: three in the first row, two in the second, and one in the third.

"How does it work?" Benjamin asks the boy.

"You have to hit the target. If you knock over four cans, you get a small gift. Five, a medium, and six whatever you like. You have four shots."

Benjamin nods, accepting the gun offered by the man.

"Which gift would you like, milady?" he asks me with a crooked smile.

"Whichever one you win."

"Choose, Bella."

He exudes confidence, so much so that my legs go limp. I look at the hanging presents and pick out a fluffy unicorn of enormous size, as Ben says.

"That one."

"Right. How many cans do I need to hit?" Ben turns to the guy again.

"All of them," he replies.

"Fair enough."

Very focused, Benjamin takes aim with the gun and pulls the trigger. The shot goes wide of the cans.

I grimace.

Benjamin speaks without looking at me: "I was just trying it out. I wanted to see how it worked."

I can't answer because what he does next is spectacular. Like a true expert, Benjamin fires, hitting a can from the bottom tier. Four cans fall to the ground, leaving only the other two on the base. With the last two remaining shots, Benjamin knocks them down, one by one, and smiles with satisfaction when the last one falls to the ground, handing the gun to the guy.

"The unicorn for the lady, please," he says.

When he hands me the unicorn, I don't even know what to say. I'm impressed, fascinated, melted, and a little horny. That is what he does to me.

"Did you like it?" Benjamin asks.

Did I like it? I loved it; he has no idea what a treat it was.

"You were marvellous." I stand on tiptoe and kiss his cheek. Benjamin smiles slightly, looking a bit embarrassed. So cute. "I love my unicorn of enormous size. Where did you learn to shoot like that?"

"I used to go hunting with my father and brother. I never really liked it, but I'm good."

Yes, I can see that.

"What do we do now?" Benjamin asks me.

"Want to go on the Ferris wheel?"

"Of course, it will be interesting."

After a few minutes in the queue, we sit on the Ferris wheel and go up. The park from above is even more beautiful. All the lights, the moving rides, the crowds of people who look like ants in an anthill. We can still smell the aroma of food mixed with marshmallows and chocolate. Benjamin looks down, smiling softly, his face flushed from the cold weather.

He is so handsome.

"I'm still impressed by so many colours." He straightens his posture. "Thank you for bringing me here. I love it."

I put the unicorn on my lap and nod. "It's nice to see you relaxed."

"I'm only now not tense. It's been a long time since I've done anything for myself. For the Duke of Waldorf, yes, but not for me, Benjamin."

He stops talking, but there's something unsaid in the air.

"Talk to me, Ben."

Benjamin meets my gaze again, just as the Ferris wheel stops. We're at the highest possible point.

"Don't worry, it's normal for it to stop," I reassure him. "You were saying…"

He sighs. "I thought my life would take one direction, and it took another. I never expected to be the duke; I never expected to have to provide for my sister. I was… just a man looking to seize the moment. I had my newspaper, so I wouldn't feel useless in society, and that was it. And then we lost Barney, then my father; Abigail was ill and, in the midst of it all, there I was. Trying not to fall apart. Trying not to feel." His words break my heart in two. Benjamin smiles sadly. "I ended up losing myself in all this. I've forgotten who I am outside the title. Who the man behind the desk full of papers is."

"He's wonderful," I say, without mincing any words, "simply wonderful."

Benjamin denies it, looking a little embarrassed. "Don't overdo it, Bella."

"I'm not. It's true. For me, Isabella Souza Kato, you, Benjamin Gerard Waldorf, the man, not the duke, are wonderful."

"Why?" he asks, turning his body slightly towards me. "Why do you say that if all I've done since I arrived is mess up your life?"

I shrug.

"Maybe that's why. Because you're a pleasant surprise. Because you make me smile, Ben."

His gaze locks onto mine. "That's great. I can be proud."

"Proud?"

He nods. "Yes. Your smile is the most beautiful thing I've ever seen."

And this is where I lose everything. The ability to speak, to think, to breathe. All I can feel is my heart racing and full.

Benjamin analyses my face, lowering his gaze to my lips, which I now realise are parted. Very gently, he brings a hand up to my face and strokes my lower lip, at the same time moistening his own. The movement is mesmerising, so much so that I feel my limbs tingle.

Ben moves a little more, getting as close as possible. Everything seems in slow motion, and I, who loves to assign songs to the moments of my life, don't know which song to choose. But I don't need them now. Definitely not. When Benjamin places his hand on the side of my face and pulls me to him, I just give in.

It's perfect.

Perfect, only that.

13

A man from the 19th century

Benjamin

Kissing Isabella is perfect. I can't define it any other way.

I didn't plan this. I didn't plan anything that has happened over the last few years. However, when I saw her looking at me, smiling at me, I couldn't resist.

I'm just a man, damn it. Right now, a very aroused man. My tongue dances with hers, tasting her sweet, intoxicating flavour. Her soft lips open to mine, wet and full. I want to feel all of her, every bit of her. I want it all. Carefully, I take the unicorn from between us and put it to one side, pulling her closer. I've imagined myself kissing her so many times over the last few days, but nothing has come close to reality.

This woman... oh, she's going to drive me crazy. My cock pulses inside my trousers as I bite her lower lip. Isabella wraps her arms around my neck, leaning in, giving me more access. There are too many clothes between us, not enough skin available, but I don't dare complain. I invade her mouth again with my tongue, explore her, and kiss her with overwhelming desire. I can't remember the last time I felt such desire. The last time I...

"*Excuse me.*"

A gasp takes us out of the moment, and I open my eyes, noticing the face of the stranger staring at us.

"Your time is up; there are more people in the queue."

I look in the direction the man is pointing, and the next couple, who are waiting to take our places on the Ferris wheel, stare at us, holding back their laughter. God, how embarrassing... I was so involved that I didn't even notice the wheel moving. I've become accustomed to observing public displays of affection these days, but being the protagonist in this is still a little strange to me.

I look at Isabella, whose lips are swollen from my kisses. Damn, I'm too aroused; I'm just wondering what it would be like to leave other parts of her swollen.

Pushing the thought away, I stand up and hold out my hand to help her do the same. Bella still looks lost as she reaches for the unicorn and accepts my gesture.

"Forgive me," I say, as we walk down the steps and away from the queue.

"Alright. What a bummer... I didn't even realise we'd come down. I was oblivious to anything else."

Yes, that's exactly how I felt.

"I shouldn't have behaved like that," I mutter. "We're in public..."

Isabella frowns but doesn't answer me. There's an intriguing awkwardness between us. I want to say something, but I don't know what, and Bella seems to be facing the same dilemma.

"Is there anything else you want to do?" she asks.

"I don't know. I… maybe we should leave."

Her eyes fill with disappointment. Hell, that's not what I wanted, but I really don't know what to do.

"Of course," Bella agrees. "Let's go home."

* * *

As soon as we enter the flat, Bella greets Duke with the best smile she can show him. But it doesn't come close to the smiles I'm used to.

Our journey home was silent. We heard only the sharp sounds of the Underground tracks, each of us lost in our own thoughts. I don't know what Bella thought about, but I can say that the time in silence brought me many reflections.

The first, and most striking, is that the kiss we exchanged meant something. In fact, a lot. I have no reason to deny that I have strong, real feelings for this woman. It's never happened to me, not like this, not even when I was in love with my mistress. I'm used to getting into bed with ladies without even knowing their names. This is something different, difficult to explain and understand. But it's real, and I strongly suspect that I'm not the only one with feelings in this room.

With that, we come to the big problem and my second thought: do I feel things for Bella? I do, but it doesn't matter. And it doesn't matter because, as soon as we find a way, I'll disappear from her life, just as abruptly as I appeared. So, any intimate involvement between us would be a very bad idea.

"Bella?" I say, as soon as she switches on the living room light and puts the unicorn aside. Duke approaches the animal, sniffing it. I continue, "We have to talk about what happened."

Bella takes off her coat and leaves it on the sofa, agreeing.

"I thought you didn't want to talk about it."

"Why did you think that?" I settle down next to her on the sofa.

"Because you kept quiet after we left, and I…" She hesitates, rubbing her face. "I don't know what to think. I'm a bit confused."

I hate to see her like this. Considering that I've been confused for almost every hour of the last few days, I'll do everything in my power to protect her from such frustration.

"Look, I apologise for the silence, but I needed to think."

"Think about what?"

"About what happened. About what I did, about the kiss."

She blinks her dark eyes, attentive to my face. "And did you succeed?"

I nod my head. "The truth is that we cannot allow this to happen again."

Bella holds her breath and doesn't speak immediately. "Do you regret it?"

"No, I don't regret it."

"You didn't like kissing me then?"

I laugh this time. "Liking… liking doesn't come close to what I felt."

"So why…"

"We can't allow it because I have feelings for you," I say at once. She looks shocked, but I won't back down. After everything she's done for me, the least Bella deserves is to know the truth. "I have feelings for you, and I suspect you're not indifferent to me either."

"You have feelings for me?"

The question sounds as if I've said something absurd. But why? I quickly remember what she told me that afternoon in Bath when we were sitting on the bench. Bella was hurt and wounded by an unscrupulous bastard who chose to abandon her when she had chosen to spend her life by his side. The guy is an idiot for letting a woman like her go.

When it comes to me, however, I refuse to accept that Bella has any doubts whatsoever. I reach for her hand, gently caressing her palm. "How could I not feel something for you, Bella?"

"You're referring to gratitude because I'm helping you."

It's not a question. God, she really has no idea.

"No, I mean you and the woman you are. The woman I admire for her strength and high spirits. The woman I find beautiful, intelligent, kind. Who attracts me to the point of driving me crazy. The woman…"

…that if I could stay here, I would choose to make mine. I'll stop before I say too much. "We can't get involved because I have feelings for you, and I suspect you have feelings for me too," I repeat. "Things I can't name, but I know they could hurt us."

"Hurt us?"

"Yes, Bella. Because I'm not from your time, and I need to get home."

My words hit her like a blow, so hard that she recoils.

"Right. For a brief, silly moment, I forgot that detail."

So did I. I thought of nothing else but her, us, when I took her in my arms.

"I acted without thinking today. I've wanted you for a long time now, but by kissing you... we're crossing a dangerous line."

She nods slowly, thinking. "What if I don't care?"

I don't understand. "Don't care?"

"Yes. What if, despite us being from different times, I want to explore what we feel? You'd go to bed with me if you could, wouldn't you?"

I feel aroused just thinking about it. Not only would I go, but I've fantasised about all the positions and perversity I'd share with her.

"I would, but we can't."

"Why not? I'm not a damsel in distress, Benjamin. I'm not even a virgin."

I'll pretend I didn't hear that. Not for her, I couldn't care less about her virtue, but just imagining another man touching her... I clench my jaw, shuddering at the thought.

"There's no honour for you to worry about," she continues. "I'm not from the nineteenth century."

"But I am, Bella."

She stops talking, her eyes locked on mine.

"I'm here in 2022, but I'm a man from the nineteenth century. It may not make sense to you, but I would never seduce a woman like you if I didn't intend to marry her. I would never treat her with disrespect; I would never put my physical needs before her honour and her heart. I have an unmarried sister, and I would kill anyone who dared to deceive her. And you... you've already been mistreated, deceived too much for my liking. Forgive me, Bella, but I don't want you to remember me as just another arse who couldn't give you what you deserve."

Isabella's eyes well up with emotion, but she takes a deep breath as if to contain her emotions.

"Do you know how often we women dream of a perfect lord like you saying words like that to us?"

I shake my head. I have no idea.

"Many," she replies. Her hand caresses mine, gently. "I didn't mean to be rude, I just... your kiss awakened something in me that I hadn't felt for a long time."

"What?"

"Happiness. Real, sincere happiness. But you're right... if we went any further, this attraction would turn into something stronger. Something irreversible."

I know that. Knowing, however, doesn't make this conversation any easier.

"If things were different, if I knew I could offer you a future, I wouldn't hesitate to make you mine."

"But there's no future, is there? As soon as we find a way, you'll be back there."

I nod. "I can't abandon my sister."

"I know you can't. I know that."

We stare at each other in silence for a moment. I bring her hand to my lips in a gentle kiss.

"Thank you for being honest," she says.

I give a little moan, grimacing. "Don't thank me. I don't even know how I did it."

"Being honourable sucks, that's the truth," she jokes, making me laugh.

"Yes, it sucks."

Bella takes a deep breath and smiles at me sincerely. "But I understand. I understand and… I want you to know that this doesn't change anything between us. Will we have repressed desires? Yes, we will, but we're adults and mature enough to deal with it."

Yes, we are. I'll have to find a way to touch myself, thinking about her in a very mature way, no doubt.

"I thank you for your understanding."

She lifts the corner of her mouth. "So gentlemanly and formal…" Bella comes a little closer. "Can I give you a hug?"

I nod, hugging her in return as she wraps her arms around my body.

"Despite everything, I loved tonight," Bella whispers. "It was wonderful."

I smile against her hair, agreeing.

Yes, it was really wonderful.

* * *

I went into my father's study and closed the door behind me.

"Sir, can we talk?"

He turned round and faced me, his eyes clouded with worry.

"Have you spoken to your grandmother?"

I nodded, moving closer.

"Yes, I did. I'm sorry, sir. She seemed very ill."

Which was another way of saying that I knew my grandmother was dying.

My father, serious as he always was, pulled up a chair and sat down behind the pile of papers.

"She's lived a good life. I just don't want her to suffer."

I shared the same feeling. My grandmother had been a strong, lively, kind woman. She didn't deserve to suffer.

"I agree."

"Your brother will be here tonight. He says he wants to talk to me, something about the war."

A chill ran down my spine at the words. Barney was my twin brother, but we were as different as could be. I knew his sense of honour and his non-conformity with what was happening in the country, with the war.

"Don't you think he..."

"I don't know, Benjamin. I hope not, but if Barney wants to fight..." my father sighed heavily, "I won't be able to stop him."

I didn't retort, although I didn't agree.

"Father, Grandmother gave me this." I showed him the cameo. My father stared at my outstretched palm, looking surprised.

"It's you, then."

I don't understand. "Me?"

He nodded. "I know this cameo. It comes from... far away. Your grandfather, my father, brought this pink stone, which you see in the silhouette of the cameo, from the Mediterranean islands. He said there was something special about it. Something... mystical. At least, that's what he was told."

Intrigued by the story, I pulled up a chair to sit down. "Tell me more."

"There's not much to tell. Your grandfather found it curious that the stone ended up with him. When he got engaged to your grandmother, he had the cameo made as a gift. She felt that the piece had something to do with matters of the heart. That one day it would belong to someone other than her. When I met your mother, I thought of giving her the cameo as an engagement present. Your grandmother wouldn't allow it. She apologised but said that the cameo wasn't meant for me."

I didn't understand a thing. "She told me she was glad it was me, but I don't understand," I said.

"We don't always understand everything, Benjamin. What's bothering you?"

"It all seems very strange to me. What am I going to do with a cameo? I'm not a woman."

"You could give it to your wife one day. I don't know."

I stood up, leaving the locket on the office table. "I don't see the point, sir. Forgive me. I'm not thinking of getting married either. I don't want that at all."

"You don't know anything about the future, boy," my father scolded me.

"I know, because it's simple. I'm not the heir to the title; I don't need to get married. I don't need all this romantic nonsense. I accepted it because my grandmother is ill. I'll give the cameo to Abigail, or—"

"No." My father reached out, took the cameo, and put it in the drawer. "If your grandmother says it belongs to you, I'll respect her wishes. If you need it one day, it's here, safe."

I laughed, even though it seemed disrespectful. "Don't worry, sir. I won't need it. Not now, not ever."

For the second time in a while, I wake up scared, with my heart about to burst out of my mouth.

I have no idea where those memories came from, but now I'm not satisfied with having forgotten them. My dream explains a lot. Why the cameo appeared in my study. The magic that the pink stone contains.

At least, that's what I was told.

Someone gave the stone to my grandfather. A sorceress? Maybe, which adds another element to my puzzle.

I get up and go to the kitchen, pouring myself a glass of water. I try not to make a sound, as I don't want to wake Bella. After quenching my thirst, I go through my things and look for the cameo, returning to the sofa with it in my hands.

I've been analysing it, just as I did before, again and again, since I woke up in 2022.

There's a connection. Now I feel like this stone should really be in my hands. But why should it? Why, when all it has caused so far is confusion and anguish?

I look down the corridor towards Bella's bedroom door. No, it wasn't just that. I'd be being unfair if I said that. Next to the woman sleeping behind that door, I felt more than that. Happiness, as she herself said.

I stare at the delicate piece again before my eyes grow heavy with sleep. I fall asleep thinking about everything. The more I find out, the more confused I become.

14

Welcome to my paradise

Isabella

A hundred per cent of women who read period novels dream of finding a noble gentleman to call their own. Well, I've found mine, and I have to say: the punishment is equal to the reward.

I'm going to change my mind about nineteenth-century good guys resisting women for reasons of honour. To hell with honour, decorum, the future. To hell with everything. In my next storyline, I'll have the two of them kissing on page five, and there's no three-act structure that can stop me from putting that climax in five per cent of the way through the book.

OK, maybe I'm exaggerating. Writing muses, forgive me, I didn't mean it like that. I'm not going to murder common sense, but I feel like it. If I can't have the hot duke because he cares about honour, I refuse to allow another woman, even a fictional one, to almost die of lust like I'm dying right now.

And how unlucky I am. I've finally found a man who cares about me, who treats me like a lady and with affection. A man who confesses, *in all honesty*, that he has feelings for me, without any fear. But also, a man who can't be mine, and never will be, because two hundred years separate us, and that's the way it is.

"Bella? Is everything alright?" The voice of Benjamin, the handsome and honourable duke, catches my attention.

"Hello. Yes, it's fine. I didn't hear you come in."

I run my eyes over him. He has just returned from his run sweaty and panting. That's great. That's all I need. This divine vision.

"How was the run?" I ask.

"Good. Exercising has helped me not to go mad." The tone of his voice is serious, enough to make me worry.

"What's wrong?"

Benjamin shrugs, sitting down on the sofa and stroking Duke's ear as he approaches.

"I've been thinking about all the films we've watched, and I can't see a solution. Nothing makes sense; I can't fit the pieces together."

I confess that this has also been worrying me. Since we got back from Bath, we've watched every possible film about time travel. We've even watched the entire Marvel franchise, all twenty-two films up to *Avengers: Endgame*. My idea, to save time, was to only watch the most important ones, but Ben liked them so much that we ended up not skipping any.

I don't know what else to do. None of the cases are like his, despite having elements in common. Not even the possible sorceress from the past who may or may not have given the stone to his grandfather.

"I know what you mean. I don't know where else to turn either."

Benjamin nods, running his hand through his messy hair. "We've tried all the films and series, haven't we?"

"From that list I got off the internet, yes."

He widens his eyes suddenly. "What about books? We haven't read any books about it."

I open my mouth in amazement. How could I forget books, dear Lord? "Wow, what a bummer. I'm a disgrace to the literary world!"

Benjamin laughs, rolling his eyes. "Don't overdo it, Bella. But we can try that, can't we?"

"Yes, of course. Let me have a look." I stretch my body and pick up the laptop I'd left under the sofa. I open the screen and the Google tab, searching for books on the subject.

"There's *Outlander*, which we've already watched… *The Time Traveler's Wife*…"

Benjamin's eyes are fixed on me. I ignore the tingling on my skin from this penetrating gaze and try to concentrate on the list in front of me. Unfortunately, most of the books have already been made into films, which means they're of no use to us.

"Look," I say a while later, "I think we can try these three. The rest didn't look promising."

Benjamin analyses the screen. "Very well. I'll read one, you read the other, and we can split the reading of the third."

"Alright, then. I'll look it up on Kindle."

Benjamin grimaces. "Is there no possibility of me reading on paper? Don't get me wrong, I understand the ease and technology of it all, but I'm, as you say, a vintage guy."

Benjamin's wicked smile makes my heart race and also makes me want to slap him in the face, begging him not to be so charming, since he refuses to have sex with me.

"Sure, let me see." Opening another tab on my computer, I search for books on Amazon.

"Two of them deliver tomorrow, so that's good. But one is out of stock, and it's the one I think could help us the most." I stop to think. "Let me see if Waterstones has anything."

"What's that?"

"A big bookshop here. There's a huge shop in Piccadilly. I always go there when I want to calm down."

Luckily, I manage to find the book in stock. "They have it. Shall we go there?" I look at the clock. "It's 2pm, I reckon we'll make it by 2.40pm at the latest."

Benjamin agrees, then looks down at himself. "Is there enough time for me to have a wash? Ten minutes at most, just because I sweated during the run."

Ah, damn. Here I am imagining this sweaty man naked in the shower. "Yes, there is. There's no need to rush; we have time."

Benjamin nods, grabs a change of clothes, and walks towards the bathroom. When I hear the door lock, I see Duke staring at me, his hairy little neck tilted to the right.

"Yes, Your Grace. Look at my situation. Am I being too obvious?"

Duke doesn't answer me. But I have the impression that he would say yes. Yes, I am.

* * *

"Welcome to my paradise," I say to Benjamin as soon as we walk into the bookshop.

The shelves, full of books with colourful, neat spines, seem to smile at me. And I smile back, like the polite woman I am.

"You really weren't exaggerating when you said it was a big shop," Benjamin comments.

"Over eight miles of bookshelves at your disposal. It's just marvellous! Smell it." I sniff the air. "Delicious." I smile, guiding Ben to the lift.

Benjamin also sniffs. Even when sniffing, he manages to be cute, playing along with my nonsense.

"The science fiction section is on the first floor," I explain. "Let's go straight there, because if I stop at the romance section… that's it, we'll lose the day."

Benjamin agrees with a chuckle, and we take the lift up to the first floor.

"We could have taken the stairs. I didn't think," I say, stepping out of the lift as soon as the door opens. "It would have been good for my glutes."

Seconds later, I look back and catch him in the act, his head tilted slightly. "Benjamin, were you staring at my arse?"

He sniffs. "No, of course not."

I squeeze my eyes shut, moving closer. He's lying to me. I know what I've just seen. "Are you sure, Your Honourable Grace? Honourable men *don't lie*."

Benjamin almost laughs but keeps his serious expression. "Of course, I wasn't. Oh, come on."

I laugh softly as I turn my gaze away and walk over

to the section on the right-hand side. I only realise he's approaching because of the whisper in my ear, which sends a shiver down my spine.

"But don't worry, there's nothing wrong with your arse. *Nothing at all.*"

His comment makes me blush from head to toe. Bastard.

"If you're not going to lose your honour, don't provoke me, milord. I can use those glutes against Your Grace."

"Pardon me." It's Benjamin who's blushing now. "I couldn't resist."

Oh yes. He can't resist *that*.

Taking a deep breath and returning to our focus, I locate the science fiction section. The book we're looking for is easy to find, so I take it down and hand it to Benjamin, who begins to leaf through it carefully. I take advantage of the fact that I'm here and have a look at the other titles. Maybe something interesting will turn up and we can take advantage of it.

"It's fascinating how a single idea can turn into so many different things," he says.

I concur, still going through the titles. "Yes, I think so too. Nowadays, I don't think there's anything that hasn't already been done. The secret is execution. Transforming ideas, to have new insights, incorporating other elements into things that already exist. For creativity, the sky's the limit."

He remains silent for a moment. "Have you thought about writing about this trope?"

"Travelling back in time? You know, I haven't. I tried it once, but I ended up going to the nineteenth century and staying there." I realise what I'm talking about only after I've said it. "Sorry, bad joke."

Benjamin doesn't seem to mind. "Don't worry, there's a good story in there if you want to get inspired."

"Where?"

"Our story…" he says. "A guy from the nineteenth century who gets lost in the future. I'm sure there's already something like that, but you have good elements to apply to the plot. Experience, which is very important."

"But I write romance novels."

"Include romance in it."

I gulp at the suggestion. Thinking about our history, as Ben said, seems like a good idea for a book. But if it has romance, and for me romance is essential, it has to have a happy ending.

My story with Ben is far from having a happy ending.

"It's just a suggestion." I think Benjamin has noticed my disappointed expression. "I thought it might help with your writer's block."

I smile, pushing away the melancholy. "Don't worry, I'd love to write a character inspired by you. You'd be the best in the Bellaverse."

Benjamin smiles, closing the book he's holding. "I'd like to read one of your novels."

I'm surprised by the statement. "I'd be honoured, but I don't have any stories translated into English."

Benjamin lets out a frustrated sigh. "Why not?"

I shrug. Laura always asks me the same question.

"I don't know, I haven't thought about it. My readers are in Brazil."

"But you could win more readers by translating. I'd

think about it. I could proofread them myself, if you want. I used to proofread for the newspaper."

"Really? I thought you were the boss."

"Yes, I was, but Howard, my secretary, was the one who showed up when necessary. In the beginning, when I opened the office, I was just thinking of having an impartial news channel. Well, as far as possible, but bold enough to expose important events, which other newspapers might not do. I ended up enjoying the work, especially the editing."

"You'd be quite an editor if you were alive today."

Ben's smile dies a little. The same thing happens to me.

"Look, if you want, there are similar books here that I can refer you to. To the ones I write, I mean." I try to change the subject.

"I want to – I am very curious about these indecorous novels."

Laughing, I guide him to the left-hand side. I know the way by heart; after all, the romance section is my safe place.

"This is the place." I indicate the shelves with my hands. "Everything is in alphabetical order. I don't know all the authors but many of them. What do you have in mind?"

"Whichever one you recommend. I just want to understand what you write."

"Right…"

It will have to be a hot period romance but with a dose of cuteness.

"This one." I pull the copy off the shelf. "I think we have the one."

Benjamin analyses the cover of a strong shirtless man with long flowing hair.

"Is this gentleman supposed to be from the Regency period?"

I nod, with a naughty smile. "Delicious, right?"

He frowns, disagreeing. "We had more manners than that."

"And, thank heavens, we've made our fanfic and improved those manners."

"*Kissing a Duke*," Benjamin mutters, reading the title. "Are you sure this is the book?"

"Yes, this is one of the most famous books in the Regency romance genre."

Benjamin analyses the book once more, sighing as he concedes, "Very well, I'll follow your recommendation."

"I hope you like it, but don't read it if you don't. If that's the case, just close the book immediately. I'm totally averse to reading without pleasure. Stories should touch our souls."

"Is that what you believe?" Benjamin starts walking beside me as we head towards the cashier.

"Yes, I've always believed that. And the same applies to writing – don't get me wrong, of course, a financial return is expected when we release a book – there's an investment there, of time, study… just like any other job…"

"Of course, it's your profession and should be treated as such."

"Exactly. But…" I hand the two books to the cashier. I notice that she runs her eyes over Benjamin, with a hidden smile on her lips. My stomach does a somersault. I don't like what I see, not at all.

"Have a nice day," she says, looking at him.

"Thank you."

I turn round quickly, and Benjamin follows me. I wonder if he realised how she looked at him.

"You were saying…" He speaks to me, and I have to struggle to remember.

"I was saying that… ah, that books are art, and art is something special. You have to… feel it, in your soul, or none of it makes sense."

Benjamin smiles, and I wonder if he thinks I'm too silly. The next moment, I have my answer.

"Just when I think you can't surprise me any more, you come along and prove me wrong. Never change, Bella." His dark eyes meet mine. "The world, no matter the era, would be a much better place if it had more people like you."

Completely touched, I hope Ben knows that I feel the same way about him.

15

All the pieces of the puzzle

Benjamin

He didn't know how to resist. Phillip was lost. He had resisted all that time only to lose his composure in a mere exchange of glances.

In a gaze that now led him to complete doom, with no chance of return.

Surrendering, he licked her, tasted her, plunged into her intimacy with all the impetus he had in him. He would make her scream his name; she was as doomed as he was. With every moan Primrose uttered, his member responded, rigid. Eager to enter her, to feel that sweet wetness squeeze him.

In the bathtub, I swallow as I look away from the pages and at *my* stiff member.

I was expecting something indecent from Lord Phillip, but this... well, I have to confess that it exceeded my expectations a little. Not that I can't handle indecency. For God's sake, of course, I can. The problem is that I'm trying *not* to be indecent. In my intention to be honourable to Bella, I've stifled every little bit of desire she arouses in me.

We've taken the situation with surprising humour. We've flirted, as we always have – she knows it, I know it – and we've just exchanged mischievous glances. It's not easy, I have to admit. It's even painful. Physically painful, my erection that's staring me in the face at the moment says so.

But I can fix it.

I sniff, putting the book aside, safe from the water in the bath. The door is closed; there's no noise outside – Bella has gone to the market, and Duke is asleep. I slide my body further into the water, finding a comfortable position. I wrap my right hand around my cock, crack my neck, and close my eyes.

The sight of Isabella staring at me with wickedness is immediate.

Like Lord Phillip and his lady, I also want to taste her. So I do. In my mind, I lay Isabella down in front of me, spread her legs, and lick her. I *really* do. My hand starts moving from top to bottom. Isabella moans my name; her legs shake. How delicious... my tongue explores every fold, every part of this marvellous intimacy. Like everything else about her, Isabella is sweet. Perfect.

The sound of the water makes me aware of where I am, but I try to stay there, with her. My hand speeds up. I suck on her swollen clitoris, alternating between slow and rhythmic movements of my tongue. The fantasy is very real. I can smell her, taste her, feel her skin. My mouth is wet with her pussy, and I can only want more. I want to fuck her afterwards. Penetrate her to the core, feel every centimetre. And then I want to do it again.

I can feel that I'm cumming, just as Isabella is cumming too.

Ahhhh... damn, that's so good.

"Benjamin, what..."

I open my eyes, my heart racing as I see Isabella staring at me close to the bathroom door. Her eyes go to my hand, still on my cock, and she blushes. Exactly as it was in my fantasy just now.

"I was..." I try to say, but I think it's pretty obvious what I was doing.

"I'm sorry, I heard you moan and I thought..."

I finally manage to react and cringe. She turns around and runs away.

Shit, that's embarrassing. It takes me two seconds to react. I finish washing, get out of the bath, and change. When I come out of the bathroom, Isabella is in the kitchen, leaning on the counter with a glass of Coke.

I approach, wrapped in embarrassment. "I feel like I should explain, but..."

"No, there's no need." Isabella puts the glass down. "I... understand. Forgive me, I heard the noise, and I didn't realise... I should have realised."

I nod, still not sure what to say. "I was on the edge."

"Yes, I understand."

"It was you, however, that I was im..." I've said too much. Isabella stares at me with wide eyes. It's too late to back out. "I was thinking about you."

Isabella lifts the corner of her mouth, blushing once again.

"Thank you for telling me."

"It's inelegant, I know, but…"

"It's not rude. I've done it too."

I was relaxed because of my recent enjoyment, but it seems that the sexual urgency has returned.

"Done what?" I can't help asking.

"I also…" Isabella hesitates. It seems I'm not the only one who's said too much. "I've touched myself and was also thinking about you."

Calm down, Benjamin. Remember your purpose.

To hell with it. I can't think of honour now. Not with the image of Isabella touching herself *thinking about me.*

I move closer, coming within centimetres of her. Bella lifts her face, meeting my gaze.

"What was I doing in your fantasy?"

She didn't expect this question. Even I didn't expect it, but I want to hear the answer.

"We shouldn't talk about it."

"Don't be a prude now, Bella. It doesn't suit you, a woman from 2022."

Bella swallows dryly, without even blinking. "What were we doing in yours?"

"I asked first."

"Well, I…"

If it's possible, I move a little closer. I can feel the warmth she exudes, the soft perfume that haunts me.

"Tell me," I whisper.

Bella moistens her lips, almost driving me to delirium.

"You were sucking me off and I came in your mouth."

Yes, you did. I remember it well.

"Give me more details."

"You asked me to lie down, and then to spread my legs," Bella says slowly. "I obeyed. You moved closer and started slowly. We weren't in a hurry. We just wanted to..." she swallows dryly, "enjoy it."

I'm about to forget everything I said the other night, like a damn scoundrel. Of course I want to enjoy it. I want to take Isabella for myself and turn these fantasies into reality.

"Bella, I..."

An annoying ringtone takes us out of the moment. I don't know whether to curse or be grateful. Isabella still looks dizzy as she checks her phone screen.

"My sister has arrived. She's on her way up."

I nod, watching Bella fix her hair and leave the kitchen. I'm hard again, so I take a deep breath and take my time, so I don't embarrass myself in front of the LeBlancs. While I wait, my wits come back to me, and I remind myself that nothing happening is the best course of action for both of us.

But is it? I don't know what to think anymore.

* * *

Laura and Pierre LeBlanc are exceptionally nice people.

Since they arrived two days ago, Bella and I have spent a lot of time with them. They've both treated me cordially, and they're polite and a lot of fun.

I believe that fun must run in Bella's family.

Tonight's dinner is at the Hard Rock Cafe. When

Bella mentioned the rock 'n' roll-themed restaurant, I didn't understand. I didn't know what rock was, or roll, or anything like that. She, as always, explained it to me with musical examples provided by the kind Alexa.

I liked the songs, but I have my reservations about some of them. I don't want to be rude and say that more of them sound like noise to me, so.... well, I won't say anything more than that.

The restaurant, unsurprisingly, is a rather noisy place. And confusing, and dark, and bright. Full of people and strange objects on display, all belonging to some rock star. According to Bella, the reservation for tonight's dinner was made a fortnight ago. It sounds like an exclusive place that today's Londoners hold in high regard.

"What about your father, Bella?" Laura asks as we all settle down at a table. She's holding hands with her husband, Pierre LeBlanc. They make a beautiful couple and exchange passionate glances without any fear. Bella had told me that they are, in her words, crazy about each other, so much so that they even work together.

She and her sister are also very different physically, I believe because they have different fathers, but I can see the similarity in the way they talk and laugh and the amused looks they exchange with each other.

"Dad's fine, but I feel he's sadder some days." Bella puts the straw in her mouth and takes a sip of her pink lemonade with basil. "He's lonely. He's dying for me to go to Tokyo and spend a few days with him."

"Are you going to?"

"I'm thinking of going next year. It wasn't in the plans, but… I can always find a way."

I'm touched by the way Bella refers to her father. We have that in common. Mr Kato has only her in the world, just as Abigail has only me. Or had... I don't know anymore. Whenever I think of her, it's as if someone crushes my chest.

"I was in Tokyo last year. I liked it a lot; it's a very modern city," says Pierre. "Do you know it, Benjamin?"

"No, I've never been there."

"But have you travelled far?"

Oh, my friend, you have no idea.

"Yes, but I end up staying in England most of the time. My tit... business demands it."

"What do you really do?" Laura asks me.

I didn't expect this question, so I take a moment to think about it.

"He's an editor," Isabella answers for me. "Of books. Benjamin has even given me some tips."

Laura opens a wide, genuine smile. "Oh, you mean you've broken through the writer's block? What a relief, I couldn't bear to see you fretting about it any longer."

"I've not really broken out of it completely, but I've had some ideas."

"Like what?" Pierre asks, taking a sip of his drink.

I remain silent, sipping my Scotch.

"He's a lord from the nineteenth century," Bella begins, looking at me, "who travels through time and—"

"Oh dear," the comment comes from Laura. "Like Kate and Leopold?"

I hold in my laughter. Apparently, Leopold is a reference on the subject among women.

"Yes, like that, but it's not certain yet. Let's change the subject."

I realise how uncomfortable Bella is with the topic. It upsets me. I've never read any of her work, but I've seen the twinkle in her eye when we're in the bookshop, or when she refers to books in general. I sincerely hope that she can overcome this block, even if it's with my lame idea of writing about our situation.

Not to mention that it would be nice to give our story a happy ending, romantically speaking.

"What are you planning to do while you're here?" Bella asks her sister.

"There's the ball, of course. We're going to the O2 to do some shopping, then I want to take a photo at Tower Bridge."

I feel lost. "Tower Bridge?"

"Yes, near the Tower of London." Laura takes a chip and puts it in her mouth.

"Ah, yes. I'm sorry," I disguise it. "I guess I'm a bit tired."

Isabella holds back her laughter. "That's where we met," she says and winks at me.

The corner of my lips lifts.

"But that's it," Laura continues. "I thought about going to Stonehenge, but we decided against it. We'll come back in the summer, and I think it's cooler to see the circle at the solstice."

Bella seems immediately struck by something. She frowns, and her gaze meets mine. "Ben, could you come with me for a moment?" she asks.

No one at the table understands the question, but I don't dare question her.

"Of course. Excuse me." I nod before following Bella through the restaurant.

She stops at an inconspicuous corner. There's a window next to it with a torn, silverish outfit of very questionable taste. The sign inside the glass reads "Lady Gaga". This lady is definitely not inspired by the Regency period.

"Bella, what's wrong?" I ask.

"My sister said something about Stonehenge that made me think."

"What?"

We've discussed megalithic sites before; Stonehenge was even on the agenda. But I didn't disappear near any giant stone.

"I think we forgot to take the solstice into account." She picks up her mobile phone. "What day did you disappear?"

"The 21st of June."

She types something into her mobile phone and smiles. "It was solstice day, Ben! That's why you disappeared. Let's think about the elements: the stone, the possible sorceress, desire, and the solstice. Yes, that must be it."

It makes sense. I mean, it doesn't, but in my case, it does.

"Does that mean I have to wait until the next solstice to repeat what I did in Bath?"

"It's possible. The next one is… on the 21st of December. My God, it's in eight days."

I'm feeling so many things that I don't even know what to think. Relief, yes, but also longing. Because I'm going to miss this brilliant woman who seems to have solved my life.

"Is that it?" I ask. "We wait eight days?"

Bella nods, but I can feel the twinge of sadness in her voice. "Yes, Ben. In eight days, we'll go to Bath and try again. But this time, I think you're really going back to the past."

No sentence has ever sounded as bittersweet as this one.

* * *

"I wanted to talk to you alone."

Sinking into an armchair with a glass of Scotch in my hand, I turned to my brother.

"I'm listening."

I was annoyed with him. With his decision to buy a commission and head off onto a bloody battlefield, leaving us behind. We were born on the same day, but we had different personalities. I was irresponsible; I wanted to live like there was no tomorrow. Barney wasn't. He was honourable. A perfect heir to a title like my father's.

"I know you don't agree with my decision."

"I don't agree."

"But I need you to understand me, Benjamin." His *voice was low. "I need to do this."*

I downed my drink, feeling my chest tighten. Squeezing.

I understood his motives. I didn't agree, but I understood. It was part of who he was. And I loved him as he was.

We all loved him. It was always like that.

"What if you don't come back?" I got up and walked over to him, my identical reflection. "What if you die there? What will become of us?"

"You'll carry on without me."

I shook my head. *"How, Barney? How can you talk about your death so naturally?"*

"Death is inevitable, Benjamin. I'd rather die out there, fighting for what I believe in, than live a life of disappointment knowing that I could have done more and didn't."

Honour. Always honour. Never the parties and the drinks. Never the women who wanted him. Never the trips with friends, the nights of gambling and betting.

Always honour.

"Brother, I can't leave if you resent me." He met my gaze. *"It's you, Benjamin. I need you to support me. I realise that this also means a lot to you, that if anything happens to me, you'll be the heir."*

"I don't want any of that."

I wanted him alive.

"I know you don't, but it's a possibility. To leave, I need you to confirm that you can do it. If I don't come back, I need you to look after our family. After Abigail, after our father. I need you to look after them and be their support while I fight for our country."

I looked away. What he was asking of me was a lot.

"Please..." Barney said again. *"Forgive me, but I have to do this."*

I pulled him into a tight hug. It felt like a final goodbye, but I refused to accept it. Barney had always done everything for us. Everything. Supporting him was the least I could do.

"Come back," I ordered.

"I'll do my best." He stared at me once more. *"Take care of them for me."*

I nodded. I would do it. For Barney, for my brother, I'd take care of them.

I stare at the ceiling, lying on the sofa, feeling...

I don't know what I feel. I hoped that when I found out how to get home, I would be happy. That's what I wanted, wasn't it? To go back to my century, my duties, my sister. To the place where I could fulfil the promise I made to my brother.

In fact, it's the only thing that awakens something good in me at the moment. With my return, Abigail will be safe, and whatever has happened to her will change. Gustave won't be a duke, and our bloodline will probably continue. Everything as it should have been from the beginning. As for me... I too will remain the same. The man who prioritises the world around him. The man who doesn't recognise himself when he looks in the mirror because he doesn't know himself, nor does he have the time to do so.

Apart from that, there's Bella. Her and the two centuries that separate us.

"Ben?"

Isabella's voice startles me. She looks beautiful, with her hair down and wearing pyjamas – trousers and long sleeves – a print of what looks like a princess on her T-shirt.

"Bella? Are you OK? What time is it?"

"Two in the morning. I couldn't sleep."

I sit down and gesture with my head for her to come closer. "Come here."

Bella smiles slightly and settles down next to me.

"Why do you think you can't sleep?" I ask. We lay our heads on the back of the sofa, facing each other.

"Thinking of you. Eight days... it seems too soon."

I swallow. Yes, eight days is really soon. It's even insulting. It's not long enough, but I suspect it never would be.

"I feel the same way. Our farewell isn't something I'm looking forward to."

Bella nods, moving a little. "What happened earlier, before Laura arrived, was..."

"Repressed desires, as you say."

She laughs. "Yes. But are we just horny?"

"You know better than that."

It's never been just lust. There's always been more between Bella and me.

She gently strokes my cheek. "What if—"

"Bella..." I mutter, just before she finishes.

Bella doesn't stop touching me. "What if we took advantage of these last days? What if we lived through it, at least to have a sweet memory?"

I understand why she's asking me that. I think about it every second. But I also realise that Bella has already suffered, that I don't want to be another man who made her cry. If I could, I'd be the opposite of that. By my side, I'd make sure she only smiled. What a difficult situation.

"I want it, but I worry about your feelings. About you."

"But I also want you. I'm the one proposing this madness."

"I don't want to break your heart, Bella."

She sighs. "I don't think there's any way out of this, Ben. We've gone too far, even if we tried to avoid it."

I think of all the words hidden behind that sentence. I think we've gone too far too.

Bella brings her face close to mine, gluing our foreheads together. I close my eyes, feeling our breath mingle. There is peace and torment inside me. Wonderfully disturbing.

"I can't stop thinking that we'll soon be separated," Bella says, and I open my eyes, meeting hers. "But I also wonder why you came to me at what was perhaps the worst moment for my heart."

I take her hand and bring it to my lips, kissing the soft palm.

She continues: "I don't mind suffering later. I'm already suffering now. But if you want us to have something besides a broken heart, good memories, if you can overcome your sense of honour, I want that too." She lifts the corner of her mouth. "Think about it, OK?"

I agree and watch her leave me alone again in the dark room. I want to follow her, to take her in my arms, to feel her, and worship her as I have never done with anyone. But I suspect that if I do, I won't be able to let go of her. And I need to do that.

For my sister's sake, I have to leave.

I've never felt such conflict between desire, duty, heart, and honour. I have no idea what to do.

Worst of all, I'm running out of time.

16

Overcoming Mr. Darcy

Isabella

I look in the mirror, laughing as I see myself as a regal lady. Tonight is the night of the ball that Laura invited us to.

"My God, look at this…" I mumble. Laura, who is also in the bedroom getting ready with me, runs her eyes over me.

"A perfect lady," she comments.

I analyse the pretty blue dress with a smile on my face. Considering that Laura told me at short notice, I was lucky to get this dress. London has a few shops that sell period gowns similar to the Regency ones, as is the case with this one. It has a beautiful straight cut, is made of a shimmering light-blue fabric, and has lace sleeves with sparkles applied to the embroidered flowers. But it's not exactly seasonal. I could easily wear it to a wedding or something.

Laura chose a similar dress but red and with a slit in the skirt. Always red, I don't know why she can't get enough of it.

"There were sixty-seven colours for you to choose from," I say, putting on the sparkly drop earrings.

"I like red; Pierre likes red; we all do. I don't see why I should choose any other colour."

I laugh, checking my bun. We did a few curls with the curling iron, but mine lasted about twenty minutes. I put on some make-up, eyeliner, eyeshadow, and light lipstick and tied my hair up in a low bun, with my bangs loose. I look nice. I don't know if I'm worthy of being the subject of a column like Lady Whistledown's from *Bridgerton*, but... pretty.

"Are we ready?" I bend down to pick up my sandals.

"Yes. But first..." Laura sits on the bed, "I have to tell you something."

I open my mouth. "My God, you're pregnant!"

My sister rolls her eyes. "Jeez, what is it with people? Just because I got married, every piece of news I tell has to be related to a baby?"

"I'm sorry, you're right." I sit down next to her. "Go on, tell me."

I know the subject is important because I know my sister and that serious face.

"Matheus got married."

OK, I wasn't expecting that. "Married?"

"Yes, last weekend. Want to know the details?"

Yes. No, I'm not interested in his life anymore. Oh dear, why do I have to be so curious?

"Tell me everything."

Laura is worried about me; that's why she's so careful. Even so, my sister isn't the type to hide things from me. She tells me that she heard from one of our mum's acquaintances that Matheus and his fiancée had suddenly decided to get married. In Las Vegas!

"Las Vegas? Are you kidding?"

"I swear. There's a photo on Instagram and everything."

"I didn't even know that was possible. What about the documents?"

"I even looked it up because I was in doubt too. But yes, as long as the bride and groom communicate their country of origin, the marriage in Nevada is valid."

I'm really surprised. "You know Matheus always criticised this kind of thing, right? He said it was cheesy and everything. I said more than once that it must be fun to be officiated by someone dressed as Elvis and he said: 'Wow, you're cheesy, Bella.'"

"It was an Elvis who married them."

I laugh, but I'm not sure I find it funny. "How bizarre…" I comment.

Laura stays silent for a minute, then asks me: "How are you?"

"I'm still trying to imagine my ex in front of a fake Elvis."

"No, Bella. I'm talking about you, about your feelings."

I frown, staring at my sister.

"I thought you'd be sad about it. Not sad exactly, but… feeling something. What are you feeling?"

Laura's words have a significant impact on me. And that's because I'm not feeling anything.

My God, nothing. I don't feel sad; I don't feel sorry for myself; I don't even want to look at the wedding photos, not out of spite, but because they don't interest me. From the bottom of my heart, if Matheus has got married and is happy, I wish him well, but I don't want to and won't waste my time finding out about his life.

"I'm fine, Laura. Really well." I smile. "He doesn't cause me to feel anything anymore. I… I think I'm finally over it. I've turned the page."

Laura smiles too, taking my hand. "Oh, Bella, I'm so happy. You're coming back. Writing again, smiling."

Yes, I really am. I've only just realised that.

"Is it linked to Benjamin?"

Laura's question takes me by surprise.

"Benjamin?"

"Yes. I've noticed the way you look at each other. There's something going on there, isn't there?"

"Oh, no." I smooth the skirts of my dress, my palms suddenly sweaty. "Ben is a friend."

"A friend?" My sister raises an eyebrow. "Are you sure nothing's happened?"

Damn. I hate that Sherlock Holmes way she has of picking up on the smallest signs.

"A kiss, but that's all."

Laura claps her hands excitedly. "Girl, but why? Have you ever looked at that man? What about the English accent?"

Yes, yes, I've noticed all that.

"Laura, it's complicated. Benjamin lives far away and…"

"Where far? Absolutely nowhere is far with today's technology."

That's right. With *today's* technology.

"Lau, don't push it. Seriously, I wish things were different, but they're not."

She tilts her neck to the side, now without smiling. "But you're in love, aren't you?"

I remain in silence. Am I? Just a second is all it takes for me to know the answer. Yes, of course, I am. It's time to admit it. How could I not be? Benjamin not only came to distract me from my broken heart, but he also put it back together. It'll break again in a week, but it's not his fault.

It's just... life, I guess. I was sincere two nights ago when I suggested we live in the moment. But I'm not going to pressure him. I expected Benjamin to simply throw his wits aside and follow me to the bedroom, but he didn't do anything of the sort. However, I know him. He's thinking about it. It's likely. For an author who was so fond of a *slow burn*, life has shown me what my poor characters go through.

I got screwed, and well done to me.

"Shall we talk to the boys?" I stand up, shaking off the countless emotions taking over the left side of my chest. "They must be ready."

"OK, but Bella?" Laura calls me, and I turn to her. "Don't deprive yourself of happiness out of fear, OK? I understand that you're afraid of getting involved after Matheus, but... be open. Life can surprise us."

A surprise from life allowing me to experience love is all I want after these last few days. I walk down the corridor with Duke in my wake.

"Your Grace won't be able to go to the ball tonight. Sorry, sweetie."

He wags his tail and gives a low bark. As soon as I enter the room, I see Pierre concentrating on his phone and Benjamin right behind him. They both stand up as soon as they notice us.

And wow. I almost lose my breath when Benjamin approaches me, dressed in character. I'd forgotten about his lord's clothes. After he came out of hospital and we bought new clothes, I had them washed at a dry cleaner and we kept them in storage. The look is perfect. The black jacket, the pearlescent waistcoat, and the white tie and gloves. He looks even taller, even more handsome than the first time I saw him dressed like this in hospital.

Maybe it's because I know what's *inside* those clothes. Because now I know his strong body, his broad shoulders, his narrow waist, and his six pack. And the cock just below it. Let's not forget that I caught Benjamin masturbating, thinking about me, a few days ago and…

Wow. Just wow.

"Milady." Benjamin bows to me and takes my hand for a gentle kiss. A kiss that gives me all the butterflies in the world in my stomach.

"You, milord, look very… hot – elegant."

He smiles sideways. "I hear you have a thing for lords."

I look him up and down. For a *certain lord*, in particular. "I love these little boots…" I mumble, making him laugh.

"You look stunning."

Oh, dear. This man…

"Wow, we're really in the Regency," Laura says excitedly. "Come on, let's take a selfie."

"Selfie?" Benjamin asks me, whispering.

I'm surprised. Since he arrived, we've been so busy with the travelling dilemma that we haven't taken any photos.

"A photo. Smile."

Laura holds out her arm with her phone camera and the four of us smile.

"Oh, that's great. I'll post it and tag you. Ben, do you have Insta?"

"Benjamin doesn't like social media."

"Hmm, a vintage man. Got it," my sister comments.

I just smile. She doesn't know the half of it.

* * *

The ball takes place at Nelson House, a Georgian house near the centre of London. As soon as we cross the threshold, I realise that all eyes are on us. Or rather, the perfect, elegant lord next to me.

"Well?" I ask him, wrapped around his arm. Laura and Pierre walk away towards the waiter with a tray of champagne. "Too different?"

I imagine it is. The song played by the string quartet is Maroon 5's latest release. The room is well lit, and not just by candles. The floral arrangements are, as Ben likes to say, stunning – white, purple, and lilac flowers. I wonder where the decorators got their inspiration. Basically, it's a party like any other, but with dances and period costumes. The best of both worlds.

"It's similar," Benjamin replies. "Maybe not completely accurate, though…"

"Come on, I want a list."

He looks around, moistening his lips. "Well, for a start, the smell. I don't smell sweat like I used to. You know, that pleasant scent of—"

I grimace in disgust. "Ew, next item," I interrupt him.

Benjamin laughs. "Alright, next. The music is different; the clothes... they're similar."

"I really thought this dress was very modern."

Benjamin runs his eyes over me. "It's beautiful. You look beautiful, Bella. I've already said that."

I blush, but I don't play modest. Yes, he's already said it, but Benjamin can praise me all he wants, and I'll believe him every time.

"There's a zip on my dress. Doesn't that bother you? There were no zips in your day," I tease.

"Why on earth would I be bothered by a zip? I think it's a brilliant invention, by the way."

"I've met people who refused to watch certain films because the costumes weren't right," I explain. "I swear, I'm not lying."

Benjamin shakes his head. "What insanity, and no sense of humour either."

"Bella!" My sister comes up to us, flustered. "Do you hear that? It's the first dance! Did you study that video I sent you?"

Oh, I didn't. Laura sent me a quick tutorial on Regency dances, so we wouldn't be so lost.

"I didn't watch it, but I doubt people here know all the steps."

"I don't know." Laura points to a boy on the other side of the room. "That one surpasses Mr Darcy in arrogance. Soon he will call us poor, filthy people."

Pierre and I laugh.

"Don't worry, we'll show him. What's the first dance?"

"A minuet." That's Benjamin speaking. "At least, if they're following the custom of the time."

"Can you dance the minuet?" I ask.

He looks at me sideways. "Bella, give me some credit, will you?"

As much as you like, Your Grace. As much as you like.

The four of us position ourselves on the dance floor, me with Benjamin, Laura with Pierre. It's not as disastrous as I imagined, but I feel sorry for Ben. He's perfect, trying to teach me the steps, turns, and jumps in harmony with the violin's melody. It's harder than it looks, but he doesn't seem to mind my embarrassment, as he laughs the whole dance, just like the other couples here.

When the dance is over, Laura can't stop laughing. "Of all of us here, only Benjamin saved himself. You can go back to the nineteenth century and you'll manage."

I tried my best to suppress a smirk.

"*Mon amour*, I wasn't so bad," Pierre protests.

"My dear, you have noble blood and that is it. But think about it, at least we're together in our lack of ability."

He smiles and pulls her into a kiss. It's not the first time this has happened, but next to Ben, I feel slightly uncomfortable.

"Shall we have a drink?" I suggest. "There's punch over there."

Benjamin nods and we move away from the couple in love. He very thoughtfully pours me some of the pink liquid that I suspect was baptised with champagne. I take a sip, feeling relief in my dry throat.

"Do they have any Scotch?" Benjamin asks.

I look round and see a waiter in the other corner of the room with what looks like a tray containing several glasses of Scotch.

"Over there," I point discreetly.

"Excuse me, I'm just going to get a drink and I'll be right back."

I watch Benjamin walk away from me, and I can't resist staring at his perfect, round arse in his tight trousers. Nothing wrong with those glutes either, but I still need to see them without clothes on. It was the only part of Benjamin that got away.

For now, I hope.

With my peripheral vision, while I'm immersed in the melody of "Wildest Dreams" by Taylor Swift, a strong blond man approaches me, looking cheerful.

"Milady! What's your name?"

Yeah, he must be a bit drunk.

"Isabella. Yours?"

"I'm Bryan…" He thinks. "I was given a title before the party, but I forgot. An earl, or a marquis."

There was a guy outside holding cards with fictitious names and titles for anyone who was interested. Considering that Pierre is a descendant of a baron and Benjamin a real duke, we didn't care much for that.

The guy comes closer to me. "Are you enjoying the dance?"

"Excuse me. Can I help you, sir?"

I look over and Benjamin is staring at the guy, his arms folded behind his back and his expression closed. Now that is a Mr Darcy. I wonder where the Scotch he went to get is.

"Hey, mate! You've certainly embodied the character," the guy comments.

Benjamin doesn't move a muscle on his handsome face. "What do you want with the lady?" he asks.

The stranger laughs. "I was going to ask the *lady*," he smiles, "to dance."

Benjamin draws himself up, moving his arms to his sides. "Unfortunately, Miss Isabella's card is full. All her dances are unavailable."

The poor thing tries to answer, but the look Benjamin gives him is enough to make him give up. He walks away, giving me an amused smile.

And I have to say that *I loved* the little jealousy scene. Loved a lot.

"I don't have my card filled out." I take a sip of my drink, talking to Benjamin. "I don't even have a card."

"But you're not going to dance with that scoundrel." He frowns. "You're going to dance with me."

"All the dances?"

"Yes, all of them."

Benjamin is sexy as a gentleman, but as a determined and jealous gentleman, he's twice as sexy. I just want to throw myself on him and rip all his clothes off.

"That would be very scandalous," I tease. "I don't know if you know this, but it's not polite to dance with the same lady more than once."

"Luckily," he takes my hand, leading us to the dance floor, "this is the twenty-first century, not the nineteenth."

I'm still laughing when the beats of John Legend's "All of Me" come out of the speakers.

"Apparently, this dance is from my time," I say.

"Teach me," Benjamin requests.

That's what I do. I take his big hands and guide him around my waist, gluing our bodies together. John Legend continues to sing as I wrap my arms around Benjamin's neck and guide the first movements. He's a quick learner, and within seconds, we're experiencing what is perhaps the most romantic moment of my entire life.

Benjamin and I dancing together at a Regency ball, or almost.

"Beautiful lyrics…" Benjamin whispers, looking at me.

"Yes, they are."

I want to know what he's thinking. What he's feeling. I wonder if it's the same as me, if this wonderful duke's heart is racing too. If it's beating for me.

With what he says next, I think so.

"I'm going to kiss you," Benjamin warns. It's not a request, nor is it a question. "But I'm still not sure about anything."

I'm not sure either, but I don't mind.

"OK."

Benjamin takes his right hand from my waist and wraps it around my face, kissing my lips. A sweet kiss, full of emotion and feeling. A kiss that I would define, in one of my novels, as a true love's kiss.

I was wrong before. *This* is the most romantic moment of my life. Here, with my perfect duke, our tongues dancing together just like our bodies. It doesn't matter what era we're from, how much time we have left, or what our futures will be like.

Here and now, I want everything from him, and

want to give everything to him, just like the lyrics we're listening to.

The evening couldn't have been more perfect. Hours later, we travel home hand in hand in the Uber, but we don't say anything. It's hard to think with my heart racing like it is now. We enter the flat, Ben giving me the go-ahead.

I'm surprised when he grips my hand tighter as soon as he closes the door behind us. It's dark, but I can see the glint in his eye. I can see the desire, which may well be a reflection of my own.

"I've tried to resist, but I can't," he says.

My heart is about to explode.

"Really?"

Benjamin nods, pressing his body to mine, my back against the corridor wall. One of his hands wraps around my waist, while the other holds my face. "Are you sure about this? Do you still think that now is enough? That sweet memories will be enough?"

No, I don't think so. Or maybe I do. I don't know. I haven't thought about the goodbye. I don't want to because it hurts. But I need him. I need Benjamin, that's for sure, even if only for one night.

"I want this," I reply. "I don't want to think."

Benjamin nuzzles our noses, whispering before finally kissing me, "Perfect. Because today, I don't want to think either. Today, all I want is you."

17

Right answer

Isabella

Benjamin lifts me up, wraps my legs around his waist, and with his hands firmly on my arse, carries me into the bedroom as if I weigh nothing.

He switches on the light and places me on the bed, never stopping kissing me. His tongue is impetuous and explores my mouth as if the world were going to end tomorrow. It's true, though. For both of us, in our little world, there isn't much time left. I scold myself. I'm not going to think about endings. Not now, when I'm finally in his arms.

Duke follows us and tries to get Ben's attention. Benjamin stops kissing me and laughs as he looks at the dog. He quickly bends down and picks him up.

"No, no, little friend. Now is my time to play, not yours."

He gently closes the bedroom door, leaving Duke outside. I don't think Your Grace protests, but if he does,

I don't hear it. Benjamin turns round again and runs his eyes over me. I've never felt so hot. I'm burning up, inside, outside, everywhere.

Nobody has ever looked at me the way he does.

We're both still dressed, shoes, boots, and all. He takes his hand to the knot of his tie and begins to undo it.

"What do you want, Bella? The lord or the rake?" he asks me, pulling off his tie and throwing it aside.

"You. I want you."

All his versions. As many as he wants to offer me.

Benjamin nods. "Right answer."

He approaches me, still wearing the rest of his clothes. Benjamin kneels in front of the bed and pulls me close. He plunges his hand into my hair and grips it firmly but also kindly. His lips touch the skin of my neck, where a trail of kisses and licks follows that leaves me shivering, completely surrendered to him.

"I'm going to fuck you all night long," he whispers in my ear, biting my earlobe, "but first I want to make our fantasies come true."

I pull away, feeling my nipples harden under the fabric of the dress. I knew he was a *naughty boy*. Benjamin's eyes are on me, and they've never been so wicked. What a delight of a man, my goodness.

"Our fantasies?" I ask, and Benjamin nods.

"Yes, ours."

I feel his hands slide the zip down the back of my dress. I imagine what it would be like if we were in his time. We'd be involved for several minutes in the difficult task of opening the countless buttons. Point for modernity.

"What did you fantasise about?" I start to open his

waistcoat, helping with a wave of my arms as he pulls at the fabric.

I'm not wearing a bra. I've always had small breasts. It's never bothered me, but people have hinted that I should consider getting silicone. From the way he looks at me, fixated on my nipples, moistening those full lips that I want to make swollen from kissing so much, Ben doesn't see anything wrong with them.

"Gorgeous…" Benjamin murmurs, pulling the dress down. The pile of blue fabric swirls around my feet, and I realise I'm only wearing my knickers in front of Benjamin.

I haven't been with anyone for a long time since my relationship ended, so I feel a bit lost. I'm not prudish about sex or shy or anything like that. I'm just… a bit intoxicated by everything that's happening right now.

"Tell me your fantasies." I continue undressing him. Benjamin helps me as I pull his shirt out of his trousers and over his head.

"They're similar to yours." His dark hair is messy from taking off his shirt. "Me, between your legs, licking you until you fall apart."

My pussy throbs with the words, with the raunchy, husky way he says them. I admire this perfect physique, touching the warm skin with my fingertips, feeling every tensed muscle and his marvellous abs.

"I want to lick every bit," I whisper, "One by one."

Benjamin smiles sideways, raising his hand to let go of my hair. "You will, but only after I've made you come."

I feel the clips come loose and my long hair fall down my bare back. Benjamin takes another moment to look at me, his hand now caressing one of my nipples, gently pinching it.

"Lie down for me." He stands up. I obey, but without taking my eyes off him. I can't stop looking at him. I want to see him all night.

Still wearing his own trousers, Benjamin approaches me and removes my panties, his fingers gently rubbing my skin. I can see that he looks surprised when he looks at me.

"What's wrong?"

Benjamin kneels down again, grabbing my hip and bringing me close. "I forget that some things are different in the future..." He touches my lower abdomen gently. "I can see every part of you."

When I realise he's referring to my waxed skin, I blush. I can't help it. "I don't even know what to say."

"You don't have to answer anything." Benjamin settles down, his face now very close. "Save your words for the right moment."

And then I feel the first lick. My God in heaven, even this man's sucking is perfect.

"Relax, darling," he asks, looking down at my folded forearms. "Leave it to me." He winks.

A little wink, about to suck me off.

I do as he suggests and give in. It's not as if I can think of anything else but this man devouring me and taking me to heaven between licks and sucks. I've dreamt about it, imagined it in my own way. Nothing corresponds to reality. Nothing at all.

Benjamin is a master at what he does. Now I understand his libertine side. He licks my folds, sucks my lips and my clitoris. He takes his time there, on the pulsating nerve. I can feel the movement of his tongue, the sound of his sucking mixed with my moans filling the room. His thumbs open me wider, exposing my whole body. I look down and see him smiling as my gasps increase and my legs begin to shake.

I'm very close, closer than ever. Benjamin notices and, pulling his mouth away just for a moment, he slips a finger into me. And then another, sucking my clitoris again, hungry, thirsty, until I'm overcome by spasms, grabbing his hair, and coming in his mouth, completely overwhelmed.

He did what he said. Our fantasies have come true.

Benjamin steps back and looks at me with a proud smile. He starts to unzip his trousers, but I stop him by sitting up on the mattress.

"No, let me do it," I say.

He doesn't refuse, coming closer.

With me sitting and him standing, I'm at the exact height of his hips. I'm still dizzy with pleasure, but I manage to open the button without difficulty, pulling down his trousers and black boxer shorts, releasing his glorious cock, which is harder than ever.

"My turn." I look at him, caressing his balls. "I want you to surrender, Benjamin."

He strokes my hair, nodding. "I've been on my knees for you for a long time, Bella."

I like what I hear. A lot. I stare at his cock, noticing every detail. The pink skin and glossy head, the purplish veins all over, the dark hairs. I touch it and spread the moisture from the tip. Benjamin moans, but the caress on my hair remains gentle. Tender.

"What do you want, Ben?" I tease, because I know exactly what he wants. My hand starts to jerk him off, up and down, again and again, feeling every centimetre.

"I want your mouth on my cock," he replies, making me smile. "Go ahead, Bella. I know you want it too."

Ah, he has no idea.

I open my mouth and start sucking him, ending the agony for both of us. His taste is delicious; his masculine scent intoxicates me. Benjamin closes his eyes and throws his head back, completely surrendering to me, allowing me to dictate the rhythm, which I do with the greatest pleasure.

I just came a few minutes ago, but I'm already on fire, wanting more of him, wanting everything I can get. I squeeze my thighs together and suck him deep into my throat, as deep as I can, and come again, repeating the movement, alternating with licks.

"Touch yourself for me, Bella," Benjamin growls softly. "Let me see you touch yourself."

Wow.

I spread my legs a little. I don't stop sucking on him as I run my hand down my stomach and find my clitoris, pressing on it. I dip my fingers in a little, feeling how aroused I am.

"Are you wet?" he asks me.

I nod with his cock in my mouth.

Benjamin smiles, his eyes locked on me as we do this. "Bella, I want you."

I take his cock out of my mouth and jerk it off again with my free hand. "I'm here."

"I want to get inside you. Let me fuck you."

I nod because I can't stand it either.

"Where's the protection?" he asks.

We talked about condoms on one of our days discussing modernity. I'm touched that Ben remembers this, even though he's desperate like me. Thinking about his question, for a moment I almost panic. I don't have a busy sex life, so condoms aren't the first item on my shopping list. Then, I remember that Cinthia is a careful girl, and there's always a packet of condoms in the bathroom cabinet.

"In the bathroom, in the cupboard under the sink."

Benjamin shoots out of the room and returns in less than a minute with the box in his hand. Duke must be asleep because there's no sign of the puppy.

"I don't know how to handle this, so…" Benjamin hands me the condom.

I smile as I open the condom and slide in the big cock. "That's it, we're safe."

Benjamin smiles, kissing me again, and lying on top of me, his strong, warm body making me aware that this moment we're living is real. He pushes my thighs apart, positioning himself between them. Benjamin penetrates me, looking into my eyes, every centimetre of him entering me.

It's as if we've been waiting our whole lives for this moment. With Benjamin, I feel at home. As if he were my home, as if… he was meant to be mine.

"My God, Bella, you're so tight…" He thrusts eagerly, going all the way in and back out again. "Are you alright?" he asks me.

I bring him closer with my arms around my shoulders. "Don't stop, Ben. Please don't stop."

Benjamin continues to penetrate me, his thrusts now stronger, more urgent. I'm so suspended in pleasure that I wouldn't be surprised if I forgot who I was. I open my eyes to find his eyes on me, his jaw clenched, focused. Benjamin takes his hand between us and strokes my clitoris, destroying what little sanity I have left.

"I'm going to come…" I confess, feeling my body tremble.

"Yes, my love. Come for me."

I can't hold it in any longer. Benjamin kisses my mouth, invading it with his tongue, and we fall apart at the same time, sweaty and eager, so exhausted and surrendered that we are unable to speak for several minutes.

Benjamin manoeuvres us both so he can remove the condom, setting it aside on the bedside table. He pulls me close, my head on his chest, where all I can hear is the rapid sound of his heart. A sound I could listen to for the rest of my days.

"That was wonderful," Benjamin says, and I look up, meeting his affectionate expression. "You're wonderful."

I stroke his clean-shaven chin with the tip of my index finger.

"You too. It's never been like this. I've never felt like this before."

"What do we do now?" Benjamin asks me.

I stroke the dark hairs on his chest, wondering what to say. The question is simple, but the answer is complex.

"Do we… make the most of it? The time we have left."

Benjamin swallows dryly, rubbing our noses together and kissing me softly. "You know that all the time in the world by your side wouldn't be enough for me, don't you?"

My eyes moisten and I feel a lump in my throat. "Yes, I know."

He kisses me once more, and once more, before we close our eyes and fall asleep, he says: "For the time we have left, I'm all yours, Bella."

I'm almost asleep when I think, *I'm yours too.* But I don't need to say anything.

I'm sure Benjamin already knows that.

18

I've found happiness, but I can't stay

Benjamin

"Are you alright?"

I looked away from my own plate and at my sister. As in recent weeks, she was still pale and thin. Her dark hair was dull, as were her eyes. So different from the girl full of life and dreams I used to know.

But I shouldn't be complaining. At least she wasn't in bed. She was trying to eat. She was talking.

"I am, Abby. Are you?"

Abigail nodded almost imperceptibly. "I've been thinking about Dad all day." She stared at the peas in front of her, playing with her fork. "Do you think he died because of guilt?"

I hadn't expected that question. Two months after my father's death, I tried not to think about him, to focus on the endless amount of work I had to do. However... Abigail's hypothesis had already crossed my mind. When Barney wanted to enlist, my father talked to him, tried to talk him out of it, even though he knew it wouldn't help. Barney was a stubborn man with strong opinions. My father knew that, so he bought his commission and said goodbye to his firstborn.

"Abby, I really think that…"

"I understand that you don't want to talk about it." Abigail sighed very slowly and met my gaze. "I understand that it hurts. But… I don't know, I think talking might do us some good."

I didn't know if I agreed. For my part, I just wanted to move on. To try. There was too much weight on my back. I didn't even see myself as having the right to complain, to feel. What was the point? Barney had died as a hero. My father was gone, leaving me the legacy of his entire life. Leaving Abigail in my care. I couldn't let them down.

"So speak up, Abby. Say what you want, I'm all ears."

Abby lifted the corner of her lips, but there was so much sadness in the gesture that I felt my heart break in two.

"I heard the butler say that Mr Spencer was here." She changed the subject.

Silently, I thanked him.

"Yes, Jack wanted to see how we were doing."

"He's your loyal friend, isn't he?"

I shrugged, but I couldn't disagree. "I think he's the only one. Well, I have other close acquaintances, but Jack is the only one I trust."

And the only one who bothered to ask how I was, even though we weren't in pleasure dens.

Another nod. "Why don't you enjoy his company and go out for a while?" Abigail suggested. "It's been a while since I've seen you do something other than working since before Dad died."

She wasn't wrong. Abigail knew me well; she knew that I liked to enjoy my nights of partying, travelling without a date to come home. However, I couldn't do that anymore. My life had changed, and I had other priorities now.

"I can't, Abby."

"Why not? Just because all this has happened doesn't mean you have to stop your life, darling."

Now she was very wrong.

"I don't have time. There's a lot of work at the newspaper; the title also demands time, apart from other responsibilities."

Abigail sighed again. "Like me? I've been quite a burden…"

Her words hit me like painful blows. Immediately, I stood up and walked over to her, pulling out the chair next to her and settling down, taking her hand.

"You're not a burden. You're my little sister." I felt my throat catch. "The only family I have."

Abby blinked back tears, her chin trembling.

"I want to get better, Benjamin. I've been sunk in melancholy, but I want to get better."

"I know you want to, Abby."

She sniffled. "I just… I didn't imagine losing them so soon. I miss Dad and Barney immeasurably."

I knew she did. I missed them too.

"Little one, you don't have to explain yourself. I understand."

Her gaze seemed lost. "I want to get better, Benjamin" she repeated. "I want to and… I must apologise to you."

"Apologise?" I couldn't understand it. My sister didn't have a single reason to apologise.

"Yes, I apologise. It's not fair on you. You're still here and you're dealing with the same situation, trying to be strong."

I nodded, bringing her hand to my lips and kissing the cool skin.

"Yes, I am. I'm not going to let anything fail us, Abby. I will honour their memory; I will protect you. You can trust me."

Abby brought her hand up to my face and stroked it.

"I hear you talking about honour, Benjamin. Honour and duty. What about your happiness?"

Once again, I didn't know what to say. "I'm happy to see you well. Don't worry about me."

Abby didn't cry, though. She straightened her posture, took a deep breath, and told me: "Dad wanted us to be happy. The three of us. That's why he allowed Barney to fight."

She was right. My father knew each of us well. In his own way, he always wanted us to be happy.

"Grandmother taught me that if you wish for something hard enough," Abigail continued, "the wish comes true. I wish you happiness, Benjamin. May we both be happy, despite everything."

I didn't answer, just nodded.

Of course, I wanted to see Abby happy. Healthy, as well. But she was being a dreamer, perhaps because she had faced so much pain.

I preferred to keep my feet on the ground. Everything had gone so wrong recently, who was to say it wouldn't get worse?

I just wanted to keep going. But I liked the discreet glint I saw in my sister's eyes. Somehow, her words were a start.

I would let Abby believe whatever she wanted to believe. I'd let her dream. If she wanted to, she could have all the hope in the world. Even though I didn't have any.

I open my eyes and stare at the ceiling, taking a while to remember where I am. The soft, sweet smell of Isabella's hair brings me back to reality. We're lying on our sides, her delicate back resting on my chest. I smile slightly, remembering what happened hours before.

I really am a scoundrel, but I don't regret what we did. It was intense, sweet, hot, all at the same time. I've never felt like this, so relaxed and satisfied. Well, at least while I can ignore what's about to happen.

Slowly, I move away from Bella without waking her. I sit on the bed, resting my feet on the floor, and run a hand through my hair. It's funny that I dreamt about my sister, the only reason I want to go back to my own time, just when Bella and I gave ourselves to each other.

The only reason. There's no denying that truth. Not anymore.

Restless, I put on my joggers and walk to the kitchen for a drink of water. Duke notices me and wags his furry tail without getting up from his bed.

"*Sshh*, go back to sleep."

He blinks and closes his eyes when I stroke his ears. Apparently, the dog didn't take offence at being kicked out of the room earlier. Not that I was worried about it.

I pour myself some water, lean my hip against the sink, and think.

I think about everything at once. Of Isabella, of the night we had tonight. My days here in London, how much they've changed me. I think about my parents, my brother. And then I think about Abigail and the intriguing lack of information about her.

I sit down on the sofa and pick up Bella's computer, opening it in my lap. Duke gets up and walks over to me, jumping up next to me and resting his head on one of my thighs.

"Let's see if we're lucky today, Your Grace," I whisper, typing my sister's name into Google.

Once again, as in all the previous searches, I find nothing but superficial information about her. Abigail Melissa Waldorf seems to have disappeared from history as if she were someone insignificant.

It kills me inside.

As I am now thoroughly awake, I decide to carry on researching. I decide to take a closer look at what I can find about the *Daily*. There isn't an infinite amount of information, but at least I can see that the newspaper has prospered. Jack's name appears from time to time among the available articles. As far as I can tell, it was Cornell's case that gave the paper its visibility. He was tried and sentenced to hang for treason and attempted murder. I wonder who he tried to kill after he was found out. There are more stories about denunciations made, some including noble ones. I can't find, however, the reasons why he went out of business.

Then, I type my own name. Each letter feels like torture; I can't explain exactly why. It's strange. I'm here, but I'm checking my past, so many years ago, but for me, it was yesterday. I wonder if the past will change when I return. If, when someone types in my name after 21 December, there will be a date of death or new relevant information.

I run a hand through my hair, putting the computer aside. I'm nervous now, restless. In a few days, I'll be dead. Not in my reality, but in this one. Just as I am in mine today, but not here. *Argh*, I get a headache just thinking about it.

"Ben?"

I look up to find Bella in the doorway, her dark, loose hair a mess. So beautiful and perfect. I think she's the most beautiful woman who has ever crossed my path.

"Did I wake you up?" I ask.

"No, but I turned over and realised you weren't in bed. I saw the light from the computer out here. Are you alright?"

Always concerned and attentive, my Bella.

"I dreamt about Abigail."

Bella presses her lips together, still reddened by my kisses. She moves closer and sits down next to me. Duke continues to lie on my lap as if I were the most comfortable pillow in the world.

"Do you want to talk?"

I take her hand and caress the soft palm with my fingers. "I often dream about episodes from the past. First, it was my grandmother, then my father, now Abigail. They all seem to send me a message. It's very intriguing."

"What are your memories now?"

"Abigail and I sat at the table after everything had happened. She wanted to heal from her melancholy. I swore to protect her; I swore to be by her side."

"And what else?"

My gaze and Bella's meet.

And she wanted me to be happy. I don't say the words out loud; I just think them. However, looking at Bella, her face crumpled with sleep, feeling the affection in every gesture towards me, I realise that I am happy. Despite everything, inside me, next to her, there is happiness.

It's an irony without equal. My sister's wish came true. I've found happiness, just as she wanted. But I can't stay. Because she needs me. Because I swore to protect her.

"I decided to look up Abigail's name again. I couldn't find anything, so I searched for the newspaper, and then my own name. It didn't do me any good."

"If it's not doing you any good, don't you think it's better to avoid it?"

She's right, it makes perfect sense, but sometimes the doubts overwhelm me so much that I just can't help myself.

"You're right. I'll calm down; we only have a week."

Bella doesn't smile. Only after the words come out do I realise what I'm saying. I stroke her soft cheek, analysing her delicate face.

"I have to go back, Bella," I whisper. "For Abigail, I have to."

Bella agrees with a soft nod. "I know you need to."

"I really hope she's alright," I confess. "I hope it's not too late."

Bella doesn't say anything; she just lays her head on my shoulder. I kiss her hair, enjoying the happiness as long as I can, trying to keep every moment of it in my memories.

"I'm going to miss you so much…" she murmurs. "And do you know why?" Bella stands up and looks at me, sighing. "Because I feel like it's going to work out. That you'll come back. I feel like it's going to be OK."

Will it? On the one hand, yes. If I go back, my sister will be safe. On the other… I'll be alone again. Without Bella.

I don't ask permission when I pull her into a kiss. Bella presses her mouth to mine, opens her lips and allows me to explore her, to dominate her. I don't know how long we stay there, just kissing, feeling each other, calmly.

As we lean away, Duke grumbles in my lap and jumps off the sofa, drawing laughter from both of us.

"Duke, today's not your day…" Bella jokes and looks at me again. "Do you want to go back to bed? I'm not sleepy anymore."

I don't dare refuse. I just take her in my arms, and we go back to the bedroom.

19

The best selfie in the world

Isabella

I wake up around 8am and feel Benjamin's breath on my neck. I'm tired, as we hardly slept last night, but happy. There's no better way to wake up than feeling his body against mine. The scent I love so much, the affection with which he holds me even when he's asleep.

I don't think I've ever felt so happy. Or sad. I'm wrapped up in a ball of yarn made up of feelings. Being with Ben is everything I dreamt of, but I can't deny that every time I remember that it won't last, I feel like crying.

I don't know how I managed to hold it together in the early hours of the morning when I found him looking lost in the living room.

I have to go back, Bella, he told me.

I already knew that. I've always known it, but knowing it doesn't make the situation any easier. Of course, I want him to stay with me. To lead his life by my side, to live this romance without haste, without an expiry date.

Unfortunately, life doesn't work the way I want it to, but the way it is. I should have learnt my lesson by now.

I look back as best I can, and Benjamin is still asleep. Slowly, I slip out of his arms and get out of bed, reaching for a pair of pyjamas in the chest of drawers. It's still dark – it always is in England in December – the day dawns after 9am. I leave the bedroom and walk to the kitchen, playing with Duke on the way, but asking him not to make a sound.

I help myself to some cereal with milk and go to my desk in the corner of the room. I haven't sat here since… wow, since the day I ran over Benjamin. In the meantime, I've jotted down all the story ideas that come to mind on my e phone's notepad. I eat a spoonful of cereal, staring into nothingness. The sound of my phone vibrating catches my attention.

I look for the device, which is on the sofa. I walk over with the bowl in my hand. The message is from Cinthia.

Cinthia: How was the ball? Send me a photo, I want to see.

I laugh. Cinthia and I haven't spoken much; she's busy enjoying everything Paris has to offer. But I did tell her that we were going to the ball, and I asked her to help me choose my dress. She also knows that Benjamin is only staying with me until the 21st. I didn't go into too much detail or open myself up to questions, but Ben and I decided to tell her that the mental confusion has passed and that he lives with his sister in Scotland but has decided to stay a few extra days to enjoy the city.

I click on our selfie, which Laura shared with me yesterday, and send it to her.

The three dots appear on the screen immediately.

Cinthia: Is that Benjamin?

Considering that she already knows Pierre from his photos, Cinthia must have realised how handsome my man is.

My… I wish…

Me: Yes, why?

I pretend to misunderstand.

Cinthia: I'm going to slap you for not telling me you were going out with a Calvin Klein model. Tell me everything, right now!

I laugh, quietly so as not to wake up my "model".

Me: OK, let's take it easy. Firstly, he's not a model; he's just really hot. Secondly, I tasted that body last night.

A million emojis and animated stickers appear on the screen.

Cinthia: That's what I'm talking about! What else? I want details.

I blush because I'm not going to give details of what happened yesterday, although the images of our libertine escapades are very fresh in my memory.

I'm going to fuck you all night.
Leave it to me.

Wow, I get goosebumps and wet just remembering it.

Me: Look, I'll just say it was amazing. The ball was amazing and he's a real lord.

A true lord, indeed. I'll send one more message:

Me: Two extra pieces of news: Matheus got married and I think the writer's block is passing.

My friend starts typing again.

Cinthia: My God, I leave for a month, and everything happens. Let's break it down: Did Matheus actually get married? When did he get married?

I summarise what Laura told me. When Cinthia asks how I'm doing, I say I'm fine. No lie – I'm indifferent to the man that was once my boyfriend. Then, she says she's happy that my block is over. I still think it's too early to celebrate, but I really believe I'm over this bad phase.

Cinthia: I hope we can go to a ball like that next year. I've never been to one, but now I want to. So, what's the deal with you and the model?

I think about the answer. The thing is, I've fallen in love, I suspect he has too, but we can't be together. Argh, what a horrible story.

Me: It's temporary. As I said, he's going to Scotland next week. It's not going to happen.
Cinthia: Can't you even try it from a distance? Paul and I are doing well.

No, darling. Believe me, we can't.

Me: It's complicated...

She doesn't answer me for a minute, going offline. I go back to eating my cereal, which is now more like a paste in a bowl. Cinthia sends me another message:

Cinthia: Honey, I've got to go. I forgot I have an extra class today. I'll talk to you later. Enjoy your man.
Me: You got it. xoxo.

I check the time in the top corner of the screen. It's 8.30am. I put the device and my bowl aside and return to the desk with my laptop in hand.

I open my computer and Word and stare at the blank page.

I take a breath and start typing. The words come out, one after the other, calmly. It seems to make sense. I don't stop to correct possible mistakes or anything. I just carry on. I don't know how long I stay there, but in the end, I have a first chapter ready.

"Bella?"

I turn round and see Benjamin rubbing his eyes, wearing just a pair of boxer shorts. I admire his bulge, his ripped abdomen, and his strong arms. Cinthia's right. He does look like a Calvin Klein model.

"Are you alright?" he asks me, coming closer. "What are you doing?"

I close the computer, smiling slightly. "Nothing. Checking social media. Did you sleep well?"

Benjamin nods, leaning over and kissing my forehead. "I didn't sleep much…" He smiles at me.

"I know…" I lean in for a quick kiss.

"What do you want to do today, darling?"

I sigh at the thought. "Well, it looks like it's going to be sunny." I look at the rays of sunshine coming through the living room window. "We can go out for a walk, if you like."

Benjamin moves away and sits on the sofa, running his hand through his messy hair. His posture is relaxed. On a scale of lord to twenty-first-century man, he's more like the latter at this point. Duke wastes no time in joining him, and Ben smiles as he strokes his soft fur. The little dog has become attached to Benjamin. I can only imagine how much he'll miss him when he's no longer here. If it's half as much as me, I feel sorry for Your Grace.

"Is your sister coming today? Or are we free?"

"Free. Laura will be leaving in two days, but she and Pierre want to enjoy some time just them."

"Why don't you show me the city?" Benjamin suggests. "I realise we haven't really walked round London yet."

"Like you did for me in Bath?"

Benjamin nods. I like the idea.

"OK, but you have to remember that I'm not from here, so I know almost nothing. But I think we can do the tour I did when I arrived. We'll get off at Waterloo station, pass the London Eye, then Parliament, Westminster Abbey, and finish in Green Park at Buckingham Palace."

"OK. It'll be interesting to pass through Parliament after all this time."

I get up and start walking towards the bathroom. "Sometimes I forget that you have a seat there."

"And that's why I like you so much."

I stop, turning to him. "Why?"

Benjamin beckons me over. I go to him, and he sits me on his lap, wrapping his big hand around my waist.

"Because you only see the Benjamin in me. Not the duke, not the rake. Just me, the man."

And I love that man.

I almost say the words, but I hold back. I suspect it wouldn't help us to exchange declarations of love. So, I just kiss him, hoping he can understand my feelings with the gesture.

"I'm going to have a quick shower. Would you like to join me?"

Benjamin raises an eyebrow and accepts the offer.

I knew he wouldn't refuse.

* * *

I don't think I've ever spent a more pleasant afternoon than today.

It begins with sex in the shower, which is preceded by oral. We have to do some manoeuvring in the cramped space, but Benjamin proves to be very skilful and efficient. A delight.

After we we're dressed, Ben and I follow my walking route, getting off at Waterloo station and walking to the Houses of Parliament. We arrive in front of it, and he frowns, analysing the tower of Big Ben.

"So, this is the famous clock…" He tilts his head.

"A curiosity I learnt: many people think that Big Ben is the name of the clock, but it's not. That's the name of the bell that is part of the clock."

He nods, still staring at the building. "And this construction is of…"

"Hold on." I get out my phone to look it up. "Oh, it says here that it was programmed into the design of the new Palace of Westminster, as the old one was destroyed by fire in 1834."

"Is Parliament going to burn down?" He looks at me, frightened.

"Yes." I touch his arm. "Please keep an eye out if you're in town, OK?"

Benjamin assures me he will, and I realise how strange this is. Here I am, in the present, giving him a spoiler from the past, but which in fact will soon be his future. God, that's crazy.

"Well, moving on," I talk again. "Construction began in 1843 and was completed in 1859."

Benjamin remains silent. Even though I know him well now, I can't understand what his gaze means. "What is it, darling?"

He sighs. "I don't think I'll see the tower finished."

I still don't understand. "Why not?"

"Because if it was finished in 1859, I'd have to be seventy-four to see it. Most people didn't live that long back then. I'll probably be dead."

Wow, what a terrible comment, but it's true. If I'm not mistaken, life expectancy at his time was very low, something like fifty-five. I feel a physical pain at the thought of this world without Benjamin. I won't think about that.

"Shall we take a selfie?" I suggest. "I realised yesterday that I don't have any photos with you, and I want some memories."

He smiles, already looking relaxed. I open the front camera and stretch out my arm. Benjamin surprises me by kissing my cheek, which makes my smile open even wider. I don't check the photo immediately, as I turn my face towards him, and Ben steals a kiss on the lips.

As we walk away, I finally look at the phone screen. Here we are, me and him, with Parliament and Big Ben in the background.

"Is it good?" He wants to know.

I nod, showing him the screen. "The best selfie in the world."

We continue on our way. We pass the abbey, and I keep my phone in my hand, looking up any things that catch our eye. I end up learning a lot of details that I hadn't realised before. We stop halfway through at Pret a Manger, a café we find on every corner here in the city. I pick up two hot chocolates with brownies and we sit there for a few minutes, holding hands as if we were just a normal young couple.

"So, tell me, do you intend to go back to Brazil?"

Benjamin asks me when we're on the street again. I ask him to stop next to a red telephone box and smile for a photo.

"I don't know," I reply, as we start walking again. "I like it here. Although I don't have a specific goal in life, working in the café is easy; I have a great flatmate; and I've settled in well. Sometimes, it's strange to be here. I look at my former friends and they're all getting married and having children. It makes sense since we're past thirty, but I don't care about that. I live my own life and that is it."

"But doesn't your family miss you?"

"They do, but we're all spread out. Laura in Canada, my mum in Sorocaba. She's very loving, but she doesn't settle, she likes to travel and so does my stepdad. Mum keeps very busy. I think that's why she and my father didn't work out. Very different from each other."

Benjamin reaches for my hand and intertwines our cold fingers. "Tell me about them."

It's not a great story. The typical case of two young people who fell in love, married quickly, had a daughter, and discovered that, in the end, they expected different things for themselves.

"The divorce was amicable; they get on well to this day. I guess I could say they're friends."

"Didn't your father remarry?"

I laugh because Tadeu Kato has been up to plenty of mischief.

"Look, he almost remarried a bunch of times, but it never worked out. I don't know, my father is focused on work. When I was younger, he'd stop doing certain things for the company so as not to be an absent father. He even refused to go on trips to go to my school's performances. But then, as I got older, he started travelling regularly. He's been in Japan for almost a year now."

"What does he work on?"

"He is an engineer. He coordinates some of the company's projects."

We arrive in front of Buckingham Palace, and I stop talking to appreciate the architecture of the place. I've been here several times, but it's always impressive. Benjamin already knows the building. The Palace has existed since the eighteenth century.

"Look, that statue in the centre," I point to a monument in front of the palace, "is Queen Victoria. This is the Victoria Memorial, and this area is called The Mall; it links the Palace to Trafalgar Square. This is where the royal family's parades take place."

And the place is packed with people when that happens. I was here for Queen Elizabeth's Platinum Jubilee celebrations at the beginning of the year. I've never seen so many people together. I even witnessed a slap fight to get a seat.

We walk up to the monument and Benjamin carefully analyses the statue of Queen Victoria. "Interesting... it looks like she really had a great reign."

"If you like, there's a film we can watch about her," I suggest. "*The Young Victoria*. It's a film mostly focused on the romance between her and Prince Albert, her husband, but it also shows a lot about how she inherited the throne."

"A romance? The queen married for love?" Benjamin looks very surprised.

"Yes. I love that story. They had loads of children, and she never remarried after she was widowed. It's a shame he died so young."

Benjamin swallows. "I believe that not all love stories have a happy ending."

I wonder if he's referring to our story. Well, Benjamin hasn't said he loves me, but I'm in love with him, so in my mind, yes: Benjamin and I are living a love story.

Unfortunately, ours won't have a happy ending either.

20

These boots are magic

Benjamin

Isabella looks at me, biting her lower lip. She finishes taking off her clothes while I analyse her, arms crossed and already naked and hard.

My gaze runs down her perfect body. Isabella is feminine, soft, and delicate. Her breasts are small, the nipples the same colour as her lips. Her belly is flat, and her bum is round, hard, and perky. A goddess. One I'm going to make the most of.

"You make me nervous looking at me like that," she comments, throwing coloured bath salts into the hot water and tying her hair up in a bun.

"Forgive me, but I can't help it." I pull her round by the waist. "Your body is delicious."

Bella gives a low chuckle as we get into the bath, her back resting on my chest, her arse pressing between my legs.

OK, this isn't going exactly as I imagined. The bathtub

is too small for two people. I can barely move. I laugh. "In 1817, I'm sure we could get up to mischief in the bathtub. They were much bigger."

She laughs too, and I wrap my arms around her as best I can, my member pressing against her hard arse.

"No problem, we can have fun in bed in a little while. Now just relax, you pervert."

I kiss the curve of her neck and do as she asks. It seems that Bella is the only person who can make me relax. And laugh. Even dream. How will I live without this woman when the time comes for me to leave?

"Tell me more about your time," she requests. "Were the baths really big? We always write bath scenes in romance novels, but I don't remember if I've ever researched this in depth."

"Well, they were taller. And a bit wider. I think we could move more easily," I tease, licking her ear.

Isabella plays with her hand in the water. "I think I'd do well in your time."

My smile dies almost entirely. "You…" I think carefully about what to say. I don't want to be wrong. "Do you really think so?"

God, I don't know what I'm doing, but I admit that Isabella's speech made my imagination cross some boundaries.

I have already thought about asking her to come with me. Despite not wanting to name what I'm feeling, trying to deny the intensity of what we share, I've considered taking Isabella into my own time. About making her my wife, about living a life by her side. I've considered making her happy.

I keep silent, telling myself that considering this possibility is silly. I've never thought about telling her. Until now.

Isabella remains silent for a moment, her hand still moving in the water. "I don't know. It's not that simple. The nineteenth century is difficult for women. It still is hard in the twenty-first century, but it was worse back then. Not to mention… I have all my family here. My father only has me."

She's basically answered the question I didn't ask. I'm glad I didn't.

I know all this, but I confess that something inside me breaks with these words. But I have no right to feel this way. Not when I'm leaving for similar reasons.

"Do you know what I think?" I kiss her neck once more, determined to divert the subject. "I think I can get up to something in this tub without having to move much."

"Is that right?" Bella tilts her head towards me.

"Yes, miss."

I place one hand gently on her neck. The other moves down her wet skin, finding a hard nipple, pinching and twisting it.

"Wow…" Isabella gasps, and I peek at her face. Her eyes are closed and she's smiling, clearly enjoying my caresses.

"Spread your legs, love."

Isabella does as I say. I slide my touch down to the middle of her legs. Even with the tight space, I manage to open up the moist folds and find her pulsating point. I tease it with the tip of my finger, pressing deftly. Isabella gasps, parting her lips. My free hand returns to fondle a breast, squeezing. I insert my middle finger into her, without stopping to stimulate her clitoris. I'm about to explode with desire, with the urge to take her into the bedroom and dive into her, but I don't stop. Even in this, we fit perfectly. Every day, I discover something new that only reinforces the idea that Bella was made for me.

"Ben..." Bella moans, and I bite a piece of skin on her neck, then suck on it.

"Come for me, Bella," I whisper, and it's as if my words are an order that she obeys without complaint.

Isabella shudders in my arms, one of the most marvellous sensations I've ever experienced. She's the one cumming and I'm the smiling idiot. I'm an experienced man. I know how to give pleasure and enjoy it. But with her... it's inexplicable. I could do this all my life. If only we had that. If only it were possible...

I can't get enough of her body, her smell, the sound of her laughter and joy. I wake up thinking about her and how sad it makes me that we're coming to an end.

"You're amazing," Bella says, and I know she's smiling.

"We are." I trail kisses along the nape of her neck.

"I'm going to have to ask you to do it again."

"I'd do anything you asked of me."

She stops and twists her head round, her expression wicked. What is she up to? "Anything?"

I nod. Bella smiles broadly. "Well... I have a fantasy in mind."

* * *

Isabella

Well then. If Benjamin says he'll do *anything* for me, I decide to test him with a fantasy of my own.

And isn't he telling the truth?

When he enters the room, wearing only his shirt, black boxers, and riding boots, I almost scream with excitement.

"What's the name of what I'm going to do?" he asks me.

"Striptease. You have to get rid of your clothes, *slowly*." I raise an eyebrow. "I want to analyse every centimetre, but the boots must remain."

"I'm practically naked, Bella."

I shake my head. "No, no. There's still plenty for the imagination."

He rolls his eyes. "Why should the boots stay? They should be the first to go."

"They stay! It's *my* fantasy, milord. Please be respectful."

Benjamin takes a deep breath but doesn't contradict me.

I get into bed, between the pillows that smell of fabric softener. I'm just wearing a pyjama top and barely there knickers, which I've chosen on purpose.

"I'm going to choose a song," I say, and he frowns deeply.

"What for?"

"So you can take your clothes off to the beat of the music. That's how you do a striptease."

"Bella, I don't understand anything."

Oh dear, what an old-fashioned guy. I open Google and type striptease into the search bar. The first result is the funniest: how to do a striptease in eight steps. Laughing, I hand Benjamin my phone.

"See this tutorial here."

Benjamin picks up the device and squints at the screen. I have to stop myself from laughing. He runs his eyes over the content, concentrating, like someone studying for an important test. Very dedicated, this English lord.

"Right," he hands me back the device, "I think I've got it."

I open Spotify and click on the first strip playlist that pops up. Britney starts singing "Gimme More", and I put my phone away.

Between the beats and Spears' giggle, I look at the man in front of me. "I'm ready."

He lifts his chin, still seeming to think. "I apologise in advance if I don't meet your expectations."

"Don't worry, I'll like it." I make a motion with my finger. "Now, show me that delicious body."

Benjamin laughs and starts to move. He doesn't dance, but he tries to keep up with the music. He runs his hand through his hair, biting his lower lip.

"The wink," I suggest.

He smiles and obeys.

Beloved father... *gimme more*!

Benjamin moves his hands to the hem of his shirt and starts to lift it up. "Is that aright?" he wants to know, referring to the speed of the movements.

"Yes, it is."

He keeps moving, his abs revealing themselves. I swallow my saliva, full of arousal. This is turning out better than I bargained for.

Benjamin pulls his shirt over his head, turning round as he lets the fabric fall to the floor. I get wetter and wetter as I observe the muscles of his strong back, the design of his arms, his hard arse.

"The boxers. Let me see your arse," I say, and he turns round.

"Calm down. I thought you wanted it to be slow."

"Come on!"

Benjamin is laughing as he turns back round and starts to take off his pants. My mouth drops open at the sight of his firm buttocks. And when he turns round, the glorious cock, which I've started to call my own Big Ben, faces me, fully erect and horny.

My God, this man is perfect. From head to toe, there's not a part of him that can be saved.

"I'm going to have to take my boots off now," Benjamin warns.

"No!" I protest immediately. "I want them to stay."

"I can't take my boxers off and keep my boots on, Bella!"

I start to really laugh because his nonchalant expression is great.

Benjamin grimaces and takes off his boots at once, putting them aside. "You laugh, don't you?"

"I'm sorry, but I couldn't take it." I continue laughing.

Benjamin throws himself at me, naked. He stops the music and gets rid of my phone. His erection brushes against my belly, and he steals an intense, possessive kiss, pinning my arms above my head.

"My turn to ask for something?" he whispers between kisses.

"What do you want?" I manage to ask. I'm already

desperate, dying for him to touch me, to come inside me hard.

He bites his lower lip as he turns me face down on the mattress, pushing my bum up.

"I want you in this position." His hand moves up my bare thigh, stopping at the fabric of my panties, which are already wet by now. "OK?"

I nod, relaxing my head sideways on the pillow.

Benjamin pulls down my panties and throws them away.

"Try to be quiet while I suck you off, Bella." He holds my arms crossed behind my back now. Firm, yes, but with the usual affection.

I feel Benjamin's tongue sliding over me, from bottom to top. He licks and sucks me, exploring my folds and my clitoris, alternating with kisses and light nibbles on my arse. I've never felt so exposed and so at somebody's mercy. So free. I moan against the pillow, rolling over a little, seeking relief from the marvellous torment Benjamin is causing me.

I'm throbbing, about to come when he pulls away and turns me round. Benjamin takes a condom from the drawer of the bedside table and puts it on. He joins me again, penetrating my body slowly, his eyes on mine.

"I've been dying to get into you, but I need to look into your eyes." He thrusts. Once. Then again. "Can you feel what you're doing to me, Bella? Can you?"

I can. If I've surrendered in this bed, Benjamin is here with me. Our connection goes beyond our bodies; it's something deeper, something unique and special. Something inexplicable that no amount of time can erase. Something that would be worthy of books, films, or plaques on benches.

I love him. I love him completely and, even if we can't be together, I want to cherish every moment, every memory of the two of us for the rest of my days.

"Bella, I'm close…" Benjamin murmurs, his forehead sweaty, without stopping moving. My heart is racing; my body is sweating; and I want to close my eyes, but I remain attentive to him, aware of every movement, every touch and gasp, every breath.

"Yes, yes…" That's all I can say because I'm close to exploding too.

He caresses my clitoris, and I start to tremble. My limbs are numb, and I'm no longer the owner of my body, the owner of me. He is. I'm completely in this man's hands. And not just my body. My heart is all Benjamin's.

It always will be. For us, there's no turning back.

We cum at the same time, shaking so much that I feel dizzy. Finally, I close my eyes, searching for air, feeling the wonderful weight of his body on mine.

Benjamin pulls out of me but doesn't move away. He kisses my neck, with such softness and affection that I get emotional.

"You're the best thing that's ever happened to me," he whispers. I turn my face to his, touching our noses.

"You too. I…" *love you*, that's what I want to say, but I can't. The words stop in my throat, jumbled and painful.

"I know," Benjamin replies, kissing the tip of my nose and pulling me to him. "I know, my love."

Still in each other's arms, we fall into a deep sleep.

21

If I could

Isabella

I wake up early, before Ben, and run to the supermarket near my house, where there's one of those kiosks where you can print photos on the spot. I want to surprise him. Benjamin is leaving tomorrow and, although I'm trying hard not to fall apart, I want him to take a souvenir of me with him. Something that, if he suddenly feels like it, he can look at again and again.

We've taken a few photos over the last few days, and I've picked out my four favourites. The first is the selfie in front of Big Ben. I've also selected the selfie with my sister and brother-in-law, a photo of Benjamin with Duke, and one of the three of us.

I scan the QR code and order two copies of each, for myself too. While I'm waiting, a lady approaches me from behind, waiting for me to finish using the machine.

"How beautiful… is that your boyfriend?" she asks, pointing to the picture of me and Benjamin.

I wish...

I think for a moment before answering. "Yes, it is."

I'll never see this lady again in my life, so I don't see a problem with lying. I can't just say that he's my lover who will travel back in time tomorrow and disappear from my life forever. I can't confess to her that he's the man I love even if it's impossible for us to end up together if I haven't even had the courage to tell Benjamin himself. Boyfriend seems like a simpler answer.

"You're both lovely."

I smile, although I bleed inside. Yes, you're right, we match in every way. I very much doubt that there is, or ever will be, anyone more suited to me than Benjamin. If it weren't for the two hundred years' difference, everything would be perfect, a fairytale. What a bummer.

The photos are printed, and I take them, saying goodbye to the little lady with a kind smile.

I'm halfway home when I feel my phone vibrate. It's my mum, video calling.

"Mum?" I answer with concern. "Is everything alright? It's 5am there."

"Hello, darling. Oh, yes, it is. Yesterday, I was very tired and slept very early, so I ended up getting up early. I thought you'd be awake."

Well, if I hadn't been, she would have woken me up, wouldn't she?

"And how are things going over there? How's Zé?" I'm referring to my stepfather.

"All fine, thank God. What about you? What about the new boyfriend?"

I frown. "Boyfriend?"

She makes a condescending expression.

"Laura has already told me that there's a handsome Englishman in your life."

I roll my eyes immediately. Laura and her big mouth! "It's nothing."

"Of course it is, your sister showed me the photo. The four of you looked beautiful. My darling, isn't the man handsome? Worthy of that TV series you love."

She keeps praising Benjamin. Although I agree with all the compliments, if I didn't know it was early in the morning in Canada, I'd call Laura right now to scold her for not minding her business.

"Mum, Benjamin is a friend," I say when she stops talking.

"Friends can become lovers."

"But not us – he's leaving tomorrow, never to return."

My mum lets out a resigned sigh. "My God, Isabella, how dramatic you are. Instead of being a writer, you should think about being an actress."

I have to stop myself from answering. It's not dramatic to suffer because the great love of your life is leaving.

I change the subject, asking how my grandmother is. My mother starts chattering about the old lady's doctor's appointments, her medication, the neighbour's cat who disappeared for two nights and returned as if nothing had happened. At least I manage to get through the rest of the call without mentioning Benjamin again.

Not that I've stopped thinking about him. No, it's an impossible task. I've spent the last few days wanting to cry, to scream, to beg him not to leave me. I really wanted to rip my heart out and throw it in the middle of the Thames to make it easier to deal with. Because I can't lose myself. I can't make it difficult for him. Benjamin has suffered enough, and I know that he's as shaken by his departure as I am. Not to mention that I'm a woman living in 2022. Abigail wasn't lucky enough to be born at a time when the world is a little fairer. When I stop to think about her helplessness, I get a little ache on the left side of my chest.

I can't condemn Benjamin for wanting to go back to protect her. In fact, I love him all the more for it.

He has to go. It's just up to me to accept it and suffer for it; there's no other way.

I hang up the phone with Mum as soon as I get into the flat. Duke welcomes me with a wagging tail, but I can sense that he's sad. I believe that animals can sense our emotions, so that must be why. As I don't see Benjamin around, I go up to the bedroom.

He's still lying there stretching, looking like he's just woken up.

"Good morning, Your Grace."

Duke barks. We both burst out laughing.

"Not you, you little dog."

Benjamin shakes his head. "Where were you?" he asks me.

"I went for a walk; I'm restless," I lie. I plan to give him the photos tomorrow. I know myself well and I'm sure I'll get a bit emotional.

"I could have come along." Benjamin stretches out his hand, beckoning me. He always wants me around, always touches me with devotion and attention. How can I live without this affection from now on?

"We can go to the park if you like. It's cloudy, but I've looked at the forecast and it's not going to rain. We could even take Duke."

Benjamin nods, kissing the back of my hand. "Give me a minute. I'm going to change."

* * *

Benjamin

"Come on, you lazy little ball."

I laugh as Isabella comes out of the flat, pulling Duke on a taut lead. My furry friend doesn't seem excited about the walk in the park.

"Where are we going to go?" I ask, as soon as I lock the door and we start walking.

"A nearby park, it's my favourite. You can see Greenwich from the other side, and it has some nice benches to sit on."

Today, 20 December 2022, is my last day with Bella. Tomorrow we'll catch a 9am train to Bath and I'll try once again to get back home.

I don't know what to feel, nor do I want to think about it. I'm holding in and ignoring as many feelings as possible. Perhaps managing my responsibilities and putting my own life to one side was training for what I'm doing now. A mere glimpse of what I would have to face. I thought being a responsible head of household, duke, and guardian were difficult tasks. But nothing, absolutely nothing, compares to the difficulty I'm having in accepting that I have to abandon Isabella.

"What's going through that brilliant mind?" she asks me as we make our way along the road.

I already know her well. Isabella is trying to be strong, trying to make things easier for me.

"I'm thinking," I reply. "A lot has happened."

She nods but doesn't continue. I've always believed that silence, depending on the situation, can be more enlightening than a long speech. That's what's happening to us now. There's nothing to say.

Or there is, but perhaps it hurts too much to do so.

A few minutes later, we arrive at the park. There is grass on the right-hand side, trees with huge trunks and dry branches, and some dried leaves on the ground. On the other side, iron benches are lined up, facing the river.

Bella lets Duke off the lead as soon as we choose one of the benches. Bouncing around, the chubby little creature starts sniffing the frosty grass and chases a squirrel he meets on the way. Bella and I settle down. As usual, there's a little plaque on the iron backrest.

"Jones Family," Bella reads aloud. "In this one, they've honoured an entire family. I confess I like the plaques for couples better."

"It's more romantic. It suits you," I say, and she nods in agreement.

"You know, I… started writing a story."

I look at her, surprised. "When?"

"Whenever I've been free. I didn't say anything because it's no big deal – I only have two chapters, and I haven't edited or revised them, but I used your idea. About time travelling."

I smile, taking her hand. I'm happy for her. Writing is important to Isabella. Her beautiful eyes sparkle every time she talks about putting pen to paper.

"Tell me," I ask.

Bella takes a deep breath, looking excited. "Well, I haven't decided everything yet. I've drawn up skeleton chapters, and I think I'm going to follow a romantic comedy line. I've never been much for drama; I prefer lighter, cute stories. But I thought about..." She stops.

"Tell me, Bella."

Bella sighs. "Well, he's a hot duke, he arrives in the future, but he has to go back because his sis... cousin depends on him. He meets a girl who has some problem I haven't decided on yet, and she helps him figure out how to get back. A few steamy scenes in between, maybe something raunchy in the bathtub. There we have our plot."

Very original, her story.

"I imagine the duke has riding boots," I tease.

Bella nods. "Of course, they're essential."

I laugh. "Basically, you'll tell our story."

She lifts her shoulders. "Slightly inspired."

"And the ending?"

"A happy ending, of course."

The tone of Isabella's voice breaks my heart.

"What will happen to them? Will she leave with him, or will he decide to stay?"

Isabella opens her mouth to speak, but we are interrupted by her mobile phone vibrating.

"It's my father. Can I have a minute?"

"Yes, of course."

Bella stands up, looking around for Your Grace.

"I'll check on him," I say, and she walks away, talking to her father. "Duke! Come here," I call, turning round a little.

Duke obeys and starts running towards me. I bend down to play with him, stroking his furry ears.

"Your Grace will be missed," I say to him, as he sticks out his tongue. "Will you miss me, Duke?"

He wags his tail.

"Look after her for me, OK? Make sure my Isabella is happy. Be there when she needs a hug. Can you do that?"

He seems to be smiling now. How silly of me to think that the dog is smiling at me.

But it's true what I say. I'm going to miss many things about this current London.

The ease of communication, the brownies. The puppy who has been my companion for the last few days, the comfortable jeans. I look at Bella, who is pushing her hair out of her face, trying to keep it out of the wind. Her. The face I'll never forget. The owner of my heart. The woman I love…

I control myself, once again stifling my feelings. But it's Isabella, *my Bella*, who I'll miss the most.

She switches off her mobile phone and comes back to me, sitting down again. The cool breeze hits us, and I can smell her soft perfume.

"My father is coming to London," she says.

"Really? When?"

"Christmas. He'll stay until the 30th. Can't spend New Year's Eve with me, but that's something." She smiles. "He says he's made a list of what we can do and what he wants to see. I'm going to be out on the streets all day."

"It's going to be good. I can tell you miss each other."

She nods. "Do you miss Abigail?"

I nod. "I do. A lot."

We both face the buildings of the Greenwich neighbourhood on the other side of the Thames. We can't see everything, as the mist covers the tops of the old towers, like in an impressionist landscape. But it's a beautiful scene.

Melancholy, but beautiful. Almost a reflection of how we are.

"That day in the bath, when you asked me if I'd live well in your time," Bella stares at me again, "was that an invitation?"

I keep looking forward. My hands cling tightly to the bench beneath me. "If I say yes, will your answer change?" I finally look at her.

"No, it won't. There's too much to consider. I can't just think about myself."

Just as I imagined, although I feel like I've just been punched in the stomach. "I wanted to… I wanted to ask you, but I thought…"

"That would only make everything more difficult." She moistens her lips. "I know, I know. I wanted to ask you to stay too."

The words are direct, harsh, and capable of knocking me over if I were standing up. I rub my eyes, suddenly exhausted.

"Would you live well here?" Isabella asks. "If things were different."

I confirm without even thinking about it. "If things were different, I have no doubt that I would be immensely happy here. With you."

Bella takes a deep breath before pulling me to her and kissing me. Her tongue seeks mine, eagerly, and I feel that in this kiss all the unspoken words between us become clear. She doesn't see herself as having the right to ask me to stay, even though she wants to. I don't see myself as having the right to ask her to go, even though I want to. However, the answer would be no anyway. Our lives are too opposite to merge. Yes, we collided, but only to split up later.

But even with all the heartbreak that this separation causes me, it was still worth it. Because I got to know her. Because of what she showed me and what she made me feel, I'll never forget.

"I want to tell you a lot of things, my love," I say, resting my forehead on hers, "but I'm afraid it will hurt us even more."

"Don't say it, then. You don't have to."

But I'm not sure I'll be able to hold on to them until the end because they suffocate me.

A while later, we return home. Isabella takes Duke off his lead, letting him go. She looks at me, coming closer.

"What do we do now?" Bella asks.

I stroke her cheek, my chest already tight with longing. "May I make love to you?"

Her eyes are instantly moved, fixed on mine. When Bella consents, just like the other night, I carry her into the bedroom once more.

One last time.

22

Goodbye, my love

Benjamin

Isabella and I lock ourselves in the bedroom for the last time.

Because tomorrow it will all come to an end.

I won't think about it now. Or I will, but I'll try to ignore it. In the time we had together, we laughed, we talked, we fucked, we embraced each other passionately.

Today, I want something different. Today, I want to *love* her. I want to demonstrate with actions what we decided not to confess in words. I want... Bella to remember me when I'm gone.

I want to remember her.

Very carefully, more than ever, I take off her clothes, piece by piece. First, the jacket, then the T-shirt. I run my hands down her back, opening her bra and releasing her perfect breasts. The nipples call to me, and I smile as I lean down to take a hard point in my mouth, my tongue playing there as I alternate sucking and licking.

Isabella gasps, dipping her fingers into my hair, keeping me there with her. I switch breasts, repeating what I've just done on the other. I'm in no hurry. At least tonight, time won't be my enemy.

Time won't mean anything. Only Bella and I matter. Both of us.

I trail kisses up her lap and neck before pulling away to remove my own clothes. Isabella looks at me, following my movements, her blushing lips parted and moist, delicious.

I take off my T-shirt, my trousers, and my boxers. My member is ready to enter her, but I force myself to wait.

"Lie down on the bed for me, my love."

She does as I ask, and I finish undressing her. I push her soft thighs apart, exposing her. I smell her, rubbing my nose lightly between her folds. I lick her aroused clitoris lightly, slowly. I taste it on my tongue, dive into her slit, suck her eagerly. Her hands dive into my hair, messing it up. I love it. I've never felt as much pleasure sucking a woman as I do with her. It's never been like this: so perfect. So real.

Isabella bends her body, her hands on the soft sheets, gripping them. I continue to get my fill of her, inserting a finger into her drenched depths, penetrating her in rhythm with the movements of my tongue.

Isabella falls apart in my mouth, letting out a low cry. I don't stop, prolonging the climax, sucking on the throbbing point until she squeezes me, and one orgasm follows another.

"Benjamin, come here," she calls me. I can't say no.

I lie down next to her, and Bella gets up, coming on

top of me. She slides down my body, her kisses and tongue tasting me, and I close my eyes, feeling her, letting her do whatever she wants to me.

The pretty face approaches my rigid cock, very eager. Isabella takes it in her mouth sweetly, just the tip at first, her head going up and down, tasting and sucking. She takes it to the back of her throat and keeps going. Once, again. My balls are squeezed, but she doesn't stop, driving me to the point of howling with pleasure.

She stops before it's too late. Bella sits on my hips and takes my cock to her pussy, rubbing it against her clitoris, the movements making her moan. She bites her lower lip as she leans over me to get the condom from the bedside drawer. I take advantage of the position and take a nipple in my mouth, sucking it firmly, biting it gently.

Bella covers me with the condom and guides me inside her. Her narrow hips begin the movement, moving back and forth perfectly. I help her, holding onto her round buttocks and dictating the rhythm.

We become more frantic, more euphoric. She rides me eagerly, her hands resting on my chest, her breasts jiggling with her rapid thrusts. I lift my back off the mattress and move my hands behind her, never stopping moving, never stopping looking at her. Bella kisses me with her tongue, sucking mine, her nails scratching the skin of my shoulders, her sweat mixing with mine.

"Ah, Ben…" she moans.

I can't speak; I'm concentrated; I'm firm. I've completely surrendered to her, giving everything of myself. All that I am.

Bella climaxes. A few thrusts later, I join her. I can still feel her squeezing my cock, trembling. I look up at her, panting. My heart breaks. There's something unsaid there.

A goodbye.

Gently, I wipe away the tears trickling down her cheek.

Her eyes are my doom. Yet, I feel saved. For Bella, and only for her, I have known romantic love. The love I said I would never feel, that I didn't want to feel. How wrong I was, how foolish…

Bella was an unexpected gift that I received at one of the worst moments of my life. She was the light in my darkness, the compass that helped me find the north. Isabella is the woman of my life. My purest and most sincere love.

She is my world. She always will be until I take my last breath.

* * *

I took my eyes off the paperwork in front of me and looked at the door. Abigail was staring at me with a half-smile on her lips.

It was the first time I'd seen her smile that week.

"Abby? Can I help you?"

"So formal," she said. "What are you doing?"

"Working."

Abigail nodded, approaching my desk. "The Daily*?"*

"Yes."

She pulled up a chair and sat down. Abigail had always been curious. Attentive and very intelligent, the most intelligent of the three of us. She was a quick learner, played the piano beautifully, and danced like nobody's business.

I, who used to be annoyed by her countless questions, missed them. I missed her curious gaze. But I missed many things.

"Tell me what's going on," she asked. "I've heard almost nothing new."

It wouldn't have been my first choice to tell my sister about the newspaper's problems. Even more so now that we'd discovered that Raoul Cornell was a traitor to the Crown. A bastard who helped the enemy army. The men who killed my brother.

"We have a complicated dilemma," I began. "A traitor, whose denunciation we're thinking of making."

Abigail nodded in agreement. "And why are you thinking? What's stopping you?"

"Lack of evidence. We have to be careful; it's a delicate situation."

Another nod. "Are you happy, Benjamin? With the newspaper?"

I shrugged, leaving the paper I was holding on the table. "I wanted it. It was my idea to start the* Daily.*"*

"Why?" *my sister asked me.*

I wasn't sure why. Because I wanted a distraction. Because I wanted to feel useful. Because I didn't know where to spend the money I had. "I don't know, Abby. I like writing. I like politics."

"You're a duke now. Shouldn't you be careful with being involved in controversy?"

I smiled. Yes, I should, but perhaps I still had the young man of yesteryear inside me. The one who didn't need to provide for anyone but himself.

"I promise I won't do anything to harm us."

"I don't worry about that, Benjamin," she said. "I know you're looking after me, that you're attentive."

My heart warmed. It was good to know that she knew.

"However, could it be…" Abigail continued.

I leant over the table, watching her face. "Yes?"

She looked down, and then at me again. Sometimes, I could hardly believe that Abby was already nineteen. That she was no longer a child, and that I would soon have to manage her suitors and promises of commitment.

"Could you have dinner with me tonight? I had dinner alone yesterday and the day before. I realise you have work, but… I'd like your company."

I had a lot of work to do; I was tired. But it was a simple, sincere request. A request I could fulfil. I held out my hand, asking for hers. Abigail didn't refuse.

"Of course. My secretary is about to arrive, and I'll let him go early. Don't worry about it."

She smiled, got up, and left the room.

And I went back to work, waiting for dinner.

* * *

Isabella

I can't sleep.

I don't know if Benjamin has slept, although he's kept his eyes closed. Just now, looking at him, I had to get out of bed to cry silently in the living room.

My head hurts from the pressure, but not as much as my heart.

As the tears fall, I close my eyes, trying to breathe. The

crying increases when I feel the embrace I'm used to, the main cause of all this.

Benjamin doesn't say anything; he just cradles me in his arms, kisses my temple, and lets me collapse. I sob, clinging to his T-shirt, enveloped in his perfume, wishing that all this isn't real, that I don't have to say goodbye to the man I love.

I don't know how long it's been, but I'm woken from my moment of despair by the ringing of the alarm I've set on Alexa so that we don't risk losing track of time.

"Alexa, stop," Benjamin says.

I sniffle, wiping my wet face. "Sorry…"

"There's nothing to apologise for. I only have you, Bella, to thank."

"I tried to hold on until afterwards, but…"

"I know." Benjamin lifts my chin so that I meet his gaze. "I'm broken inside, love, but if I allow myself to fall apart…"

"I know, I know. Don't worry."

Benjamin doesn't seem to know what to say. Since I'm a mess, I take the opportunity to give him my surprise.

I get up and open my desk drawer, taking out an envelope with a red bow.

"Look, it's no big deal, but I wanted you to take something to remember me by." I hand him the envelope. "These are my favourites. I hope you like them."

Benjamin accepts the parcel and undoes the bow, carefully taking the photos out of the envelope. I see his Adam's apple move as he analyses our images as if I had just handed him the most precious treasure.

Crying as I am, I feel like collapsing again.

"That's... everything." Benjamin looks at me. "Thank you, Bella."

I lean over and kiss him on the cheek, asking to be excused to go to the toilet. It's about time, I can't delay any longer. We have to leave, or we'll miss the train at the station. Benjamin has prepared a rucksack with his own clothes. He'll change as soon as we get to his old house; that way we won't attract anyone's attention on the way.

After we leave home, we journey silently. What can we say?

I'm trying my best not to start crying again, trying to imprint inside me the sensation of my fingers intertwined with his, his masculine scent, and the warmth of his body next to mine. However, I already know that Benjamin is engraved on me. Tattooed, permanently.

The walk from the station to the museum is equally unnerving. The cheerful streets, full of people and decorations, and the sweet smell of the stalls do nothing for me. I'm oblivious to anything other than the emptiness echoing in my chest. I want to walk slowly so that we never reach our destination. I want to pull him away and run, to change our sad ending, to give our romance a different ending.

A happy ending, in which I ask him to be mine and Benjamin is able to accept my request.

We turn onto Brock Street, and he stops in front of the house. Benjamin looks at me, his expression serious. "It's time."

I nod because there's nothing to do. We enter the museum still holding hands.

The same girl who attended to us the other day smiles at me. I buy the two tickets and go up to the second floor.

We enter the study, and Benjamin glances down the corridor before discreetly closing the door. As soon as he does, he takes his rucksack off his back with his clothes inside. "I'm going to change."

I'm not offering to go out; there's no need. We're past that point. Benjamin gets dressed slowly. He takes off his jacket, T-shirt, and jeans. He puts on his own trousers, and I say playfully, "You'll arrive in boxers in the nineteenth century."

He lifts the corner of his mouth. "I won't give up my boxers."

Our smiles last only seconds. He continues dressing, without haste, his breathing controlled as if trying not to cry. When he's ready, Benjamin taps his hand on his jacket pocket. "It's here," he refers to the cameo.

I swallow back the tears as I approach. "Do you have the photos?"

"In the other side of the jacket," he confirms.

I nod, noticing a spot of white fur on the dark fabric lapel.

"Duke... he sheds hair from time to time."

Benjamin doesn't try to smile as he pulls me into an embrace. I can feel his heartbeat in my ears as I rest my head on his chest. A tear rolls down my cheek. Damn it, I won't be able to hold it back.

Just a little longer, I think. For him, just a little longer.

I move away from Benjamin and take a step back. "Go and look after your sister. I... hope everything's alright."

Benjamin's jaw is clenched, his sad eyes almost making me collapse again.

"If it doesn't work, I'll—"

"It'll work," I interrupt him. "I know it will."

He rubs his eyes and I realise he's shaking. Benjamin swallows, turning towards the centre of the room. He gives up just a second later. His gaze meets mine again and it's as if time has stopped.

Time. Our great enemy, but also the one responsible for uniting us.

"I love you," he says, with impeccable composure. "I love you with all the strength of my soul. With all my heart."

I don't know what to say; I can only feel it. My soul aches and rejoices at the same time, listening to the sweet words I've longed for. Words that reflect what I also feel. What we feel, together, for each other.

"I know we said that confessing in words would be worse. I know that maybe I shouldn't be doing this." Benjamin approaches me, taking my hands. "But I believe that you deserve to know. That, after everything you've been through, you deserve to know how much you mean to me, how much you've made me happy."

Benjamin closes his eyes and kisses my knuckles, very slowly. I don't know how I'm still standing.

"Our love is impossible," he tells me, "but it's real. Every touch, every word, kiss, and look. It's all real, Bella."

He takes me in his arms and kisses me as if it were the last time. Because it is. I'll never taste him again, his tongue on mine, the peace his embrace brings me.

Between us, all that will remain are memories. I thought that would be enough, but it's not. It hurts, a pain that I don't see any way of overcoming.

"I love you," Benjamin says again. "You were responsible for showing me true happiness, my love. I'll never forget you, Bella. Forgive me for not being able to choose you."

But he did choose me. Even though Benjamin is leaving, I know he chose me. He chose to give me his heart. He chose to love me for the time we had. Even if it wasn't enough, he chose me.

Crying, I find the strength to speak. "I love you, Benjamin. Thank you for putting the pieces of my broken heart back together. You showed me that I don't believe in love in vain. What we lived was real. It always will be, no matter how much time passes. I'll never stop loving you."

He looks at me one more time. The last time.

"I have to go, darling."

I relent, taking a step back. Despair takes hold of me. I feel my throat closing, my legs giving way. I won't be able to stay here, watching as he disappears.

"Ben, I can't."

He nods instantly. "Go on. It's OK."

I cry some more, completely devastated. "I love you," I say.

"Me too, my darling."

I can see that Benjamin is suffering as much as I am. I gather all the courage I have and leave the room, closing the door behind me. I should leave, but I can't. My feet are planted on the floor. I can barely breathe, so I close my eyes, trying to calm down. Trying to ignore the pain.

When I open them, I don't know how long afterwards, the discontent is real. I feel it. I turn round again and push the door open, slowly, afraid. Afraid of what I already know has happened.

Everything is confirmed when the door opens fully.

Benjamin made it back. He left. The room is empty. Completely empty.

Just like the place where my heart used to be.

23

And now, life goes on

Isabella

"Darling, shall we sit over there?"

My father points to an empty table in the corner of a dining room at the Victoria and Albert Museum.

"Sure, that's fine."

We approach the round table in a room whose decoration looks like a work of art. Paintings of the months of the year and the signs of the zodiac line the walls with arches and gilded details in contrast to the marble columns. And we're only here for a coffee break.

"I'll get us something. What do you want, princess?" my father asks me.

"A hot chocolate and a pear cake."

"OK."

I watch my father walk away and sigh. When he's away, I can stop pretending to smile and make pretty faces. Not that I'm not glad he's here. I am. My father is in good spirits – we've been out and about a lot in the last few days since he arrived in town. We've been to Windsor, the Tower of London, and Parliament. We passed through Camden Town and Abbey Road, where a woman took our photo crossing The Beatles' pedestrian crossing.

However… I'm still broken inside.

In the place where a heart used to live, I feel only emptiness. It hurts, and every time I think of Benjamin and how much I miss him, I feel like crying.

Like now. One second with him in mind, and my throat is closed, my eyes moist.

I see my father approaching holding the tray and I shake my head, trying to stifle my emotions.

"There. There was no queue."

I smile, accepting the mug and plate of cake.

"This place is refined, huh? I had no idea," my father comments.

"Yes, it's one of the best museums in the city."

"I really like it."

I nod, taking a sip of the chocolate, although it's hard to swallow. I try to eat a piece of cake, and my stomach is upset. My father, who is very perceptive, frowns as he looks at me.

"What is it, Bella?"

I try to chew some more. "Nothing."

"Darling, I know something is happening." My father reaches for my hand. "You're sad; I know you. Is this about Matheus?"

I blink, not understanding. "What?"

"I heard he got married. I spoke to your mum before I came here, and she told me."

Wow, my hometown's gossip grapevine is efficient.

"It's not about him," I say. "He's in the past, Dad. I'm over it."

"So, what happened?"

I can see that my father isn't going to let it go. I put the plate away and straighten my posture, trying not to collapse.

"It's another man. A…" – wonderful man who I love and who left me forever – "guy I was with, and it didn't work out."

My father scratches his grey hair, nodding slowly.

"But from the looks of it, it's making you suffer."

I wipe away a stubborn tear that escapes and runs down my cheek.

"Isabella, you can't let the end of a relationship affect you like that. The first time, I understood. You had hopes for the guy and he didn't reciprocate. But that can't always happen. No broken relationship can be responsible for extinguishing your light."

It's very difficult to agree, but I try. From a normal point of view, considering what he knows, my father isn't wrong. Maybe I shouldn't have gone on this adventure after my relationship in Brazil ended. But you know what, at this point, I don't care. I do care that I've finally found someone who really loves me, who wants to be with me and can't. *That* matters to me. That's what's killing me.

"I know, Dad. It's just… difficult. I liked him a lot; he did me a lot of good."

My father takes a deep breath, takes a sip of his coffee, and eats a piece of cake. "Can't you work it out?"

"No. Unfortunately not."

"Right, then, a New Year's resolution: to move on."

I meet his caring, loving eyes. I can't help but smile a little. "Practical like that?"

"Yes, practical. You can even allow yourself to cry, get a little drunk, do whatever helps you. But then, life goes on."

That phrase should probably be my mantra.

I have to admit that there will be no other solution. Although it hurts, although I miss Benjamin every day, yes, it's true that life will go on.

He's moved on. Benjamin isn't even… no, I refuse to think about it. It's too painful.

"Bella?" my father calls me. "Did you understand what I said?"

"*Sim, senhor,*" I confirm. "Thank you, Dad. I'm really glad you're here."

He smiles warmly and pulls me into a tight hug. Despite everything, I'm not alone. There's one reason I couldn't go with Benjamin: I have a life here. Family, friends, people who love me and are here for me.

My father is right. I'll get over it. I have to get over it; there's no other choice.

* * *

One month later

Sitting at my desk, I stare at the refined white piece of cloth in front of me. A tie from Regency times.

Benjamin's tie, which he ended up forgetting.

"Time is ticking, isn't it? It's almost the end of January," Cinthia comments, lying on the sofa.

I sigh. "Yeah…"

But not quickly enough. A month after Benjamin left, and it still seems like yesterday that we said goodbye. I've stopped crying every day, at least. Thinking about him, however, is still part of my sad routine.

"What are you doing later? I was thinking of going to the pub."

I still don't feel excited enough to go out. In recent weeks, I went with her to the cinema and to an Indian restaurant nearby, but today, I really have other plans.

"I'll pass, darling."

"You can't stop your life, Bella."

Cinthia has been by my side in my worst moments. They've improved over the last month, but they still happen.

"I know, it's just that I really have to write."

She stands up and turns to me, excited.

"Tell me the story."

I swivelled around to face her.

"It's a time travel book. A sweet romance. The guy, a duke, comes to the future but has to go back to look after his sister. He meets the girl and there's the dilemma."

"I love it! It's going to be great. But there's a happy ending, right? For God's sake, don't separate the two of them."

I try to smile. "Of course, I'm not an evil author. It has a happy ending; I just don't know how yet."

She stands up, leaving her phone on the coffee table. "Good then. If you're going to write, I won't insist. I'll see if I can find some company for tonight. I'm going to the loo."

My friend leaves the room and goes into the bathroom, closing the door.

I stare at the tie again, running my fingers lightly over the fabric. I pick it up and bring it to my nose. I can still smell his perfume. The left side of my chest starts to ache again, but I stay there for a few seconds with my eyes closed.

Finally, when I put the fabric aside, I look at our selfie in the picture frame on the table, Ben's beautiful smile showing all the happiness we were feeling.

I love you. Our love is impossible, but it's real. It's as if he's whispering the words in my ear.

With a tight chest, I open my laptop on the document I had already started.

I don't know if this will work, if I'll change my mind in a few minutes, or delete the file the day after tomorrow. All I know is that I feel the *need* to write, to put into words the memories that I treasure in my heart.

I click on the top bar, where the document name is labelled "new book" and type in the new title instead.

My heart races, a tear runs down my cheek, but I like what I read. It feels right.

I pull my hands away, my eyes fixed on the words on the screen: *Falling on a Duke.*

24

My wish came true

Bath, England
December 1817
Benjamin

Sitting behind the desk in my study, I stare at the photo in my hands with a tightness in my chest. Isabella's smile is still the most beautiful thing I've ever seen.

My heart is broken. *Broken.* Who knew?

It's been three days since I came back from the future. Perhaps it was the very specific wish, but I woke up in the same room, on 7 December 1817. That means I was away for six months.

In the meantime, a lot has happened. Abigail didn't tell anyone that I was gone. Not immediately. Instead, she asked our coachman, with a false note in my name, to take her to London, with the intention of asking Jack Spencer for help. My friend was quick to help her and accompanied her to Bath to check on my disappearance.

While they were looking for me, he took over the paper at the request of my secretary, Howard, who no longer knew what to do about the denunciation of the traitor to the Crown. Fearless and reckless as he is, Spencer gave the order for publication. The fact is that when I returned, I found Abigail desperate because the damned Cornell, who had spent months in hiding after the denunciation, had ordered my friend to be kidnapped in search of revenge.

We managed to rescue him, but the surprises didn't end there. As soon as I got home and thought I could pour myself a shot of Scotch to relax, I discovered that, before the kidnapping, Jack Spencer and Abigail were leaving for Gretna Green. To get married in a hurry.

Two knocks on the door catch my attention. I hide the photo under the pile of papers, straightening my posture and rubbing my eyes. I need a break; I'm just an ordinary man.

"Come in."

Jack Spencer opens the door and gives me a naughty smile, the kind that wins over the women he chooses to seduce.

"Benjamin Waldorf, His Grace, returning from his unexpected disappearance ready to assume his responsibilities."

Jack's tone is good-humoured. It always is. But I don't feel like smiling right now. Not in the slightest.

"You can wipe that smile off your face, Spencer."

He raises his hands in front of his body. "I come in peace. I know we have to talk, that things with Cornell have got a bit messy, but—"

"Messy? Peace…" I laugh humourlessly. "Peace would be to return and find things just as I left them."

Jack closes his eyes a little. "You're being ungrateful, Waldorf. I did my best to manage your affairs during the almost *six months* that you were away doing who knows what."

I haven't told anyone the reasons for my disappearance. I changed the subject, dodged questions, said I was tired, did what I could. I don't think anyone would believe me.

"You're forgetting my sister. You've done your best to get on with her too."

I get up and walk over to him; he's still standing by the door. Jack and I are the same height, but he's slightly stronger because he's a boxer. I've always beaten him at fencing, though. Jack is a bit too rough for the sport.

"Tell me, Spencer. Were you busy dealing with my business when you decided to seduce Abigail?"

He clenches his jaw. "I didn't…"

"You didn't seduce her? Don't lie to me, Jack." I take a step forward, sticking close to him. "I know you and the perversities that please you. Do you really think I don't know what's behind that marriage proposal? That unexpected escape to Gretna Green? Are you going to look me in the eye and lie that you didn't take my sister's virtue?"

Jack breathes heavily, without looking away. But there's an answer in that silence. I'm right. He seduced her.

"Unbelievable…" I mutter, walking away.

"It's not like that, Benjamin."

"And what is it like, then?" I turn round. "Explain it to me."

"Abigail came to me for help because you had disappeared, and she didn't know where else to turn. She was desperate. She came to me at night, tired and cold. So first, before you give me these ready-made sermons, answer me: where the hell were you? Why did you abandon her?"

"I didn't abandon her." I face him closely again. "What happened was beyond my control. I would never abandon my sister. I would do anything to protect her."

Even giving up the woman of my life. The woman I love. I won't say those words. They hurt, and I don't think Jack would understand.

"Well, you weren't here for the last few months." Jack doesn't hold back. "I was."

"And so you felt entitled to take advantage of her."

Jack clenches his fists at his sides, letting out a frustrated sigh. "I didn't take advantage of her, damn it! Yes, I seduced her, but she knew what she was doing. You don't know the whole story."

"And what's the whole story, Jack? Tell me, what is it?"

Spencer runs a hand through his hair, clears his throat, and answers me: "I'm in love with Abigail, Benjamin." He lifts his shoulders. "I love her."

I wasn't expecting that. Not at all. I don't even believe what he's saying. By God, he's Jack Spencer.

"I don't believe it."

"But it's true."

"I know you, Jack. We've known each other for years.

Do you really want me to fall for your love story? We're talking about my sister, you prick. About her future, about her happiness."

He looks angry now. "What should I do? Make up a dirty story so you'll believe me? If I'm telling you that I love her, that Abigail is my—"

"Enough!"

Our attention shifts to the door, where Abigail stares at us, frowning.

"What are you doing here?" I ask.

Abigail turns up her nose at me and crosses her arms. "You're discussing my future without my presence, Benjamin. I believe I deserve to be part of that conversation."

"Abigail, I am talking to this…" I look at Jack, and he rolls his eyes, "this man about his deplorable behaviour towards you."

Abby lets out a frustrated sigh. "Oh, for God's sake, I'm not a child."

"I'm responsible for you!" I retort.

"Not in the last few months," Jack mutters, and I glare at him.

"I don't care about your responsibility," Abby continues. "I just want you to listen to what Jack has to say."

"Mel, calm down. Benjamin is angry, but—" Jack starts to say, but I interrupt him.

"What did you say?"

They both stop talking, looking at me with surprised eyes.

"What did you call her?" I ask again.

Jack looks confused and looks at my sister, who understands first.

"Ah. Mel." Abigail lets out a giggle. "You know I never liked Abigail, so Jack started calling me Mel as a joke and we got used to it. You know, Abigail *Melissa* Waldorf."

My heart races and I'm speechless. I'm transported back to that afternoon in Bath when Isabella and I sat on one of the benches.

The sign read: *Mel and Jack: Two souls who met and lived a long life full of love.*

Could it have been your friend? Isabella had asked me.

I can't believe it. Yes, it was my friend. With my sister. Jack and Abby loved each other for a lifetime. They were happy for a lifetime. Jack is the happiness that Abigail wanted to find.

"Waldorf? Are you alright?" Jack asks, snapping me out of my trance.

"You look pale." Abigail approaches. "What's wrong?"

Everything. Simply everything. I just found out that my sister was safe. That she's going to be happy. That she doesn't need me. That... I'm free if I want to live my happiness too.

My head is in an unbridled whirl. Today is 10 December, which means that in less than two weeks, there will be another solstice. If my sister is safe, there's nothing to keep me here. Just as there's no reason to believe that I won't be able to use the solstice to travel through time a third time.

Hopefully, the last time.

I don't know how much time has passed in the future. I don't know if Bella will be free, but I have to try.

"Abby, let me talk to Jack," I ask her, my throat feeling dry. "I'll talk to you in a minute, I promise."

Abigail exchanges a look with my friend and nods, leaving the room.

Without saying anything, I walk over to the sideboard and pour us two shots of Scotch. I hand Jack a glass and turn mine round.

"So, you love my sister," I say.

Jack runs a hand through his hair. "That's what I'm trying to say."

I laugh at his manner. Bollocks. Of all the men in the world who could marry Abigail, the last one I would have thought would fill that role would be Jack Spencer. Now, however, looking at him... I think I was wrong.

"Forgive me, I beg you. What you've done for me over the last few months has been a lot. But it's you, Spencer, so..."

"Hey, I understand." He turns his glass round too. "Well, I don't understand this sudden change of mood, but your reluctance is understandable. If I had to trust myself... I don't know if I would. I'm also grateful that you saved my skin. But I'm being honest. Dealing with the newspaper, looking after Mel during these months... they've changed me, Waldorf. Abigail makes me want to be better. To be the man she deserves to have by her side."

I understand the feeling.

"I suppose... I have your blessing to marry her?" Jack asks me, leaving his glass on my desk.

"That's what she wants, isn't it?"

Jack nods his head. "Yes, it is."

I take a deep breath, ready for the second part of this conversation. "Jack, I... I have to go."

Spencer doesn't understand me. "Go where?"

"Away. Far away. Indefinitely."

He continues to stare at me in amazement, not understanding.

I try to explain. "My last few months have been... peculiar. I ask you not to ask me any questions, but just believe that I didn't disappear of my own free will. However, the only reason I came back, once I could, was my sister. Now she has you and..." the memory of Isabella makes my chest overflow with hope, "I need to get back there."

Jack takes a deep breath. He walks over to the sideboard, pours himself another, thinking. "A woman." It's not a question.

"Yes."

"Why not bring her here?"

"I can't."

Spencer turns the glass round, running a hand through his long hair. "You're really not going to tell me where you've been, are you?"

I shake my head.

My friend nods and continues. "What do you need, Benjamin?"

I sigh, staring into the leaden eyes. "Just look after her. I'll talk to my sister. I won't act without talking to Abigail, but... look after her, Spencer."

There are still other matters that I have to take care of before I leave. The newspaper, which I'm also leaving in Jack's care, a will, other paperwork. However, I can think about that later. Abigail is the priority. If she's well, I know I can leave with my heart and conscience at peace.

Spencer agrees with me, taking two steps forward and holding out his hand to me. "Don't worry, Your Grace." It's still strange for me not to hear Duke's bark when people call me that. "I'll take care of her. Better still, I'll love her and make her happy."

I smile, accepting the gesture. "I know you will, Spencer. I know you will."

* * *

A few minutes later, I leave Jack behind and walk out of the study towards the music room, where I know Abigail is waiting for me. My sister is sitting by the piano, her delicate hands fingering the white keys.

"You finally finished your conversation with Jack," she tells me.

I cross my arms behind my back. "With Mr Spencer, you mean. You're not married yet."

She widens her eyes, attentive. "But we will be, won't we?"

I nod and approach her, and she moves to give me space on the piano bench. I sit next to her, without touching the instrument.

"Remember when I tried to teach you and you ran away?" she asks me, making me laugh.

"I wasn't a keen music student. Barney filled that role."

She laughs too. My God, my sister is laughing again.

"He was. Barney was good at everything he did. I miss him every day."

"Me too…" I mutter. "Do you really want to marry that arsehole?"

She laughs again. "Ah, Benjamin. If you only knew… when you disappeared, I almost went back to the same dark hole I was in before. Almost. I got too close. And then I refused. I raised my head, got into the carriage, and set off for London, determined to find you. Jack was the only one I could think of to ask for help. And as the weeks went by, as we looked for you, well… we…"

"You fell in love," I finished for her.

My sister nods, smiling.

I look at her, and I can see how different she is from the girl she was when we lost Barney and my father. Abigail is flushed; she looks healthy, poised. She no longer has dark circles under her eyes. Her eyes shine now; they sparkle… joy. Love. I saw the same sparkle in Isabella's eyes when she looked at me.

It's such a relief to know that she's OK. That she's happy and will be happy. A relief that frees me. Not because Abby was a prison. I would never resent her for making me stay here, for needing my protection. But now I can choose Isabella. And I can allow myself to be chosen by her too.

"Darling, I have a request to make of you," I begin, taking her hand.

"Tell me."

It's hard. As much as going back to Isabella is all I want, that my happiness lies in the future, saying goodbye to Abigail forever is painful. She's my little sister, my family.

"Over the last few months, I've been away against my will."

"What happened, Benjamin?"

"I don't think telling you will make any difference."

"Why?"

"Because I don't think you'll believe me. I wouldn't believe it myself."

She pouts, unconvinced.

"Would you believe me if I said I'd travelled forward in time?" I shoot.

She frowns, tapping my forearm with her hand. "Come on! I'm talking about something serious, Benjamin."

As I thought, telling the truth won't make any difference to us.

"Please trust me. If I don't want to tell you everything, I have my reasons. I've never lied to you, and you know me well."

Abigail sighs, eventually nodding. "Right. Keep going."

"During my time away, I met someone."

"A woman?"

"The woman of my life."

Abigail grins from ear to ear. "Who is she? Why isn't she here?"

"Because she can't be. The only way for me to be with her is to leave. But I'm not just talking about living far away, Abby. If I leave, if I manage to leave, I won't come back. Not ever."

She takes a few seconds to stare at me in confusion.

"I don't understand, Benjamin. Why forever? What's stopping you from bringing her here, from coming back?"

I realise that the information I'm giving Abigail is insufficient.

"It's not possible, Abby. If it were, we'd find a way, but our situation really doesn't allow it. For me to be with her, to be able to love her, I have to give up my life."

"And that's what you want," Abigail says, "because you love her."

I nod my head in agreement. "Yes, I love her."

My sister runs her delicate hands over her face. "Is it the only way?" she asks me again, a little emotional.

"The only one. I wouldn't go if I didn't know you were safe. That you're fine, that you're happy, Abby. And you are – you will be for the rest of your days. You'll be happy; you'll live for many years, and…"

"You seem to know my future." She laughs nervously.

I shrug. If she only knew…

"Maybe I know."

Abigail takes a deep breath, then another. Overcome with emotion, she asks me: "Will you be happy?"

My throat feels tight, and I swallow my saliva with difficulty. "I believe that's the only way I'll be happy."

A tear runs down Abigail's cheek. "And you're asking my permission to be happy?" Another tear. "Benjamin, do you know how much I've wanted this? After everything we've been through, everything we've lost, we're finally happy."

We really are, aren't we? Not yet, but I will be. I can almost feel the happiness in my own hands.

"Forgive me for not being able to explain more." I bring her hands to my lips. "I love you. I'll miss you every day."

Abigail wipes my damp face. Only then do I realise that I've been crying too. She smiles. Her face has never been brighter. So at peace.

"No more suffering," she whispers and hugs me, wrapping her thin arms around my neck. "Let's just be happy. That's what they wanted for us."

Mom, my grandmother, my father, my brother. Yes, she's right. That's what they wanted.

"When are you leaving?" Abby asks me as soon as we part.

I pull myself together, straightening my posture. "On the 21st day of the month."

"Which means I only have ten days to get married."

I'm confronted by her mischievous expression.

"We can get a special license, no problem."

Abby claps her hands and stands up. "Good. I'll let Jack know." She takes my hand once more. "I want you to give me away at the altar," she declares. "Will you do that?"

"Of course, future Mrs Spencer." I kiss her hand affectionately. "It would be an honour."

25

Falling on a duke

London, England
June 2023
Isabella

I loved it! I'm suspicious because I love time travel stories, but what I felt reading the story was indescribable. Isabella came back inspired.

Exciting, touching, surprising. Only these words could describe this beautiful story.

I spent all night reading; I couldn't put it down. Exciting.

Written with feeling and sensitivity. Congratulations to the author.

"So?"

I look away from the laptop screen and find Cinthia staring at me with anxious eyes.

"Well, so far, the reception is excellent." I move round in the swivel chair in front of my desk. "One person complained that it was too sweet, but that's part of it." I laugh. Nothing I'm not used to by now.

"*Yay*, I knew it would be a hit." Cinthia claps her hands twice.

She's told me as much several times in recent months.

Last week, I released my first book after a long hiatus: *Falling on a Duke*, a time travel romance with a guaranteed happy ending.

It was a very difficult story to write. Not because of the writer's block. I overcame that completely. But because of the inspiration: Benjamin Gerard Waldorf, the man who constantly inhabits my mind and heart.

After he left, I thought I would never stop crying. I thought about what my father said when he was here: no failed relationship can extinguish your light. I knew he was right, but it was hard to believe. I allowed myself some time to grieve, to try to get over the loss. I grieved, cried, listened to songs, and looked at our photos, feeling my heart bleed. I realised that only time could do anything for me.

So, through Benjamin and the memory of what we lived through, I focused on my story.

When I wasn't working in the café, I was writing. I studied, edited, and rewrote chapters. The words got bigger and bigger. Writing helped me to heal. To get used to the pain. I used it as a source of strength to keep going. When I finished, I felt relief. A silly pride. I cried again, this time with joy. As if I had done my duty. As if… the book was my honourable act, for a man of unparalleled honour.

"I'm happy with the messages," I say, closing the screen, "but the book is already out in the world. My part has been done; God knows I've put my heart into this story. When people tell me they can feel… that's the point, you know? To feel."

Cinthia sits on the sofa, running her hand through her dark curls.

"And… did you tell him?" She nods, pointing to the picture frame on the desk with the photo of me, Ben, and Duke.

My friend isn't the type to push me, so she didn't pepper me with questions all the time about Benjamin. But she's been my shoulder to cry on over the last few months, and she knows everything I've suffered.

"I didn't tell him, but he knew I had started the story."

"Call him, Bella."

I laugh without humour. For Cinthia, Benjamin is still the man who lives in Scotland with his sister.

"I can't, darling. And you know… it's better this way. Since we're not going to be together, it's better not to talk. It hurts less."

It doesn't really. In fact, it hurts a lot more. Starting with the fact that Benjamin is dead, considering he's back in the nineteenth century. I had a few desperate moments when I googled his name to find out what had happened. If he had married, if he had produced heirs, if he'd been happy.

The information remains the same as when we did the research together. His name is listed as the Duke of

Waldorf with a date of birth but not of death. I found it so curious, and then I started to panic, thinking about the possible reasons why that had happened. Could Benjamin have arrived in another year, a random third period? What if he disappeared, but didn't make it back to the house? What if he got injured or ill?

I shake my head lightly, chasing the thoughts away. My heart already feels like it's tied up with a tight string just thinking about such possibilities.

"But Bella," Cinthia continues, "you dedicated the book to him. Why not show it to him?"

I sigh sadly, holding back the lump in my throat. "I'll think about it, OK?"

My friend realises my sadness and gives up arguing.

I hear my phone ring and see my mother's name on the screen. I answer the video call and find her smiling at me.

"I want to know, did you send it?"

"Good afternoon to you too, Mum," I tease.

She rolls her eyes. "Isabella Souza Kato, answer me."

"Yes, Mum. Although the book is already self-published, I built up the courage and sent the manuscript to the traditional publisher. They said to expect three months for a reply. Now we have to wait."

She celebrates on the other side, whooping proudly. "That's it! It'll all work out, you'll see."

I hope so. Ever since I told my mum and Laura that I was writing again, they have been active participants in the book process. They did one round of beta reading, and then another, as well as pointing out any plot holes, ideas, and details I could add. I'm always very open to these suggestions, especially as they enrich the work, even those that I don't feel apply to a particular story. But my mum fell so in love with the couple – unsurprising since I was one hundred per cent inspired by Benjamin – that she encouraged me to finally send it to a publisher I follow and admire a lot. In other words, we're excited and anxious to receive an answer.

"Let's hope, it's in their hands now," I say.

"You'll see. In a year's time, we'll be celebrating its publication. I can feel it."

Well, if my mum feels it, who am I to argue?

"Darling, I have to go. I just rang to find out."

"OK. Everything OK over there?"

"Yeah, yeah. Zé and I are starting to plan a trip to visit you. Cross your fingers."

I cross my fingers in front of the camera. "Crossing."

My mum laughs and says goodbye. "Kisses, my love."

"Kisses." I hang up the call with a smile on my lips.

"You look lively," Cinthia comments, still on the sofa.

"My mum wanted to know if I'd sent the book to the publisher. I told you she encouraged me to do it," I explain, since I spoke to my mum in Portuguese.

"It's going to be great, Bella. I'm rooting for you."

"Let's wait."

Cinthia stands up and reaches into her jeans pocket. "I was thinking of going to Subway for a sandwich. Would you like one?"

"Yes! Let me get my card." I stand up, but she stops me with a wave of her hand.

"Don't worry, I'll pay. I'll be back in about fifteen minutes."

"OK. I'll have the usual: meatballs, cheese, lettuce and mayonnaise."

Cinthia writes down the ingredients on her phone. "Italian bread?" she asks me.

"That's right."

"Alright, I'll be right back."

As soon as she's out the door, I look at Duke, relaxing in the corner of the room with his hind legs back. He's huge, that little animal.

"I'm going to the bedroom to do nothing. Do you want to keep me company?"

Duke doesn't even move, which means he doesn't want to.

I walk into my room and see my bed in disarray. I don't make it every day, much to my mum's chagrin, but today it's too hot to lie under the covers. I open Spotify and put on the playlist I made for my book. I've put together all the songs that meant something to me and Benjamin during the time he was here. No one will ever know the true meaning of each one, but inside I feel like I'm sharing some of that love with the world, albeit in secret.

John Legend's "All of Me" starts to play. I feel a lump in my throat, remembering when we danced at the ball, how Benjamin kissed me and gave himself to me that night.

So real, yet so impossible.

I put the pillow back and spread the quilt on the mattress. In the living room, I hear Duke's paws scrabbling and euphoric barking.

"What are you up to, Your Grace?" I ask, still arranging

the bedspread, my eyes riveted on the task at hand. "Your Grace?"

"Yes, milady?"

I pause. That voice. My limbs freeze, my heart feels like it's going to burst out of my mouth. Am I delirious?

I leave the quilt as it is and turn round. No, I'm not delirious. Standing in the doorway, in his jacket, pearlescent waistcoat, white tie, and riding boots, Benjamin stares at me with his arms folded behind his back and a smile on his face.

My God, how did he get in here?

"Ben?" My eyes are already moist by now. "You…"

"I'm back," he says. "I'm back, my love. I've come back to you."

I have so many questions, so much to say, but nothing matters now. Not when I have my man back, in one piece, just as I remember him. Not when he came back to me.

Benjamin walks over to me, closing the door behind him. He lifts me onto his lap and kisses me, with such intensity and love that I can feel every little piece of my heart knitting back together.

In his arms, I'm home, and I want him to know that he is too.

We take off our clothes without any delicacy, desperate. If this is a dream, I don't want to wake up. Benjamin lays me down on the quilt I've just made. My every memory is revived to the sound of John Legend's romantic lyrics.

Benjamin kisses me, touches me, moves his hands up to my breasts, moves his mouth down to my nipples, sucking them reverently. I look at him between gasps, at every bit of him, still afraid that this is a dream.

"It's real, love. I'm here," he says, kissing me again.

We move apart just to reach for a condom. Then, Benjamin enters me, slowly, completing me as I squeeze and pull him to me, wanting it all, wanting him to feel how much I've missed him, how much I love him and need him.

I'm alive again, I realise. For the last few months, no matter how hard I tried, it was just breathing. Just waking up, walking, eating. But it wasn't living.

Now it is. And if it's up to me, it will be until the end.

Our bodies merge, sweat, tremble. Benjamin thrusts more fervently, and I tilt my hips, opening up, letting him take what he wants, what he needs.

We enjoy it with hearts beating fast, complete, full. The song now is "Halo" by Beyoncé. And it really is as if we're glowing. As if our love were so sublime, our happiness so great, capable of making us shine.

He cradles me to his chest as soon as our breathing calms down. Without control, intoxicated by what we've just shared, by what has just happened, I begin to cry softly.

"*Shh…* easy, love." Benjamin caresses my bare back.

"You came back to me," I whisper.

Benjamin pulls back slightly, lifting my chin up to look at him. "I'm back."

"What happened? How did it happen?"

He takes my hand and intertwines our fingers. We fit perfectly together.

"I want to talk about it later, tell you everything. But in short, I got there, and things were fine. Not immediately, but they were. Abigail is safe; she'll be happy. So, I was able to come back, to take hold of my own happiness."

"When did you get there?" I ask. My God, I have a million questions.

"Around six months after I disappeared. Around the winter solstice."

"And then you wanted to come back to me."

He nods. "I wore the cameo." He caresses my face. "You know, when my grandmother gave me this cameo, she told me that I was the chosen one. She said that one day I would understand. She was right – today I do get it. I don't know the exact reasons that brought me to you. Whether it was something mystical, magical, cosmic. The first time, I had no choice. But how lucky I was, Bella, to be hit by you and your scooter."

I laugh, even through my tears.

"It's different now," Benjamin continues. "You are my choice. I chose to be here; I chose to beg you to accept me into your time and into your heart. I've always wondered why so many bad things have happened to me over the last few years. Why I had to suffer, why Abigail had to suffer. I believe that I was being prepared, transformed into an honourable man. A man who can, on a very small scale, consider himself worthy of you. And, perfect as you are, the path to finding you brought happiness not only to me but to my sister too. It was all written."

Yes, it was.

"I can't believe you time-travelled for me again."

"I'd travel to the end of time if I had to, darling. I love you. I want to make you happy, fill you with love, hear your laughter, and smell your sweet perfume until my last breath."

I steal a kiss from him. I'll spend my life doing that.

"What about you?" he wants to know. "What's happened?"

I sniffle, wiping away a tear. "I wrote the book. I spent all those months writing our story. I dedicated it to you," I confess, making him smile. I get up just enough to reach my phone and open the e-reader. I click on my book, looking for the dedication page.

Benjamin smiles as he picks up the device. "I can read my name, but what's written next to it?"

"To Benjamin," I read to him, "with all my love. This story would never have existed without you."

He swallows, overcome with emotion. "I want to know everything about it," Ben says.

"I'll tell you about it. You know what? I'll translate it so you can read it. The readers really liked it. I was reading the reviews for Cinthia and…" My eyes widen. "My God, my friend is coming back from Subway and…"

"No, she's not," Benjamin says. I don't understand and he explains himself: "I met her on the stairs. I think she recognised me from the photos and let me in. After she looked me up and down, *including my boots*, she said you wouldn't mind eating afterwards."

I laugh now. Out loud. "I said that these boots are something else…"

Benjamin pulls me to him, my breasts pressing against his strong chest. "You never told me. What happened at the end? Did he stay or did she go with him?"

I smile, my eyes moist again. "He stayed."

Benjamin strokes my cheek with his thumb and asks me: "Was that a wish?"

"A dream," I reply.

He brings his face close and whispers, before kissing me: "A dream come true, then. Marry me, Bella. Please be mine."

Such a gentleman, such a lord. So perfect.

"Yes, I will marry you."

Benjamin takes my lips and sweeps me off my feet, sealing our love in a kiss that has the flavour of eternity, of certainty.

Here, and for the rest of our days, we are real. He is real. No longer a duke from the past, but a man in the present. A love in the present. My love.

EPILOGUE

An eternalised love story

Bath, England
Two years later
Benjamin

"These are the documents." I hand the pile of old newspapers to Miss Johnson, the lady in charge of the Waldorf Museum. We're at the reception desk and, apart from the two of us, there's just one guy analysing the crystals on display in the right-hand corner of the room.

She looks at the pile behind her glasses and nods. "Right. So here we have…"

"These are samples of the most important stories in the *Daily Bath* up until 1840. And here, the marriage certificate of Abigail Melissa Spencer, formerly Waldorf."

What I'm handing over to the woman is the collection I've gathered since I returned to the future. Well, the present, rather. As soon as I adapted to the changes (I moved in with Bella, Cinthia, and His Grace, Duke, the dog), I started working as a waiter at events held in the halls of a university in the city. Bella continued at the café and managed to get published with the Brazilian publisher she wanted. Her publisher had a contact, who had a contact, which turned out to be useful for me to get a job in publishing.

We moved into our own flat a year later. We got married soon afterwards in a simple ceremony that was attended by Bella's parents and Laura and Pierre. Our honeymoon was in Scotland, a place that Bella used as inspiration for her next novel. Following the success of *Falling on a Duke*, the publisher is keen to publish a new period series set in different parts of the UK. Bella has also translated the book into English and already has a readership in the language. I was proudly the book's editor.

Despite knowing that Abigail lived a long and happy life with Spencer, I was bothered by the lack of information about her for the generations of today. So, I dedicated myself to a personal project, visiting libraries and old collections in search of documents that could demonstrate the legacy built by my sister and Jack. I even met a descendant: their great-great-grandson, Ian Spencer. We follow each other on social media.

"I have to admit that I was excited when my boss told me that we would be receiving more documents about the Waldorfs, especially coming from a direct descendant," the young lady tells me, looking at the sheets on the counter. "And the *Daily* is famous in the city, even after all this time. The case of treason they denounced is historic."

"I'm here." The soft voice makes me turn my attention away from the woman at the desk to appreciate my beautiful wife. She approaches me and gives me a kiss on the cheek, greeting the lady in the room.

"I see that the papers have already been delivered."

"Yes, they have. Mr Waldorf is very kind to give these treasures to the museum."

Bella pushes her hair out of her face and tucks it behind her ear. "Now they're in the right place, aren't they, my love?"

"Yes, they are now."

"Shall we go, darling? I want to go and buy some fudge before we catch the train," Bella says.

"Let's go." I take her hand.

We say goodbye and leave the house that had once been my home behind. Bella and I walk side by side, turning the corner from Brock Street towards the railway station.

"How are you feeling, my love?" I ask.

She smiles, looking down at her belly, which has already grown a little. "I feel great, just a bit more tired than usual. And I'm craving sweets more, so I'm warning you that we'll be buying more fudge than usual today."

I laugh. Bella is five months pregnant with a baby girl. We've decided to call her Melissa, in honour of Abigail.

"Buy as many sweets as you like." I bring her hand to my lips and kiss it. "We won't be coming back to Bath for another few months."

"Aren't you coming to see the newspaper exhibition?"

I shake my head. "No, Miss Johnson told me they'd send photos. From now on, I'm all about you and this little princess. I want to assemble the bedroom furniture and put up the wallpaper soon."

"Oh, that's lovely. It's not like you asked me to prepare a bath for Your Grace when you arrived," she teases me with a poke in the ribs.

"You'll never forget that, will you?"

"Never. But don't feel embarrassed. You've evolved significantly. You're a perfect twenty-first-century man now. My man."

I stop and pull her to me, rubbing our noses together. "Yours?"

Bella nods, running her hand through my hair in a gentle caress. "All mine."

I kiss her, breathing in her soft perfume, because there's no arguing about that. All hers. Forever.

Acknowledgements

When I started my journey as a writer, I never imagined I would get somewhere. It was fun at first, and then it became work, until I finally realised that writing was what I really loved to do. Today, after years of hard work and dedication, I am so lucky to have an amazing readership in Brazil, but I was graced with even more. *Falling on a Duke* being published in English shows me how life can surprise us.

Of course, I was never alone.

First, I would like to thank God for His light and wisdom.

Thank you to my loving family and darling husband who have always supported me from day one and believed I could take this step to publish my book in a language other than Portuguese. You are my daily inspiration. I love you and I would not be anyone without you.

Thank you to all my friends. I won't mention names because I am overwhelmed and afraid I would forget someone, but you know who you are. I am so grateful to have you in my life.

Thank you to the Meetcute Book Fest in the UK, the

lovely romance event I had the honour of attending in 2024. It was after that wonderful afternoon that I decided to give it a try, and the fellow authors I spoke to afterwards, asking them how to proceed, were all so supportive and kind.

Thank you to the team at The Book Guild, who believed this book could reach the shelves, for all their hard work and support.

Finally, thanks to you, darling readers. I hope you spent a lovely time with Benjamin and Bella (and, of course, with His Grace, Duke, the dog).

If you want to reach me on my Instagram (@stefanynunes_), I would love to chat with you.

About the Author

Stefany Nunes is Brazilian, graduated with degrees in Letters and Brazilian Law and has been an avid reader for as long as she can remember. A great lover of romance novels, she always created stories in her head without putting them on paper. After moving to London, inspired by the city's atmosphere, she finally found the courage to fulfil her dream of writing.